I0761854

SAVING MCNAMARA

LOU ZITNIK

ALSO BY LOU ZITNIK

Blues in Paradise, short stories

Magic Words in the Palace of Desire

My Daughter

Saving McNamara is a work of fiction. All incidents and dialogue, and all characters with the exception of some well-known historical figures, are products of the author's imagination and are not to be construed as real. Where real-life historical persons appear, the situations, incidents, and dialogues concerning those persons are entirely fictional and are not intended to depict actual events or to change the entirely fictional nature of the work. In all other respects, any resemblance to persons living or dead is entirely coincidental

for AMY SELF

EPIGRAPH

"He had 50 cents in his hand and a bullet in his head. We'll have film."

— VAN AMBURG, CHANNEL 7 NEWS GANG, 1970S

Mutter this with William Munny, out of Missouri,
in silhouette against the sky's clotted blue:
"It's a hell of a thing killin' a man."
Here's a sun settled on a dark horizon
of Golden Rule, where we must understand
that killing's hard, for most of us, to do —

— JOSEPH STANTON, FROM "UNFORGIVEN" IN *IMAGINARY MUSEUM,* 1999

CONTENTS

PART I

OLD LIFEGUARDS TELLING STORIES

McNamara, remember him? Robert Strange, the accountant who ran the war in Vietnam? Born right here in San Francisco.

Big Mac?

That's him. The killer with the wire-rim glasses and slicked-back hair.

He tried to kill me. You rescued him?

1. ARMY JEEPS AND A MISSING WISE MAN

Time: December 25,1967
Location: Hilo, Hawaii

Four hours later and twenty dollars richer, Sarah Costa woke to tires skidding on wet asphalt. She grabbed her grease-stained uniform, slipped it over her head, and ran out the door, into the orange glow of a lone streetlight.

Barefoot, she reached the bridge and leaned over the concrete railing. A jeep was stuck in a swirl of white water, its driver standing on the seat, holding a bundle over his head and shouting, "Help! Save the baby!"

For a second, Sarah thought to call for help. But the streets were deserted, the houses dark, so she closed her eyes and jumped. Landed on her feet, then her butt, and slid downhill, picking up speed, until water rushed up her skirt and a bundle dropped into her arms.

Pressing it to her chest, Sarah looked up at combat boots, pale legs, boxer shorts, a soft belly, dog tags swinging on a hairless chest, and a pink face shouting, "Soldier, you're out of uniform."

A spotlight swept down from the bridge, searching the swollen stream, and settled on the soldier in his underwear. A man's voice called from the light, "Are you okay, LT?"

The driver jumped down to her and held a finger to his lips. "Say nothing, soldier. I'll take care of this." His breath stunk of beer and cigarettes as he jerked the bundle from her arms. He shook it, held it to his ear, and frowned. "Dead," he sighed. "I couldn't save him. Killed in action."

"LT? Is that you?"

"He's drunk," Sarah shouted. In his arms, a plastic baby Jesus reached for her. An icy hand grabbed her wrist, and the LT said, "Tell them I'm wounded."

Sarah grabbed the bundle and left the boxer-short soldier puking into the stream. At the top of the trail, a stocky soldier in fatigues jumped from a jeep and asked, "Is he okay?"

"He's drunk."

He waved two soldiers down the slope.

"He's bleeding." She pointed at her forehead. "You should call an ambulance. And the police." She held up the plastic Baby Jesus. "He stole this." When he tried to take it from her, she pressed the baby to her chest. "I know where it belongs."

He had a young man's voice, soft and reassuring. But in the headlights' glare, she saw pale and worn. His uniform had two stripes on the sleeves, a corporal, like her father in his old photographs. "Call the police," she said, holding the plastic baby close.

"Can't do that, sistah. We're shipping out in a couple of days. LT's coming with us."

"Are you drunk, too?"

"Not me, ma'am."

A sliver of light appeared along the horizon. One soldier was helping the lieutenant up the hill. The other sent to help was hooking a cable to the Jeep.

"You okay?" The corporal's hand settled on her shoulder. "You shouldn't be out here. You're soaked through. Go home."

She pulled away, and he gave her a close look. "Hey, do I know you?" he said. "From Hilo High?"

"No."

"And the pancake place? You work there."

"Maybe."

"Matsui," he said. "Folks call me J.J." He moved closer. "Three years varsity football." He smiled. "See?"

She saw black hair cut short, dark eyes, full lips, and broad shoulders. A boy hiding in a uniform. "I'm calling an ambulance," she said. "And the police."

The corporal grabbed her elbow. "Can't let you do that. We're shipping out for Nam in a couple days, and he's going with us. He's weak, but there's worse."

She shook her arm free. He held out his hand, and when she didn't take it, he said, "We've been training on the mountain. You know?"

She knew but didn't say so. Her father had pointed at the old Quonset huts every time they drove over Saddle Road. It was none of this soldier's business.

"Got a little crazy last night," he said.

"Did the LT hurt you?"

"Who? Him?" She shook her head. "No way."

"We'll take care of everything. There's a church around the corner with a manger scene. We could take it there for you, sistah."

"I know where this belongs." Too tired to talk, Sarah walked by him. When she looked back, two soldiers were tossing their lieutenant's limp body into a jeep. She kept walking. She had worked a double shift on her 18th birthday, and she had a flight to catch. Her first flight.

In her yard, she used the garden hose to spray the mud off her polyester uniform and the plastic baby. Shivering, she ran to the tool shed and slipped into her father's field jacket, zipped it to her neck. Still barefoot, she walked up the hill, turned the corner, and didn't stop until she stood in the neon glow of the blue sign that promised: "Jesus Is Coming Soon."

In front of the church, a life-size mother and a life-size father knelt at an empty cradle. Plastic camels and two plastic wise men stood in awe as Sarah gently laid the baby on plastic straw. Before she left, she picked up two empty beer cans near the Virgin's feet. "Jesus is back," she said and ran for home.

Later, when the taxi honked, she was waiting in boots, jeans and a blue palaka shirt. She grabbed her father's jacket from its nail and dragged her duffel bag to the driveway. The taxi driver behind the wheel of an old Chevy waited for her to shove the bag in the back seat. Then said, "I could've done dat, sistah."

"No problem." She could handle.

"Good jacket," he said. "I had one of dem. Last long time."

She zipped up the field jacket.

"AC too cold for you?" the driver asked over his shoulder. "You gotta toughen up for dah mainland, sweetie."

When they passed the bridge, she looked down at the stream. The Jeeps were gone, the soldiers with them. Now there were busted-up banana trees, rocks, and beer cans. Sarah didn't tell the driver about the accident or the drunk soldiers. She didn't want words to make them stronger in her memory.

The driver turned on the radio and heard a DJ say, "Viet Nam," before he could switch stations. "Heard enough war news to last a lifetime," he said.

Sarah looked out the back window and watched her home disappear. The Beatles were singing about love. It was all they needed.

2. TATTOOS AND MISS JANE

Time: January 1, 1968
Location: San Francisco

Home for the Costa family was a single-story on Northridge Drive in Daly City. Their three-bedroom shared a floor plan with a hundred others in the neighborhood. But Mr. and Mrs. Costa were more than satisfied. For him, it was like living in the city without living in The City. Thirty minutes in his Chevy Handyman and he'd be at Guerrero Brother's Butcher Shop. Eight hours and thirty minutes later, he'd be home.

For Mrs. Costa, their home was warm and comfortable, easy to clean, quiet and peaceful. The perfect size. And only a short walk to a cliff-side park with an ocean view.

Now, as they sat down to watch the Rose Bowl, Mr. Costa told himself to be thankful. Football and his wife's cooking were in the air. Thanks to Simpson, the running-back from Galileo High and City College, USC was leading Indiana, 7-0. Mr. Costa liked Simpson, but part of him didn't feel right enjoying the game. His oldest son was in Vietnam. A marine in Vietnam.

"If you're going to smoke," Mrs. Costa said, "do it outside before the kids come home."

He reached for his cigarettes. They were still in his shirt pocket, a nasty habit he had picked up in the Navy, dropped after his wedding, and picked up again after David had dropped out of college to enlist.

"Don't worry," Mrs. Costa said. "Terrence will drift off and they'll be late, but Sarah will make sure he finds his way home. That young lady is a blessing."

They smiled as Curt Gowdy predicted Simpson's future in the NFL. The running back would be a star. There was no doubt about it.

The Rose Bowl was over by the time Terrence parked on Northridge Drive.

"Sorry," Sarah said.

"No problem," Terrence said. "It takes years to adapt."

They had been swimming in the bay. Terrence had powered through a mile in thirty minutes. Sarah had lasted five minutes. Now they were sitting together, bundled up, shoulder to shoulder, in his brother's 63 Ford Falcon.

"Acclimate," she said.

Looking at her, Terrence saw a girl in combat boots, thick socks, jeans, and a long-sleeve checkered shirt. Her field jacket was zipped to her neck and her watch cap pulled down over her ears. Looking at him, she saw a boy in black loafers, white socks, pressed slacks, and a white dress shirt. His newsboy cap was pulled on his forehead, his eyes hidden behind brown Ray-Bans.

When Sarah told him she liked his outfit, he said "his threads" came from a pawnshop in the Haight, but he was no hippie. "You can get anything you need in a pawnshop," he said. "Anything."

Sarah nodded. She didn't know any hippies and had never been in a pawnshop or the Haight, wherever that was.

"My father has a shirt like yours," Terrence said. "I think it's in his footlocker with his army stuff."

"Palaka lasts forever."

"Listen." Terrence turned on the radio, turned it off, turned it back on, and said, "Listen, man. I gotta tell you something. Just between you and me, okay?"

"Okay," Sarah said, brushing her hand along the Falcon's dashboard. "This is one nice car."

"I'm taking care of it for my brother."

"We should be good to it."

"Right on."

Sarah watched a police car drive by.

"Don't worry about them. I have to tell you something." Terrence slipped his glasses down his nose. "But you can't tell my parents. They worry too much."

"About what?"

"Everything. They worry about everything."

Sarah nodded. She liked her aunt and uncle. They had helped her, and she wanted to help them. Her aunt was a skilled organizer and a generous cook. Her uncle was soft-spoken and a steady worker.

"Never mind," Terrence said. "Listen, what I was trying to tell you...I'm in love with a girl, I mean a woman."

Sarah nodded. She was on the mainland and had plenty to learn about swimming in cold water. But she knew all about boys in love.

"She's older."

Better, Sarah thought. Her cousin needed older.

"Not much older, a few years, that's all. Maybe four."

"That's nothing," Sarah said. She wasn't lying, but she wasn't certain.

"Don't tell my parents."

She nodded.

"Promise?"

She nodded.

"And I'm getting a tattoo. By Lyle Tuttle. A devil dog."

"You can get anything you need at a pawnshop."

"Exactly."

They stopped laughing when the radio jumped from music to news. O. J. Simpson had scored another touchdown at the Rose Bowl. Marine reinforcements were being sent to Khe Sanh.

"We'd better hurry," Sarah said. "We're running late."

As they walked to the front door, Sarah smelled roast turkey and the wind off the ocean. While Mrs. Costa kissed her cheek and hugged her tight, Sarah apologized for being late. In the kitchen, Mr Costa loaded her plate with turkey, stuffing, and green beans. "To bulk up for cold water swimming," Terrence said, handing her a second plate with mashed potatoes, gravy, and iceberg lettuce smothered in blue cheese dressing.

In the living room, Sarah sat between Terrence and Mrs. Costas on the couch with her two plates on a TV tray. Terrance ate pumpkin pie and vanilla ice cream as his main course. No one mentioned missing the game until Mr. Costa, sitting in his recliner, said that USC had won by two touchdowns. Both scored by Simpson.

Terrence said he was growing a goatee. Sarah thought it would take plenty work, and Mr. Costa said, "It'll take years."

"Quiet," Mrs Costa said. "Terrence, turn it to Channel 7. They'll have the war news."

"We can watch for David."

Sarah ate turkey while the Costa family stared at a reporter in army fatigues crouched under whirling helicopter blades. He pressed his helmet to his head as he shouted into a microphone. A battle was raging near the Cambodian border. The North Vietnamese had broken the New Year's truce, and the wounded were being evacuated.

Sarah watched men being lifted onto stretchers. A soldier knelt over something hidden under a green poncho. As the helicopter lifted off, the poncho fluttered to life and took flight, revealing….

Sarah turned away.

Mr. Costa said it was the army fighting, not the Marines, so David was safe.

The scene switched to a man in a business suit behind a desk in

New York City. Calmly, seriously, he reported nearly a half-million American soldiers in Vietnam.

Mrs. Costa turned off the TV.

After dinner, Sarah helped wash the dishes, then walked with Terrence and Mr. Costa to the end of the street. They stopped at a chainlink fence blocking a steep drop into the ocean. Mr. Costa lit an unfiltered Camel, and said, "Let me give you some advice."

"Oh, no," Terrence said.

Cigarette hanging from his lips, Mr. Costa rolled up his sleeve, revealing a hairy forearm. "You see this? Better remember it, Terrence Costa. You too, Sarah Costa."

Sarah saw a mermaid, with a swirling green tail and naked breasts, wrapped around three fading words: "Born to Love."

Smoke poured from his father's nose and mouth as he said, "That's my warning to you."

Sarah wasn't sure what he meant. "About love?"

"Of course not," Mr. Costa said. "About tattoos."

"Stop it, dad. Don't listen to him."

"I tell you," Mr. Costa said. "What you do when you're young stays with you. Like this tattoo stays with me. See how silly it looks on an old man? A grown man with a mermaid on his arm."

Sarah didn't understand. She liked tattoos. Not like her uncle's, but she liked tattoos.

"Anything else?" Terrence asked, knowing there was always something else.

"Study hard," Mr Costa said. "Work hard. And stay away from demonstrations and love-ins. No drugs or politics. And respect the police."

"I can do that," Sarah said.

"Wait. Most important…"

"Don't say it," Terrence begged.

"What?" Sarah asked.

Her uncle took a long drag on his cigarette and held it in. “Whatever else you do,” he said, “promise me this.” He exhaled long and slow. “Stay away from Miss Jane. You hear me? No tattoos and stay away from Miss Jane.”

“No problem,” Sarah said, searching the horizon, trying to see Hilo through chainlink. She didn’t know anyone named Miss Jane.

3. A GOOD SAMARITAN

Time: Spring, 1968
Location: San Francisco

Sarah held her breath as the Falcon jumped a speed hump and landed between two police vans. A sign stenciled on the cinderblock wall warned: “Parking For Emergency Vehicles Only.”

“Is this legal?” she asked.

“In an emergency,” Terrence said, resetting his Ray-Bans. “I’ll leave the key under the seat. The campus will be a mess today. If you need the car, it’s here. Don’t worry.”

Sarah wasn’t worried. She had survived five months at San Francisco State and was days away from completing her first semester. If anyone needed to worry, it was her cousin. He was smart and respectful, funny and easygoing, but loose around the edges. A film major one day, a journalist the next. Outgoing and secretive. Slipping off at night, returning early and quietly in the morning. Claiming to be a beatnik, then an anarchist. Discovering jazz, then rock and roll, back to jazz and classical, then country and folk. He was, as his father had warned, not someone who should tattoo a permanent message on his arm.

“Typical spring weather,” Terrence said, hefting his gear bag from the Falcon's trunk. As he started uphill, his shoulder sagged under its weight.

Sarah zipped her field jacket to her neck and pulled her watch cap over her ears. "What's in the bag?" she asked, falling in behind him.

"My lunch. Avoid the Quad today, and stay away from the Admin Building."

Sarah unzipped his bag and dug past notepads, candy bars, and two cameras before she found the Thunderbird. "For lunch?" she asked.

"The Nikon's for stills. The Kodak Super 8 for movies. Newest of the new."

"They look new. From a pawnshop in the Haight?"

"Not exactly. Why all the questions?" He zipped the bag shut and kept walking. "Synchronize watches. I have to be at work by 3. Or Miss Jane will kill me."

Sarah checked her watch, a Master Navigator, a Bulova her father had bought in 1946 and worn proudly until her high school graduation. "Like me," he had told her, "war surplus and made to exacting Government Specification."

Now it was 11:30. Cold and foggy. And Terrence was running uphill, through students in wool overcoats, flapping ponchos, and puffy down jackets. "Go the other way," he shouted back at her. "Skip the Quad."

From behind card tables, students thrust petitions at her.

"Admit minority students."

"Support the Black Student Union."

"Stop the war!"

"Impeach Reagan. Solidarity."

A heavy woman in a field jacket reached for her. "Sister, have you heard about the Orangeburg Massacre?"

A man in a suit and tie demanded, "Fight the radicals! Get LeRoi Jones off campus."

Sarah kept moving.

"Join the Students for a Democratic Society."

"Help the poor."

"Serve the people."

Most of them were older than Sarah. There were only 700 freshmen at SF State. The rest of the 20,000 students were what Terrence called "revolutionary job seekers." Transfers from city college splitting their lives between part-time work and part-time classes, chasing a degree that promised a decent job downtown.

A student nurse wearing a white uniform and a helmet with a Red Cross in a white circle handed Sarah a picture torn from a newspaper, a close-up of a South Vietnamese official pointing a .38-caliber pistol at his prisoner's head.

"We have to be human," the nurse begged. "We have to stop killing."

Sarah handed it back and followed Terrence's newsboy cap bobbing into a crowd at the center of the Quad. From the speaker's platform, a micro-phoned voice launched into a scratchy rendition of "Testing. Testing. Testing!" Followed by a clear call for "Solidarity. Peace. Serve the people!"

Behind Sarah, the nurse said, "The Panthers."

Terrence was climbing the steps to the platform, pointing his movie camera at six men dressed in black leather jackets.

"The FBI," the nurse said, pointing at two men near the crowd's edge.

Unlike the students, the two men looked as if they had stepped out of a Sears catalog in matching nylon windbreakers and Wright slacks. Their Giants baseball caps were a nice touch.

The crowd pushed Sarah into the arms of a young man wearing a black beret. He held her a second, smiled under his dark glasses, then hurried up the shaky steps, past Terrence, to the speaker's platform.

Terrence shot through a roll of film as two men forced him down the steps into Sarah. "I'm going to the sit-in at Admin!" he shouted, pointing her at the library. "You go that way."

Sarah tried, but the crowd caught her, turned her around, and swept her back to her cousin. When a man in a faded letterman's jacket knocked Terrence to the ground, she helped her cousin to his feet, slipped the heavy bag off his shoulder, and held it against her chest as a crush of students herded them up the steps and into the Administration Building. The doors slammed shut, trapping them in a hallway filled with shouting students.

"Sit in!"

"Sit in!"

"Sit in!"

"Everyone stay calm and peaceful. Don't break anything. The pigs will use it against us."

"This is for justice. Stay calm. Leadership this way."

Terrence held the Super-8 over his head, filming students sitting on the dean's desk.

"Get the pigs off campus!"

"Pigs out!"

The students shoved desks and chairs against the wall and sat crossed-legged on the floor. Chanting, "Admit minority students. 400! 400! 400!"

Terrence kept moving, dragging Sarah with him, until he found an empty room at the end of the hall. When he turned on the light, they faced a copy machine the size of a VW. "A Xerox 7000," Terrence said. "Prone to fires. I spent a semester of work-study with one." He pushed aside the curtains and forced open a window.

Sarah looked down at a man in dirty overalls and a black beret hiding behind a flimsy hedge.

"Hey," Terrence called down to him. "Can you give us a hand?"

The man pointed at two ranks of uniformed policemen as the first line shoved through students and the second line swept away the stragglers.

The man held up a shopping bag. "Take it," he said. "Give it to one of the brothers. I'm locked out."

Sarah leaned out while Terrence gripped her belt until she yelled, "Pull me up!"

They opened the bag and found two loaves of French bread and a thick salami. "Revolutionary groceries," Sarah said. "Toss in your Thunderbird."

"I'm staying," Terrence said. "You're going."

"No way."

"Can you cover for me at work? If I miss another day, Hathaway is going to fire me."

"Who?"

"Get on the ledge. Hurry! I told her all about you. She's a tall chick, skinny with long black hair, if she didn't dye it yesterday." He helped her climb onto the windowsill. Her heavy boots dangled in the air as Terrence said, "She's at Fleishhacker Pool. The second floor of the Bath House. Past the Zoo. You can't miss it. Tell her I sent you. Say you're my cousin."

"I am your cousin."

The grocery man looked up, and Sarah dropped into his arms.

They tumbled into the bushes. Found their knees, and saw riot police in black boots and cavalry pants.

"It's like Battleship Potemkin," the grocery man said. "The steps scene."

Sarah wondered what he was talking about. "Are you a Black Panther?" she asked.

The big man laughed. "Not me. I'm no hero." He took off his beret and stuffed it in a side pocket. "Nice meeting you, young lady. I'm heading back to Oakland. Thank your boyfriend for me."

"He's not my boyfriend."

"Good. Too skinny. But I like his hat."

"He's a journalist."

The big man smiled and shook his head. "Sure he is, and I'm Malcolm X."

Whistles blew, megaphones blasted orders to disperse. A woman holding a baby, both of them crying, ran by the bushes. A white helmet with a red cross rolled across the concrete. Sarah felt her grocery man from Oakland lean in close to say, "I'm running that way. When they come after me, you run the other way."

"It's the TAC Squad," Terrence shouted, movie camera to his eye.

Sarah watched the line of shiny black boots reach the sidewalk.

"Run, girlie," her rescuer from Oakland said, crashing out of the bushes.

A policeman heavy with riot gear pointed a baton. Three policemen broke from the line, chasing the revolutionary grocery man uphill.

"Stay where you are," Terrence shouted.

Sarah stood up, brushed off her jacket, and stepped out. With her back straight and head high, she walked into the double thick line of riot gear. "Excuse me, officers," she said. "Please, I'm late for class."

The lines parted, and she stepped through untouched, then glanced over her shoulder. Terrence waved from his window. Malcolm X was gone.

The Falcon was where Terrence had left it. Two motorcycle policemen were blocking the exit. They watched her walk downhill, climb into the Falcon, back it into a U-turn, and drive to the gate.

When she rolled down the window, the tall policeman said, "How's it going up there?"

Sarah shrugged. "It's a love-in."

The policeman laughed. "Funny. Where you going?" He checked the plates, looked in the back seat, said, "Could you open the trunk? Jerry, call in the plates."

"Give me a sec. I'm trying to light this smoke."

Sarah opened the trunk, and they stared down at a case of Anchor Steam Beer, a jug of Gallo wine, swim fins, two soggy bathing suits, three ex-large bags of tortilla chips, and a pile of damp beach towels.

"Looks like a party," the tall policeman said.

She smelled gun oil, leather and Aqua Velvet. She said, "Anchor Steam is the best."

"I'm a Hamms man." The policeman closed the trunk. "Sorry for the delay, ma'am. Things getting nasty these days. Hell, the other day we found a pipe bomb under one of our cruisers. You hear about that?"

Sarah shook her head. "You know the way to Flycatcher Pool?"

He laughed. "Fleishhacker Pool."

"That's it."

The policeman pointed toward the ocean. "Head for the Great Highway. You'll see the pool on the left. Can't miss it. Big pool by the zoo."

"She good," the smoker said and waved her through with an unlit cigarette.

4. MOONLIGHT AND SEA MONSTERS

Time: Spring 1968
Location: Fleishhacker Pool, SF

Cracked asphalt led to an outdoor pool long enough to float a cruise ship and a concrete bathhouse decorated with fake columns and sea monsters.

Aware of her promise to Mr Costa, Sarah parked in front of a hand-painted sign warning "No Entry!" But the doors next to it were unlocked, and a double-wide stairwell led to the second floor, where Sarah found a woman sitting behind a steel desk.

"Like it?" the woman asked, holding up a pink bathing cap decorated with plastic sunflowers. "I wear it to distract the kids. It keeps their tiny minds off the water temp." When she stood up, the woman's terry-cloth bathrobe fell open, revealing more than Sarah wanted to see. "You're Sarah, right? Terrence said you'd be coming."

"Miss Hathaway?"

"Never mind that. Call me Miss Jane if you like formal."

Sarah felt long fingers take her hand, apply slight pressure, then slip away. "It's your cousin's little joke from the TV show. A character in The Beverly Hillbillies?"

"No." Sarah shook her head.

"Wouldn't help." She spread her arms wide, revealing more of herself, including a tiny tattoo above her belly button. "See? I don't look anything like Miss Hathaway." She followed Sarah's eyes. "It's a peace sign. Brit language for Nuclear Disarmament. You're for peace, right?"

To change the subject, Sarah pointed at the initials embroidered on the robe's lapel. "PH?" she asked. "Your real name?"

"Oh, those. No." Miss Jane picked at a golden thread. "A present from Little Miss Rich, one of the volunteers. Donated to lost-and-found. Poor little Patti didn't like terry cloth."

Sarah smelled something burning. Miss Jane's office seemed to stretch forever, one side lined with blackboards, plastic tables, and folding chairs. The other side flooded with light from floor-to-ceiling windows. In the corner, a bathing suit was smoking on a rusty space heater. "Is that catching fire?" Sarah asked.

Miss Jane tossed her robe on the desk and rescued the smoking swimsuit. As she stepped into it, she asked, "See any burned spots?"

Sarah shook her head. The baggy suit, whatever its original color, had faded to grey and looked thick enough to be a sweater. "You can swim in that?" she asked.

"Hell, no. Who said anything about swimming? This is graduation day. Any minute, the kids will be swarming out there for their ritual dunking in ice water. Believe me. Count to ten. Count to ten. Turn blue."

"Terrence said the pool is heated."

"He's funny!" Miss Jane picked up a transistor radio. "It used to be. In the old days, the boilers could heat seawater to 75° in minutes, and the filters caught most of the dead fish. Not anymore."

"The pool is beautiful."

"It's a thousand-foot white elephant. No more 10,000 swimmers a day. Now we're down to toddlers blowing bubbles." She stretched the flowery cap over her thick black hair and tried a few sloppy jumping jacks. "Gotta get psyched up," she sang. "Cold is all in the head."

Sarah thought she might be 25, maybe 30. It was hard to tell with the goofy sunflower cap and the jumping jacks. "You should wear a wetsuit," Sarah said.

"While the kids shiver and shrink into raisins? Not cool. Terrence said you used to be a lifeguard? Was he telling the truth? He tries to."

"In high school."

"Did you rescue anybody?"

"Once. But not really. He was drunk and faking."

"Great. But you look fit. Wait." She dug through a cardboard box and dug out a bright red nylon one-piece. "No cooties. Take the suit and my robe. Sit in the highchair at the shallow end. By the old rescue boat that doubles as a flower pot."

She tossed the bathrobe to Sarah and ran down the stairs, shouting over her shoulder, "Don't let any of the kids wander off."

In Patti's robe, from the lifeguard chair at the shallow end, Sarah watched adults in heavy coats lead a line of squirming knee-high children wrapped in bright beach towels to the pool's edge.

Miss Jane, waiting for them in waist-deep seawater, waved to the first child, waved again. The boy threw off his towel and jumped into her arms. As Miss Jane backed into deeper water, she held the boy away from her, his face buried in the water. He kicked so violently that the parents had to step back to avoid being splashed. Miss Jane lifted him by his armpits, gave him a big smile, and cooed, "Count to ten." Then she let go, and the boy sank, blowing bubbles.

The parents chanted, "One, two, three." And the shivering girl next in line broke for freedom, running along the pool's edge toward the deep end, her towel flying behind her like Superman's cape.

To the sound of counting parents, Sarah jumped, ran, and scooped up the escapee. As she carried her back, she offered the advice her father had given her before dropping her into Kawamoto Pool. "Be a big girl. It's only water and it wants to play."

Later, after all the sinkers had survived their dunking and been cheered for surviving six weeks of basic hypothermia, Sarah and Miss Jane stood under cold showers. Sarah liked the room's dark green tile and twenty ancient shower heads, especially the two which worked.

"So tell me," Miss Jane said, rubbing dish soap into her long black hair. "Are you sleeping with him?"

"I'm not sleeping with anybody."

"Terrence?"

"That's not funny. He's my cousin."

"Not against the law in this state."

"He said you were his girlfriend."

"Now, that is funny. Has he asked you to help with his… What's he calling it this week?"

"Journalism. Not yet."

"Good. Don't do it. He's going to get himself in trouble." Miss Jane faced into the shower head, drank, then spit. "I heard you swam the cove."

"Not exactly." A week ago, when the water temperature had reached a surprising 60°, she had started off strong, veered slightly off course, made a sudden turn, lost track, and beached herself at the Maritime Museum. "He told you?" Sarah asked.

"He tells me everything."

"He talks too much. I'm freezing."

"That's for sure." Miss Jane stepped back from the cold water. "Wait for it," she said. "Wait." The shower heads coughed, choked, then blasted the two women with warm water. Miss Jane turned her back to it, letting it wash through her long black hair. "You'll like his brother," she said. "Your older cousin. Quiet. Very good looking." Hidden in steam, she said, "I love him. We're going to be married."

"Congratulations."

"If they don't kill him."

Miss Jane walked into the office wearing Levis, an SF State sweatshirt, and pink bedroom slippers. “Terrence called,” she said, tying her bun. “Your college president has resigned. Oh, and Terrence is in jail. No need to hurry. No worries. He’ll be out in the morning.”

“Should we call his parents?” Sarah asked.

“Are you kidding? Not me. They’d flip. I like them, but they don’t like me. Let’s have a drink. You can call later.”

“I’m not good at lying.”

“You’ll learn. Give it time. Let Terrence handle it.”

They sat on cots in the moldy first-aid room. Miss Jane drank Gallo wine from a paper cup while confessing that she had lived at the pool rent-free for the last two years. “Trying to save money for graduate school.”

“Saving is good,” Sarah said, zipping her field jacket.

“You’re right.” Miss Jane picked up a gallon jug and poured wine in a second cup. “Rents are going up. This used to be a blue-collar city.”

Sarah nodded. There was no need to explain. She understood rents.

Miss Jane said she wanted to be a social worker, which meant she'd have to rob a bank to stay alive. “It’s a vicious circle,” she said.

Sarah said she was looking for a job. Her aunt and uncle would let her live with them forever, but she didn’t feel right.

“You can live here. There’s plenty of room.”

To change the subject, Sarah said, “I met Malcolm X at school today.”

“You’re funny.” Miss Jane handed her a paper cup. “Drink up.”

Sarah tried her first sip of wine. Shaking her head, she left the cup on the desk.

As they climbed the stairs, Miss Jane said her last name was Mirikitani, then quickly added, “This city is crawling with ghosts.”

She stopped for a gulp of wine. "Not even they can find cheap rent," she said, climbing again. "Take Aquatic Park. The city needed room for housing, so they dug up thousands of bodies and dumped them in Colma. A mud flat south of here. Then they used the old tombstones to build the breakwater at Aquatic Park. No new houses, and you're swimming with dead people."

"In Hawaii…" Sarah said, wanting to tell Miss Jane about gravesites and construction crews. But Miss Jane cut her off, whispering, "Shhhhh. There's one living in the women's locker room. Follow me."

Miss Jane drank more wine as she climbed the stairs. And when they reached the roof, she walked to the edge and tossed her paper cup at the parking lot.

Sarah saw the ocean sparkling in foggy moonlight. A fire engine, then an ambulance rushed north along the Great Highway, their sirens singing.

"Out there," Miss Jane said, pointing at the sea. "A hospital ship on its way to the Korean War sank just outside the Golden Gate. In water so shallow, the rescuers could see it resting on the bottom. Thirty people drowned. They live there now."

Sarah's father had told her the same story, but Sarah didn't tell her new friend. She didn't want the memory mixed in with wine-talk. Instead, she gazed at the dark sea.

"Some nights I hear them crying," Miss Jane said.

Sarah closed her eyes and heard sirens.

5. FOG AND ICE

Time: December 24, 1968
Location: San Francisco

Years later, when the young woman asked how it felt to be alive in 1968, Sarah remembered flying downhill on a block of ice.

The young woman, a history teacher eager for answers, confessed that if she had been alive in 68, she would have marched against the war. Screamed at Nixon, cried for Kennedy and King, and voted twice for Shirley Chisholm. Had Sarah done anything like that?

Sarah wanted to tell her in 1968, the Public Health Service Hospital had seven stories. The morgue was in the basement. The Army research center on the top floor. And in between, there were nursing stations, operating rooms, and beds for 500 patients. Everything connected by linoleum and marble floors that needed to be scrubbed and made to sparkle by Sarah Costa, mop in hand, drawing soapy figure eights.

Enjoying the memory, Sarah let herself run by the red-letter warning on the research center's door: "Restricted Area. No Admittance." Sweating in jeans and field jacket, she hurried down the hall to the emergency exit, stepped out, and zigzagged down the fire escape.

Miss Jane was waiting for her in the parking lot, dressed in her holiday attire: Chuck Taylor high tops, a new pair of bedazzled jeans, and a thick orange SF State hoodie. “For completing two semesters with perfect attendance,” Miss Jane said, hugging her friend, “the new college president sent you a Christmas present.”

“They do that?”

“Not really. But as your reward, Governor Raygun’s stooge closed the campus to keep everyone safe from an education. No more wading through angry demonstrators and equally angry policemen.”

Sarah didn’t care about the new college administrator or the cowboy actor who had turned governor. They could do whatever they wanted as long as she had a job and they didn’t interfere with her plans. “Who’s this?” she asked as the Falcon’s radio jumped into something rocky, ragged and repetitive.

“Grateful Dead.”

“Do they ever stop?”

“When you’re grateful to be dead.” Miss Jane zipped up her hoodie. “Which reminds me. We’re parked on a mass grave. Back in the day…”

“My supervisor told me.”

“I’d like to meet her. Do you know anything about that research center on the top floor?”

“I mop floors, mostly in the maternity ward. We got babies. Plenty of babies.”

“Really? Because I’ve been thinking about babies.” Miss Jane scratched her head, thought for a moment, then whispered, “Do you think you can sneak me into the Research Center? If not, I’ll take a peek at the babies.”

The hospital’s back door swung open, and Terrence stepped out, shoving a shopping cart down the loading dock, his trench coat flapping in the wind. Sarah blocked the cart before he crashed it into the Falcon.

"Three 35-pound blocks," he said. "Can't find them anywhere else in the city. I got a friend in the kitchen."

While Sarah lifted three blocks of ice into the car's trunk. Jane snatched a greasy brown bag from the cart and peeled it open. "Donuts? What, no apple fritters?"

"All gone," Terrence said. "Those nurses eat lots of fritters."

Miss Jane rode shotgun, Sarah sat in the back, and Terrence swung a U-turn out of the parking lot and into the fog. "We've got ice," he said, "a dozen donuts and plenty of booze. It's a party."

Miss Jane produced a jug of red wine. "Gallo Hearty Burgundy. A buck and a quarter a gallon. Hey, stop. We're going the wrong way."

"So soon?" Terrence said.

Sarah pulled her watch cap over her ears as the Grateful Dead continued to repeat.

"Lost already?" Miss Jane asked. "When was the last time you went icing?"

"The night David enlisted." Terrence turned on the high beams, and the fog threw the light back at him.

"Turn around," Miss Jane said.

Sarah rolled down the window and inhaled pine trees as the Falcon crossed the double-yellow line, turned left, then right, and drove down a narrow road, hitting potholes and tree roots before it stopped. Lines of white headstones quivered in the moonlight.

"The National Cemetery," Miss Jane said. "You brought David here to celebrate?"

"No way. I must've missed a turn."

"I'd like to be buried here," Terrence said

"Now?" Miss Jane asked.

"We should leave them in peace," Sarah said.

"Agreed."

"Agreed."

They drove in and out of the fog, picking up speed, crossing busy roads. The headlights gave way to shadows and wooden buildings boarded by chain-link fences. Miss Jane lit a fat joint and said, “The Presidio.”

“No way. I didn’t see any gates. Can’t be.”

“The Presidio.”

“No way,” he said, a second before an MP with his hand raised stepped in front of the Falcon. Terrence hit the brakes, Miss Jane tossed her joint out the window, and the MP rested his hand on the holster at his hip.

Behind him, a chain-link fence topped with barbed wire surrounded two buildings with bars on the windows. Above the gate, a sign claimed: “OBEDIENCE TO THE LAW IS FREEDOM.” The MP motioned for Terrence to roll down his window.

“I want a picture of that sign,” Miss Jane said, reaching under the seat. “Where’s the camera?”

“Stop it,” Terrence hissed.

The MP pointed his flashlight into the Falcon.

“Good evening, corporal,” Terrence said. “Sorry, we’re lost. The fog, you know. Where are we?”

“The Presidio Stockade.” He eyed Miss Jane, pointed the flashlight at Sarah, and asked, "What are you doing here?”

“Looking for a golf course,” Sarah said.

“At this time of night?”

“Icing,” Terrence said with a smile.

From the guardhouse, a thin soldier stepped into the light, the single bar on his cap flashing gold. “Get those civilians out of here,” he ordered. “Now, corporal!”

Ms Jane pressed the Instamatic’s shutter release, and Sarah saw the flash bleach the lieutenant’s face white. “Go!” he shouted.

A series of jagged S-turns led to foggy silence. Miss Jane screwed the top down tight on the wine jug. Sarah felt the Falcon shudder as they passed a tiny church with a proud little steeple and a larger-than-life-size nativity scene. On the radio, Otis Redding was singing about a dock on the bay.

Terrence said, "They shot a prisoner back there a few months ago."

"Shot?" Miss Jane said.

"Dead," Terence said. "A deserter,"

"Dead?" Miss Jane said.

They passed a long row of two-story apartments that looked tired and rundown, "Military housing," Miss Jane said.

Terrence pressed forward into a well-lit neighborhood of huge homes balanced at the edge of a steep cliff. "Sea Cliff," Terrence said.

Sarah was lost. She had learned her way around the city by riding the Muni, the city's mixture of streetcars, buses, and cable cars. But none of them had taken her this way, where a fat Santa pointed at a gaudy pile of presents under a sparkling Christmas tree.

After a few turns, a straightaway, and more turns, Terrence found a lonely road lined by pine trees. On the radio, Lesley Gore started to sing about a party, her party.

"This, my friends," Terrence said, "is the most exclusive golf course in San Francisco."

"And only took two hours to find it," Miss Jane said.

He parked on the narrow shoulder, scratched his wispy goatee, and said, "Don't worry. I'm a member."

They unloaded ice blocks and shoved them through the pine trees onto a grassy slope. Terrence went back for the donuts, Miss Jane for the wine, and Sarah for strips of cardboard.

Terrence said that Sarah should start with the bunny slope. Or she could live dangerously and take the pro course. "It's steeper. You can always bale out in the sand trap," he laughed.

"You've done this before?" Sarah asked.

"Sure. With David." Terrence tilted the wine jug back, swallowed three times, and handed it to Miss Jane.

"On the other side of the road," Miss Jane said, "is the Legion of Honor. When they were digging the foundation, they found a grave with 800 bodies."

"Let's ride," Sarah said.

They stood around Terrence's block of ice. "First," he said, "place the cardboard on the ice to keep your butt dry. Then sit on the cardboard with legs straight, feet off the ground, and we push. You'll be icing. But first, more wine."

They passed the jug while Sarah used the Instamatic to click a shot of her two friends. "How do I stop?" she asked.

"You can't," Terrence said.

"Drag your feet," Miss Jane said. "If all else fails, roll off and let the ice go," Miss Jane said.

Terrence rolled down the Falcon's windows and turned the car radio as loud as the knob would go, sending a deep-throated voice into the night, promising they were minutes away from the extended version of the Grateful Dead's Dark Star.

Sarah reached for her ice.

"Wait. Me first." After two jumping jacks followed by a long drag off a joint, Terrence said, "Okay, sisters, check this out." He pressed his chest to his block of ice, straightened his legs, and flapped his arms like wings. "Launch me, ladies!"

Miss Jane and Sarah each grabbed a wrist, tugged, ran, slipped and launched Terrence downhill, belly-boarding into a strip of fog, screaming, flying toward the trees at the cliff's edge.

"The little brother," Miss Jane said.

Picking up speed, Terrence grabbed at the grass and dragged his legs. Held on and rolled, shooting his block of ice at the cliff

Sarah watched it hit a tree, bounce off and skid to a stop.

"Is he hurt?" Sarah asked as Miss Jane held her back.

Terrence struggled to his feet, raised his hands over his head, and shouted, "That's living. You hear me? Living!"

"I prefer a more sophisticated approach," Miss Jane said. She positioned her cardboard, sat on it, and crossed her legs. Lifting her feet off the ground, she shouted, "Sarah, initiate thrust."

After a hard shove and a short run, Sarah sent her friend flying downhill and watched her gracefully navigate between two sand traps, angled right, picked up speed, dragged an arm, and coasted to a gentle stop on the green, stood up and offered a beauty queen's wave.

Sarah shook off the cold. Opted for bare ice. And felt Terrence's boney fingers dig into her shoulders as he rushed her downhill, laughing. When he let go, she flew by Miss Jane. Picked up speed. Flew through fog. Heard waves breaking against the rocks, closed her eyes and leaped into the night.

Would the young history teacher understand that? Could she see them standing by the old Falcon? Hear Terrence saying, "You gotta be careful, cuz. You could've been killed." See him stick a tiny pink candle in a maple bar and say, "Stand here. I'll take the shot. You and Miss Jane holding it. And don't blow out the candle until I tell you."

"Make a wish, birthday girl," Miss Jane said.

The candle flickered, held, then blinked out.

"No worries," Sarah said. "I made my wish."

6. FIRST SIGHTINGS

Time: October 11, 1969
Location: San Francisco

Ten months later, Sarah was struggling to escape the wetsuit she had rescued from a garage sale. The thick neoprene fit her like a strait-jacket, so Ms Jane had to stand behind her and tug at the rubber neckline until Sarah could break free.

“What was that?” Sarah asked, toes digging into the wet sand to hold her steady.

They had been surfing off Golden Gate Park. A long paddle in a strong rip had carried them to deep water, where they had stopped to catch their breath. Straddling their boards, feet dangling in dark water, they had felt the ocean moving thick and slow as the whale broke the surface between them, its curving back spraying sunlight before slipping under as quickly as it had appeared.

"What was what? Never seen a whale?" Ms Jane asked, tugging the thick rubber off Sarah’s shoulders.

"Yes. Humpbacks. Beautiful. But not that."

"A Grey. On its way south.

The fighting whale, but it's cool, won't touch you."

"Not that," Sarah said, jerking one arm free, then the other. "I mean, you crossed yourself.".

"Five years of Catholic school," Ms Jane said. "A reflex. Funny."

"St Joseph's School for me."

Sarah hefted David's longboard onto her shoulder and followed Ms Jane across soft sand to the parking lot. As they shoved their boards onto the Falcon's rusty racks, Ms Jane said, "I don't believe any of it."

"Me neither," Sarah said. "I think."

"What does that mean?"

"I'm not sure." Sarah wrapped herself in a beach towel, sat in the Falcon's back seat, and tried to think. Her two friends sat up front, sharing a hot dog for breakfast. She wasn't surprised. For two years, she had been watching them eat whatever was within easy reach. But now she was studying to be a nurse, so she said, "Hot dogs will kill you."

"The sooner, the better." Ms Jane found a half pint of Jim Beam in the glove compartment, gave it a long look, then shoved it under the seat. "I have to keep my wits about me," she said. "The Zodiac is still looking for slaves to serve him in the afterlife."

Terrence handed Sarah a greasy paper bag. "Try this."

"What?"

"It's-It," Ms Jane said through a mouth full of hot dog and bread. "Ice cream sandwich."

"You hodads," Sarah said. "Ice cream for breakfast?"

"Not just ice cream," Terrence said. "It's It. The San Francisco treat. Can't find it anywhere else but Playland. Right across the street."

Ms Jane closed her eyes and moaned, "Dark chocolate, oatmeal cookies and vanilla ice cream."

Sarah bit off a tiny piece of frozen, sugary, fatty, empty calories as a DJ on KSAN reported that President Nixon, their 37th President, had a plan for peace with honor.

"He'll get us all killed," Ms Jane said.

Sarah bit into chocolate ice cream and cookie dough.

"I'll take peace without honor," Ms Jane said. "How bad can it be? You'd feel bummed out for days or weeks or years, then you're fine. You're alive. And you didn't kill anybody."

"What about your honor?" Terrance asked.

"I've managed without honor so far."

"What about the communists?"

"Live and let live," Ms Jane said. "Unless they're coming for my ice cream or hot dogs. That's where I draw the line."

The breakfast of champions, Sarah whispered to herself and bit into It.

Two hours later, soapy clean in fresh Levis and her blue palaka shirt, Sarah was standing at a jewelry counter, while a short, stocky clerk with a flattop and thick glasses tried to hand her a watch.

"Funky name, right?" he said. "The Zodiac. That's why it's on sale."

Sarah turned and headed for the door.

"Forget the name. It's waterproof," he added quickly. "At $160, you can't beat it."

"Sorry, excuse me. Just looking." She waved goodbye and found Terrence next door at Frank's Coffee Shop. "You're crazy," she said and sat down across from him in a red vinyl booth.

"It's not him."

Terrence leafed through a Zap comix and asked, "Did you see the Zodiac?"

"I saw a man selling Zodiac watches." She tore the flimsy mag from him, flipped through the faded pages, and tossed it back. "What's so funny about bushy beards and funky feet?"

"I'm thinking, Nurse Sarah."

A bright red motorcycle hopped the curb and stopped on the side-walk. Ms Jane swung her leg over the gas tank, wearing black jeans, a leather jacket, and a black beret, and stepped into Frank's. "Why this place?" she asked, dropping into the booth beside Terrence. "It smells like the pool's locker room.

And the only other guy is behind the register."

"That's why I picked it," Terrence said.

"He thinks the jeweler could be the Zodiac."

"No way."

"I don't joke about that sicko," Terrence said.

Ms Jane looked up to see the counterman offering her a black coffee. "Not you, honey," she said. "He's talking about the guy next door."

"You mean the Zodiac?" the counterman said.

"Do you have ice cream? It's-It?" Sarah asked.

"What? Sorry. No." The counterman turned to Ms Jane. "Nice bike, sister."

"Try Ms Jane," she said.

"A 450, right, Ms Jane? The CL? You take it off-road?"

"Give us some room," Terrence said. "I've been thinking."

The counterman left, and Ms Jane reached inside her leather jacket and offered Terrence a half pint of Jim Beam. "This might help. Beam you up."

"Where'd you get that?"

"It's yours."

Terrence waved it off. "When David comes home," he said, "I promise not to talk about serial killers."

"He's seen enough of them in Vietnam," Ms. Jane said.

"That's different."

"They're going to try Lieutenant William Calley for 21murders," Ms Jane said. "It's not serial, but it's mass."

"Who?" Sarah asked

"Calley," Ms Jane said.

"You can't be convicted of murder during a war," Terrence said. "Everybody is already murdering everybody. Think about it."

Sarah tried. Ms Jane shook her head. Then Terrence followed a gulp of strong black coffee with mental stimulation. "When David comes homes, we'll swim from Alcatraz. The four of us. That should help him forget the war."

"If the Indians don't occupy the island," Ms Jane said.

"Never happen. The Feds will be all over that."

"Indians?" Sarah asked.

"To Alcatraz," Terrence said, lifting his coffee cup.

"To good stuff," Ms Jane said.

"It's It," Sarah said.

From the back of the motorcycle, Sarah hugged Ms Jane so she could see over her shoulder. The wind in her face was a bonus.

"I got to get out of here," Ms Jane yelled, darting the Honda past a trolley car, up a hill, and down a winding road to a cross street blocked by demonstrators. "This city is driving me crazy."

As Ms Jane zigged and zagged through the crowd, Sarah smelled marijuana smoke, closed her eyes as they sped by a line of police cars, and opened them as the motorcycle roared into a tunnel that led to Aquatic Park.

Terrence was waiting at the Maritime Museum, filming the front line of the protest march. Men in Army fatigues and a woman in the blue-and-white uniform of a navy nurse marched under a banner calling for peace. Behind them, protestors shouted, "Stop the war! Peace! Free our brothers. Free the Presidio 27. Stop the war."

Ms Jane turned off the engine and tossed Sarah the keys. "Take it home," she shouted and blended into the marchers, chanting with them, "Peace! Peace! Peace! Hell no, we won't go!"

Under dark skies filled with the promise of rain, Sarah walked to the Dolphin Club's dock, sat down, and closed her eyes, waiting for quiet.

That night at Fleischhacker, in the empty classroom Sarah had been renting as a bedroom, Sarah stuffed her microbiology textbook into a backpack. Then she rode Ms Jane's motorcycle up Balboa to Arguello, turned left, and kept going until she found Julius Kahn Park.

She liked this little park in the Heights. It was her discovery. And she enjoyed sitting at the top of the rusty slide, wondering what it would cost to live in the townhouse neighborhood facing the Presidio.

On a nurse's salary, she could do it. Maybe. If she worked hard.

She was sitting there when a dark figure ran from townhouse shadows, crossed the street, and stopped to look back. Then turned and ran by the slide toward the Presidio's trees.

Sirens broke the night as a police car swept a circle of light along the townhouses. When it was gone, two long hairs in bell bottoms hurried across the street and stopped at Sarah's slide.

The woman was wearing a poncho, the man an army field jacket. He cupped his hands in front of his face. The woman leaned into him and struck a match. "That scared the shit out of me," she said.

"Bummers." He inhaled the joint to life.

"Did you see the poor guy, the taxi guy?"

He blew smoke, nodded. "Couldn't miss it."

They looked back at the street.

"My first body," the woman said.

The man coughed smoke.

"You must've seen them in Vietnam," the woman said.

Sarah noticed the man's black combat boots.

"I was lucky. In supply," he said. "In air-conditioning. Only saw body bags."

They passed the joint back and forth, back and forth, silent until the woman yelped, "Ouch. Burned my lip!" She dropped the roach and pressed it into the grass with her bare foot. "I wish we didn't see that body."

"Zodiac," the man said. "I bet it was the Zodiac. Let's go."

Certain they were headed for the ocean, not the trees, Sarah slid down to Ms Jane's motorcycle and rode into the Heights. She stopped at the intersection where three policemen were huddled near a parked taxi. The driver-side door was open, a man's body hanging out, his fingers touching blood in the street. The police waved at her to keep going.

Days later, she read in the Chronicle that the taxi driver's name was Paul Stine, 29, a graduate student at San Francisco State, studying to be an English teacher. He had been shot in the head. A Zodiac victim.

Sarah crossed herself.

7. NO ESCAPE FROM ALCATRAZ

Time: January 1970
Location: San Francisco Bay

"We're here," Terrence said.

Ms Jane kept rowing, and Sarah rowed with her, deep strokes along a rocky shoreline. Past a cement wall, abandoned foundations, and a watchtower, they rowed in the morning fog.

David woke up in the stern of the Whitehall. He had arrived that morning with assurances that his doctor had cleared him for light duty. His orders would arrive in a matter of days if not weeks. He was taller than his brother, with dark eyes and a gentle smile, but Sarah thought him too thin for his frame.

When Ms Jane first saw him, she had bear-hugged him, kissed him on both cheeks, and stepped back to ask, "What? They don't have sun in Vietnam?" She had reached under his sweatshirt, felt his ribs, then turned to Sarah. "What do you think, Nurse Sarah? Maybe we should beef him up for a few weeks before he tries this."

"It's up to him," Sarah had heard herself say. Now they were gliding over dark water in the middle of the bay.

"How far are you going?" Terrence asked, standing in the bow, rocking the boat. "The Indians. Remember?"

"Sit down. I know what I'm doing." Ms Jane stopped rowing and let the boat drift. Sarah heard voices, something slipping into the water. A seal? Then Ms Jane whispered, "Ship oars." And the boat brushed along a buffer of old tires hanging from a cement dock. "We're here."

A circle of foggy light fell on a spray-painted sign: "Indians Welcome." Below it, "Government Property!" had been crossed out and replaced with "Indian Property."

A man's voice shouted, "Indians?"

"Not today," Ms Jane called back. "Only swimmers."

"This is Indian land."

Closer now, Sarah saw three men in jeans and field jackets.

Ms Jane called, "We're here to pick up a friend."

"That's me." A tall woman in army fatigues and a leather jacket stepped out of the fog. "Over here."

Sarah held the boat steady and watched the woman toss her gear bag to Terrence. She took off her cowboy boats and, with a camera swinging from her neck, dropped into David's arms.

"Whose this?" Terrence asked.

"Lois Lane," she said. "Photo-journalist."

"Is that your real name?"

"Close enough. And you must be the little brother."

"She's with me," Ms Jane said, using an oar to push the boat away from the dock. Sarah pulled hard on her left to point the bow at the city.

"Thank you," the journalist shouted at the dock, then turned to Ms Jane. "And to you. Mucho thanks, sister. It's harder to get off that island than it is to get on it." She offered David a silver flask. "For luck."

"Maybe later."

The journalist shrugged. "It helps," she said and swallowed twice.

"It'll be light soon," Ms Jane said.

Terrence checked his watch. "Plenty of time. Twenty-five

minutes before the tide shifts. Fifteen minutes more before it really moves."

Lois Lane capped the flask and squinted into the fog. "The Coasties usually show up around seven to circle the island. Man, this fog is thick." She pointed her Nikon at David, asked, "Mind if I get a few pics?" And clicked off three shots before he had a chance to say no.

"Why did the Indians let you on the island?" Terrence asked.

"It's not an island," she said. "It's an idea. That's what they told me."

"You're not an Indian," Terrence said.

"Thanks for telling me." She turned to David. "You must be the older brother, right? Back from the Nam. How's the world treating you?"

"None of your business," Terrence said.

They drifted into the fog as Ms Jane handed the journalist her flowered swim cap. "For luck," she said. "You'll need it. The water's 55."

"No problem."

Sarah watched David strip down to khaki swim trunks and saw the fresh scar from his knee to upper thigh.

"Coasties. Tide. Hurry," Ms Jane said.

The journalist passed her camera to Terrence, asked him to stash it in her gear bag, then, still holding the swim cap, stripped down to a heavy grey bathing suit with Fleishhacker Pool stenciled across its chest.

Terrence held up a short-barreled revolver. "What's this?

Lois shrugged, her skin turning blue. "A little souvenir from Vietnam." She tugged the flowered cap over her ears. "It's freezing."

"Funny souvenir," Terrence said.

"It's my lucky charm, college boy. I was in country for 10 months. Your brother understands."

"Where?" David asked.

"With Ewell's 9th in the Delta. Did some time with the Americal in Son Tinh."

"It's a .38. Not loaded," Terrence said, still holding the revolver.

"Snoopy, aren't you, little man?" the journalist said. "Toss it in the bay. I don't need it anymore. I've been waiting for a chance to dump it."

Ms Jane grabbed the gun and the gear bag. "Listen up," she said. "If you can't keep up, I'll haul the straggler out and catch you later. The fog should burn off soon." She checked her watch. "You've got twenty-five minutes."

Sarah strapped on her goggles.

David and the journalist slipped over the stern and disappeared under the black water. Terrence dove off the bow, rocking the boat. They surfaced a few yards from the boat, the journalist spitting water, David eggbeater kicking until his chest was out of the water. "I think I see the Ghirardelli light," he shouted.

Sarah jumped in. Water rushed up her nylon suit, pressed against her chest. When she surfaced, she spit into her goggles, rinsed them with salt water.

"Line up," Ms Jane ordered. "No cheating, Terrence."

"See you in 20 minutes." Terrence ducked underwater and came up stroking toward the city. David nodded to Sarah and Lois, then he swam after his brother. The journalist held out her hand to Sarah. "Good luck, honey."

"You've been drinking," Sarah said. "You won't make it."

"Geronimo!" the journalist shouted, stuck her face in the water, and popped up, smiling. "I mean Geronimo in a good way, a respectful way. Don't worry about me." She stuck her face in the water, tried three wild three strokes, and rolled on her back, screaming, "Jesus, it's fricken freezing!"

The brothers were three body lengths ahead of them, swimming along the fog's edge. Sarah buried her face in the water and swam with long easy strokes, trying to control her breathing and set a steady pace, forgetting the cold and her hands disappearing into the murky water. When she looked up, the journalist was spitting water and yelling, "Jesus, those boys are fast."

"Don't worry about them," Sarah shouted. "They'll burn out. Stay close."

"Thanks."

"This way."

"I can't see a thing."

"I'm following them."

"Go. I'm right behind you."

Sarah felt strong. The row out had helped, and the cold water was pumping her full of adrenaline. But she forced herself to go easy, settle into a steady rhythm and breathe every third stroke to save her strength. She relaxed her arms during recovery, keeping her elbow high, reaching long and pulling hard, not letting the cold rush her.

When she looked up, Terrence was leading. David, a few yards back, was shouting something at his brother. Terrence kept swimming, heading straight for the blue glow of Ghirardelli, gambling that the shortest course would be the fastest. If he wasn't quick enough, he'd have to fight the tide or miss the opening and be carried out the Golden Gate.

She looked back, saw the journalist wave. Where was Ms Jane? Way back, a white cutter with red running lights was skirting the fog. The journalist waved again, tried a few strokes, stopped and waved.

"Shoots," Sarah said as she felt the tide waking up, pushing her, telling her to hurry. David was swimming toward her, head up, lifeguard style, keeping his eye on her and kicking hard. "Can you catch him?" he shouted.

"No problem."

"He's too fast for me," David said. "Can't catch him. He'll miss the opening." For a second, they were face to face. "I'll go back for her," he said, then ducked under and swam toward the struggling journalist.

Sarah turned to the shore. "Shoots," she said, searching for Terrence. Shoots! She buried her face in the murky, oily, stinky water and swam hard and fast. Shoots!

8. OPIHI PICKERS

Time: January 1970
Location: Underwater

Years later, Sarah could still see David standing at the nurses' station, back straight, almost at attention. Part Marine with a buzz cut, part civilian in a striped rugby shirt, loose Levis, and Vans deck shoes.

The doctors passed without comment. The nurses offered quick smiles as David apologized for being the messenger. Their abalone trip was off. His brother had run off with Jane and Lois Lane to interview a radical pastor in Ukiah. Someone named Jim Jones.

"They didn't invite you?"

"Not my idea of fun. And you?"

"They know better," Sarah said, thankful that Lois Lane had finally been useful.

David hesitated. "If you like," he offered, "we could take the Falcon. There's plenty of gear, enough food for weeks. Jane begged me to go. She wants me to pick up two bottles of her favorite Brut. From the source, whatever that means. She said you'd know."

"I do," Sarah said. "And I can help with the driving."

On the drive over the Golden Gate, Sarah watched sailboats circling Alcatraz.

David said, “It was my fault. I should never have tried it.”

“You saved Lois.”

They were over the bridge when David said, “I was going back no matter what. I couldn’t finish. Thanks for taking care of my brother. He’s like me. Gets carried away. You know?”

“I know. I mean, I know him.”

David laughed and told her how difficult it had been for Jane and him to lift Lois Lane into the boat. “She recovered fast enough when the Coasties arrived. Asked them what they thought about the occupation of Alcatraz. Snapped pictures.”

“Did Jane still have the gun?”

“Thanks for taking care of my brother.”

“I tried.”

Sarah had caught Terrence easily enough, but he had refused to change course, so she had ridden the tide with him, past the cove, the World War II warehouses, and the Marina, where a tiny sailboat had saved. “An auntie saved us,” she said, “in a Sabot.”

“A wooden shoe?”

Sarah nodded. “We had to hang off the sides.”

“Terrence told me you caught a ride.”

“If you call being dragged to shore by an eight-foot sailboat, inch by inch, a ride. We’ll do better next time. When you get back.”

“When I get back.”

They passed the houseboats at Sausalito and the prison at San Quentin before David said he wished he had a second chance. He’d be a corpsman, a combat medic. He had met some great nurses in Nam. “You picked a good profession.”

“Mopping floors?”

“I mean it. Good as in doing good. Saving people.”

In silence, David followed the highway to Santa Rosa, turned left, and left Napa behind. They drove along the Russian River until he pointed at a break in the trees. "That poor man's wine country," he said. The infamous Korbel Winery."

A tour guide, a young woman who looked too young to drink, led them to a cool cellar full of champagne bottles. "These bottles will be flipped over by a machine to bring the yeast to the top, where it can be siphoned off." At the door to the tasting room, she told them that Korbel had been brewing champagne in the bottle since 1882. "To keep the price reasonable, ladies and gentlemen. In California, that's a challenge we have met."

At a table for two, Sarah sat across from David while he tasted two glasses, one Brut, one Extra Dry. He said he liked Coors better. Sarah told him Adolf Coors was on Ms Jane's blacklist. "Good for her. I'll switch. Any beer is fine." He paid $12 for two bottles of Brut and said, "I love Miss Jane."

They waved goodbye to the winery and followed the Russian River to the ocean. Turned north and reached Fort Ross in the dark. David said he knew the way with his eyes closed. He parked so close to the ocean Sarah could feel it inside her.

"Let's see what we have," David said, opening the Falcon's trunk.

Sarah saw sleeping bags, wetsuits, goodie bags, snorkels, weight belts, and a cooler. When she opened it, she sighed and shook her head. "Terrence must've done the shopping." There were two six-packs of Coors, a loaf of white bread, two pounds of bologna, and a family pack of chocolate-covered donuts.

That night, they sat on the cooler, eating bologna sandwiches washed down with Coors. After a chocolate donut, David described the dive site, starting with the beauty of kelp beds. "It's a rugged shoreline with limited entry and exit points," he said. "So stick close to me. And there could be sharks. We'll stay shallow, but sometimes the Whites come in close to hunt seals.

Sarah nodded. She wasn't afraid. She had seen plenty of Tigers in Hawaii.

She slept on the Falcon's back seat, wrapped in a Merry-

Christmas turtleneck she had found under a pile of swim fins. It smelled of cigarette smoke and reached to her knees, but it fit under her field jacket and kept her warm. David, wrapped in his brother's sleeping bag, slept outside in the moonlight.

After a breakfast of chocolate donuts and chocolate milk, David held up his abalone iron, a leaf spring cut to twelve inches with black tape wrapped around one end for a handle. "The key," he said, "is to slip the iron under the shell before they clamp down."

"I can do that," Sarah said, telling him that her father had taken her to his secret trail in Hamakua when she was nine. They'd slept in the car and climbed down the cliff face in the morning to scoop Opihi off the rocks with a butter knife. "The waves never caught us."

"With a butter knife?"

"Plenty for Little china hats, no bigger than a quarter. We'd eat them raw. Little brothers to abalone. Taste like butter."

"Sounds dangerous."

"Not for us."

"Here, you have to measure first. See if the abalone meets the limit, about the length of my hand." He handed her the ab iron. "See? It's marked on the iron. Be gentle. If they clamp down, you'll have a hell of a time peeling them off the rock without injuring them."

Sarah thought he was kidding her.

"If you cut into the abalone," David said, "it'll bleed to death, and if it's under seven inches, you can't bag it. Best to measure before you pop it. Keep it alive until you're ready to eat."

"Got it. Will do." Sarah turned her back to him as she squeezed into her wetsuit. It was her surfer suit, thick and buoyant, so she needed ten pounds of lead on her weight belt to help her stay down.

"That should do it," David said.

Terrence had borrowed his father's old hood, used once years ago before being tossed in the attic. It was a loose fit for Sarah, but better than nothing. To keep her feet warm, she wore her surf booties. And to protect her hands, she wore a pair of Ms Jane's motorcycle gloves. David showed her how to sterilize his father's old snorkel by blowing beer through it.

Years later, when the young history teacher asked about the men "in those days," Sarah saw David carrying his fins and goodie bag across the rocky beach. At the water, he checked her weight belt to see if it could be released quickly and told her she was lucky. He had never seen the ocean this calm, not even during the summer. "The kelp beds can be like spider webs," he said. "If they latch on to you, stay calm, don't twist and turn. Make a hole with your hand as you kick slowly to the surface. The kelp will open up if you treat it right."

Holding her fins, she stepped between softball-size rocks slippery with kelp. When she was knee deep, she stretched out flat and pulled herself along the rocks until she could slip her feet into her fins, bite down on the snorkel, and kick to deeper water.

When David jack-knifed through the canopy of kelp, she followed him, pinching her nose to equalize the pressure. At the bottom, she grabbed a rock and looked up at the light cascading through the kelp, making stained-glass windows like in a church, like St. Joe's underwater.

David reached between a crevice, pried loose two abalones, and kicked slowly through kelp branches and spinning otters until he reached the surface.

She kicked along the bottom until she found an abalone in the open, jammed her iron bar under the shell, and popped it free. As she kicked for the surface, short on air, remembering to measure, she let the ab drop through the kelp.

At the surface, David spit out his snorkel. "I've got two big ones," he said. "We better head in. The seals are on the rocks."

"You go." Sarah sucked air through the snorkel, then jack-knifed into the kelp. When she reached the abalone, she measured it, then looked up. From an opening in the kelp, from a circle of sunlight, David peered down at her, signaling an OK? She held up the abalone and kicked for the surface.

That night in the moonlight by the campfire, they drank champagne from the bottle. Held pieces of abalone flesh over the fire. And let it melt in their mouths like butter while the ocean broke against the rocks, salty, rich, and dangerous.

9. ISLAND OF ANGELS

Time: February 16, 1970
Location: San Francisco

Ms Jane offered Sarah a pair of red bell bottoms and a see-through turtleneck blouse. "Guaranteed just like Janis Joplin's."

Sarah opted for thick socks, jungle boots, a clean pair of Levis, and her blue palaka shirt. In her canvas pack, she carried a pound of Monterey Jack cheese, a miniature salami, a loaf of sourdough, and two apples. Ms Jane added a bottle of Zinfandel and a corkscrew.

At the door, she handed Sarah two tickets for the ferry to Angel Island. "They're good for today. One of my sistahs is working." She pressed a manila envelope into Sarah's hand. "Give this to our friend Lois. She'll be at Ayala Cove." The envelope was addressed to Ms Lois Smith, Vancouver, Canada.

Sarah folded the envelope, stuffed it inside her field jacket, and climbed into the VW bus. She was turning the key when Ms Jane reached through the window, offered a neatly rolled joint, gave up, and tucked it behind her ear. "Talk to him," she said. "He trusts you. He'll listen to you. Don't let him go."

Sarah slid the window shut.

Three wrong turns later, one of them that led to the Golden Gate

Bridge, Sarah found David waiting patiently on the steps to Lettermen Hospital. He ran to the VW, his rugby shirt buttoned to his neck and his jeans hanging loose over black boots. As he climbed in, he smiled at Sarah, then slipped off his sunglasses.

"What did the doctor say?" she asked.

"Army doctors. They're a trip." He pointed at the exit sign. "I'm good to go. That way."

They sat shoulder-to-shoulder, David's buzz cut an inch from the roof liner. Every day she saw David, he looked stronger.

"A hundred percent," he said.

Sarah found her way past the yacht harbor to Terrence's secret parking spot. They ran the rest of the way, Sarah surprised by how fast David could move. Halfway to Fisherman's Wharf, she noticed him flinch when he stepped off a curb. But he kept going, and they ran up the gangplank seconds before the ferry shoved off.

On the top deck, they stood together, watching the city grow smaller. When David went looking for coffee, Sarah remembered the manila envelope, dug it out of her field jacket, and found a magazine that looked like it had been mimeographed and stapled together by hand. Faded black letters on the cover announced: "Up Against the Bulkhead." When she opened it, she found a small white envelope addressed to David and stuffed with twenty-dollar bills. She counted thirty of them before she heard a young woman's voice on the scratchy intercom say, "Ladies and gentlemen, we'll soon be passing Alcatraz Island." A voice in the background shouted, "22 acres of angry Indians."

David handed her a styrofoam cup of coffee. In return she gave him the magazine. "I've seen this before," he said. "Vets against the war. Better not let the MPs catch you with this." He laughed, scanned a few, and tucked it in his back pocket. "From Ms Jane, right?"

Sarah nodded.

"She's a good friend," he said. "Always."

Sarah leaned back and watched seagulls circling in the salty wind. She closed her eyes and concentrated on feeling his shoulder touching her. He put his arm around her, and they sat facing the

Golden Gate until a scratchy voice on the intercom announced, "Angel Island. The Island of Angels. The second largest island in the bay. Roughly 3 square miles."

The island looked quiet and peaceful, with three sailboats anchored in a small cove.

Years later, Sarah would return to the island. By then, it had become a destination with tourists, paved trails, a restaurant, a store for souvenirs, and bicycles to rent. A shuttle service promised to take tourists to every historical site on the island.

Now, though, only Lois Lane and a young man were waiting at the dock. "Down we go," David said.

Sarah grabbed her pack and followed him down the gangplank to Lois in her cowboy boots, black slacks, and a grey turtleneck sweater. Next to her, the skinny young man looked lost in sandals, blue jeans, and a shaggy black overcoat.

Sarah bent down to double-knot her boot laces while David hugged Lois, shook the stranger's hand, and walked with him to the trailhead marker.

Lois waited to shake Sarah's hand and say she had three tickets for the ferry to Tiburon. "I want David to go with us," she said. "Did you talk to him?"

"No. And I'm not going to." Sarah handed her the envelope with the money.

"They'll kill him," Lois said, stuffing the envelope in her back pocket. "You know that."

"Who's they?"

"What difference does it make?"

Their eyes met, and Sarah was certain Lois was trying to help, might even think she was telling the truth. But David was waving to her, shouting for her to hurry.

Lois hugged her, wouldn't let her go, and said, "We'll wait here for the last ferry to Sausalito. If David misses it, tell him goodbye for me. We're heading for Mexico." Finally, she let go. "Talk to him. Please. I've tried."

Sarah left her there, ran past the young man in the overcoat, and walked with David until they couldn't see the dock, then told David that Lois was headed for Mexico."

He laughed, "By way of Canada."

They walked together, decided not to visit the Civil War buildings, hurried past the concrete slabs that used to be Nike Missile launchers, and stopped to rest where they had a view of the Bay Bridge. Sarah peeled off her jacket and wrapped it around her waist as the sun rose higher in the winter sky.

She was glad David liked to hike in silence, pacing himself the same way he swam, smooth and easy. When she wanted to stop, she stopped. And if David wanted to keep going, he would wait for her further down the trail. Together, they reached Fort McDowell.

Years later, Sarah would pick up a brochure that said the barracks, hospital, Quonset huts, and chapel were being restored to help preserve the memory of the soldiers who had served in two wars. When she was with David, there were no brochures, only empty wooden buildings with locked doors.

A half-hour more on the trail, they found another chain-link fence and a rusty sign warning that trespassers would be prosecuted.

"Ms Jane says there are ghosts here," David said.

"She sees ghosts everywhere."

"She said we would have to climb the fence."

David found a gate, gave it a gentle push, and watched it swing open. "So much for the honorable Ms Jane," he said.

They followed a narrow path nearly hidden by weeds and found a two-story building with shuttered windows. "It reminds me of the buildings on the Presidio," Sarah said and peeled off a strip of dirty yellow paint,

The front door was hanging loose on rusting hinges and didn't stop them from stepping into a room as big as a basketball court. Two rows of thick metal poles reached from floor to ceiling.

Thirty years later, her young teacher friend would show her a book with black-and-white photographs of the same room. Bunk beds were attached to the poles, stacked three high, with men staring into the camera.

David stopped to brush his hands over the cracked paint on the walls. Chinese characters appeared from under thick dust. Birds fluttered along the ceilings.

"Angels," David said, looking up.

Sarah touched the Chinese figures and felt hands carving thoughts in hard wood. Outside, the wind blew through eucalyptus trees.

"The immigration center," David said.

Sarah told herself to remember the rotting floors, the broken toilets, the sinks along the wall, the anger and hope in poetry on wood.

Later, the young professor, the history teacher, would give Sarah the numbers. From 1910 until 1940, the government detained 175,000 Chinese and 60,000 Japanese in what research called "Adverse and oppressive conditions." The young professor had found a translation of the poems and pinned one to her office wall:

"If the land of the Flowery Flag is occupied by us in turn,/The wooden building will be left for the Angel's Revenge."

Later, Sarah sat with David outside on dry grass. In the shadow of Monterey Pines, they turned their backs to the detention center and shared bread, cheese, and dark red wine. David said it was his favorite. Sarah liked it better than champagne.

The food made them sleepy, so they closed their eyes and let the sky press down on them. Her back on the warm earth, Sarah felt the voices inside her calling, telling her this was the last time she would see David.

She woke him, and together they ran, jumped from the dock to the ferry while the passengers lining the rails cheered. The last ferry to Tiburon had departed an hour ago.

On the way home, they drove toward the sunset. Parked at Golden Gate Park and shared a concrete table at Stow Lake. Ate sourdough bread and drank from a fresh bottle of Zinfandel. And later, lying on wet grass, they gazed at the stars, trying to stay awake. And David asked if she would take care of his brother. Keep him safe. Don't let him go.

And Sarah was reaching for him. Touching him. When the explosion tore through the night.

10.COUNTING DAYS

Time: February to December, 1970
Location: San Francisco

The next day, Terrence called to say they had been lucky. The bomb had exploded on the windowsill of the police station at the east end of Golden Gate Park. Close to Stow Lake. One policeman had been killed, and seven others injured. Terrence was certain it was the Weather Underground.

In the background, Ms Jane shouted, "They don't know. It could've been the Rainbow Party, the Southern Patriots, the Red Feather Party, or the Panthers."

"It was the Weathermen," Terrence said. "Believe me, I know."

"He doesn't." Ms Jane took the phone. "We're not lucky. None of us."

Sarah, ashamed to say the explosion had made her want David even more, could only say, "Tired."

"It's the city. This war."

"What was his name?"

"Who?"

"The policeman."

"We don't know."

Sarah closed her eyes.

Two days later, David left for Vietnam. Sarah closed her eyes and found herself standing alone on a crowded sidewalk. People cheered as messages written on tiny scraps of paper fell from a red sky. But when she caught one and tried, she couldn't read the words.

The next day woke her, and she made plans. She would take a summer course and five courses in the fall. She would graduate early. The next day at the college library, she discovered she could still read. She studied first, then searched the stacks of newspapers for the latest news and found the policeman's name. Sergeant Brian McDonnell.

In March, three members of the Weather Underground blew themselves up in Greenwich Village while constructing a bomb. They had planned to show Americans what war felt like.

In April, President Nixon ordered the invasion of Cambodia to counter North Vietnamese aggression. An editorial described dominos falling, claiming to know which country would fall next. Black-and-white photographs froze marchers demanding peace, college students burning draft cards, and veterans on capital steps ripping medals from their chests.

In May, the National Guard killed four students. Eleven days later, police in Jackson, Mississippi, killed two more.

In June, President Nixon extended the 1965 Voting Rights Act and lowered the voting age to 18. The war continued. It would be over soon, Terrence assured her. No one would be left behind.

In July, "Close to You" by the Carpenters reached #1 on the charts. Sarah wondered if the Grateful Dead heard the news.

In August, the ocean in Aquatic Park reached 59 degrees. In the concrete bleachers, Ms Jane stripped down to her thick wool bathing suit, and in between bites from a half-pint of Old Grand-Dad, she sang opera loud, "Today we sank 418 containers of nerve gas in the Gulf Stream."

Toes in the water, Terrence whispered, "I'll enlist."

Waiting without thinking, Sarah slipped into 59 degrees and kicked along the bottom, digging her fingers into the silt, stirring up muddy clouds.

In September, Chevrolet introduced the Vega. Ford introduced the Pinto. Jimi Hendrix choked to death, and Congress gave President Nixon the authority to sell arms to Israel.

In October, Janice Joplin died of a heroin overdose. The North Vietnamese rejected a Nixon peace offer. Lieutenant Calley went on trial for the My Lai Massacre. In the library, Sarah studied the paper lieutenant in uniform and told herself he looked familiar, like a hundred other young boys. She left him at the top of the page and moved down to a report that a week had gone by for the first time in five years without a combat fatality in Vietnam.

In November, President Nixon announced a gradual troop withdrawal. Ms Jane said there was no such thing. Terrence said, "He'll be home soon."

In December, two days before Christmas, workers finished the north tower of the World Trade Center, making it the tallest building in the world.

On the first day of the new year, Sarah woke up on the Costa's couch. They had driven off to face the New Year in Big Sur, with their last instructions to Sarah, "Let us know. Anything about David."

On the television, soldiers fired into tree lines, slogged through jungles, lit grass huts on fire. Exhausted men hid behind sandbags, ate from tin cans, smoked cigarettes, and pointed at clouds of burning napalm. Soldiers loaded body bags into helicopters. In the background, President Nixon's voice promised increased bombing "Until the North Vietnamese agree to negotiate."

The footage jumped to B-52s dropping streams of bombs. Sarah turned off the TV and closed her eyes. She had finished her exams and needed to sleep. Wanted to dream. Deserved to see confetti she could read.

She woke up to the wind blowing off the ocean. At the window, telephone lines were shaking and newspapers were scattering in the street. A taxi parked in the driveway, and an old man in green slacks and a thick blue sweater stepped out. He glanced at the house, at his clipboard, and walked across the tiny patch of grass to knock on the door. When Sarah opened it, he asked, “Is this the Costa residence?”

Sarah nodded. She was Sarah Costa. The man held out a clipboard, asking her to sign on the bottom line. She heard him say, “Sorry, ma’am. I don’t enjoy doing this, just part of the job. Sorry again, ma’am.” He handed her a telegram, turned, and hurried to his taxi.

The message had been cut into strips and pasted onto a yellow background, starting with, “We regret to inform you.” Sarah skipped down until she read “Missing in Action.”

PART II

MISTAKEN IDENTITY

Kinda. It was 1972. We were on the ferry to Martha's Vineyard. Nasty water. Not as bad as this bay but rough, with wind chop, cross currents and ripping tides. East Coast dirty water. And this young guy, our age back then, he finds Big Mac and pretends to be part of the crew and says Mr. McNamara you have a phone call.

11. COCKTAIL HOUR

Time: April 2001
Location: Hilo, Hawaii

When Celeste Blake still cared about such things, she had an office with a view. It was cramped and stuffy and up two flights of sagging stairs in the old Hata Building. But the union paid the rent. She could sleep in the worn leather recliner. And the desk was made of steel.

She was standing on it, forcing a screwdriver into the window latch, when she saw a stranger climbing the stairs in board shorts and a t-shirt, most of her face hidden by a baseball cap and sunglasses. By the time Celeste realized her mistake, the woman was knocking on her door.

Yesterday, Celeste had seen her introduced to the faculty in heels and a dark blue pantsuit. The union's chief negotiator had noted her twenty-five years of organizing with the United Farm Workers. Added the West Virginia teachers strike in 1990, the Hormel meat packers strike in Minnesota in 85, and the Garment Workers strike in NYC in 82. And finished strong by raising his voice to say, "Now Ms Sarah Costa has returned home to give back to her community as a special advisor to the union president."

Now, Celeste jumped down, shoved her bike against the wall,

tossed her workout clothes into a footlocker, and stepped over her surfboard to open the door. "Come in, Ms Costa," she said and remembered the maile lei. Slipped it off the nail next to the door and draped it over the woman's broad shoulders, hugging her tight, Hilo style, and saying, "Welcome home. I'm Celeste. Celeste Blake."

The special advisor remained mainland stiff until Celeste let go and stepped back. Then Ms Costa held out her hand and offered a smile. "Call me Sarah."

Celeste guessed she was in her fifties. A sturdy woman with a gentle grip, she was a hand shorter than Celeste, fifteen or twenty pounds heavier, with wide shoulders and dark brown eyes. Her hair, cut short and streaked with grey, looked as if she had dried it with a towel and left it uncombed, like a surfer would, all adrift.

Ms Costa lifted the lei to her face, inhaled, and said, "Hilo maile. So sweet the smell. My father gave me one just like it for high school graduation."

Celeste wanted to call her auntie and ask why it had taken her so long to return to the island, but she chose professional. "Come in. Please. This is the office," she said. "I'm here to help in any way I can. Whatever you need, Ms Costa."

Ms Costa stepped over the surfboard and ran her finger along the recliner's cracked leather. "The union has gone all out for us, Celeste."

"We're oceanfront."

"Perfect," Sarah smiled. "Are you a professor?"

"Instructor of history. First year on tenure track."

"Of course. You're too young and healthy to be a professor, but you're a brave young woman to be a union rep without tenure."

"No one else volunteered."

Ms Costa scanned the office. "Is there a bathroom?"

"Down the hall."

"A cot?"

"The recliner."

"Room for another surfboard?"

"Not a longboard."

Both women laughed, and Ms Costa said, “I used to surf the harbor, but that was thirty years ago.” She looked up at the window. “Can you see the water from there?”

“Kinda. Sometimes. And we'll catch the breeze if I can pry the latch open."

"Nice." Ms Costa patted the desk and said, “The union made reservations for me on the other side of the island.”

“That’s a two-hour drive. I mean, you know that.” To cover her mistake, Celeste explained that she lived with her family in Volcano. Ms Costa could sleep in the office. There’s a microwave and a hot plate. A sink and a cooler with ice. She could walk to Pesto’s for Italian or Reuben’s for Mexican. The laundromat and KTA were around the corner. “I’ve slept in the recliner,” she said. “It’s a winner. Perfect to check the surf in the morning.”

Ms Costa pointed at the bicycle. “I haven’t seen a Schwinn Varsity in years. Still good for getting around town, right?”

“It’s my race bike.”

“Oh,” Ms Costa picked up the bike. “Heavy.”

“A present. My dad’s old bike.”

Ms Costa nodded, touched the handlebars, and said, “I can shower at the canoe hale or Kawamoto Pool. The laundromat is new. Let’s get my stuff.”

Celeste followed her down the stairs to a rental car, where Ms Costa hauled an army duffel bag from the trunk. When Celeste offered to help, Ms Costa hefted the canvas bag onto her shoulder and said, “No need.” As she climbed the stairs, two at a time, she asked over her shoulder, “How’s the strike?”

Celeste hesitated.

“The teachers sticking together?”

“Mostly.”

“Sometimes organizing faculty can be like herding coked-up cats."

Celeste nodded. “There may be one or two.”

“No worries. I like cats."

She sat on the recliner, dug into her duffel bag, pulled out a pint of Old Grand-Dad, and twisted off the cap. "Any glasses?"

Celeste handed her a coffee mug, plain white with a thick handle, and said,

"Nothing for me. I'm training."

"So am I."

"There's a bottle of white wine in the cooler," Celeste said. "If you want something lighter. The Honolulu folks left it."

"I don't drink wine. Long story." Sarah poured an inch of Grand-Dad into the mug and checked the depth with her finger. "I allow two inches a day. Sometimes more." She sipped Grand-Dad while Celeste finished prying open the window. A hint of ocean breeze carried jazzy piano music up the stairs from Pesto's.

"What are you training for, Ms Costa?"

"A swim from Alcatraz to Aquatic Park. Barely a mile."

"How long have you been training?"

"Since 1968."

Both women laughed, and Celeste jumped to the floor, sat on the desk.

"What about you, Celeste?"

"The Iron Man, in October. Three-mile swim, hundred-mile bike, and a marathon run." Afraid she had been bragging, she added, "I don't plan on winning. Just finishing. I mean, if the strike is over."

Ms Costa capped the whiskey. "Don't worry. It'll be over. If it were only college profs, you'd be in trouble. But no one likes their grade school kids out of school for long. Have to hire child care. Who can afford that? We're two weeks in. I give it a week, maybe two more."

Celeste said, "I'd give up salary increases if the state promised to lower tuition."

"Keep that to yourself."

"If tuition keeps going up, we'll force these kids out. They're living on student loans, 90% of them. They'll never be able to pay that money back."

"One thing at a time."

"My mom and dad told me they went to college for almost free, less than $100 a semester." Too late, Celeste realized that Ms Costa must have lived through those times. Unlike her parents, had she become like current leadership and faculty, concerned only about money, salaries? And if Ms Costa was sure the strike would end soon, why had she volunteered to help? Was she another union official on a free trip to Hawaii?

"Your parents sound like good people," Ms Costa said. "You have to introduce me."

"No worries." Celeste nodded but changed the subject, saying she was almost thirty and had been off the island only once. "For graduate school at Manoa. They offered me a teaching position in Honolulu at Roosevelt. But I wanted to come home. I could never leave this island."

"You're a Hilo girl." Ms Costa stood up and pointed at the desk. "May I?"

Celeste nodded, and Sarah climbed onto the desk to look out the window. The wind had died, the water smooth and deep blue. Two tugs were dragging a red-and-white cruise ship toward the open ocean. It would be dark soon.

"Why did it take you so long to come home, Ms Costa?"

Sarah jumped down. "Did you say you're a fast swimmer, Ms Blake?"

12.POWERED BY SPAM

Time: April 2001
Location: Hilo

Sarah Costa was biting into a malasada when she saw a pickup truck cut across traffic, jump a speed bump, and stop inches from Celeste Blake. The driver rolled down his window and smiled. "Good morning, young lady. You could get hurt stepping in front of a truck."

"You can't cross the picket line."

"What picket line?"

Behind her, the striking faculty had stepped aside, offering the truck a direct route to the campus parking lot. While Celeste turned and talked the professors back in line, Sarah stepped up and gave the driver a closer look. He was her age, maybe a few years older. His bloodshot eyes and weathered skin suggested much older, too many cigarettes and too many long nights.

"Professor Matsui," he said, holding out his hand. "Administration of Justice."

It was her first day, so Sarah gave his hand a gentle shake. "You came at us pretty fast," she said, eye-to-eye until he let go.

"Bad cross traffic. Had to speed up to get through it, or I'd still be out there waiting. Happens every morning here. Hilo traffic. Had to say hello to my old friend and the new union lady from the mainland."

"That's me."

"Here to solve our problems?"

"You have problems?"

"Don't we all?"

"Don't listen to him," Celeste said, handing Sarah a malasada. "He talks too much. And knows too little."

The professor offered another quick smile. "You're my favorite," he said, shifting into reverse. "Take care of my friend, Ms Costa. She's one of the good ones." He snapped a military-style salute as he backed his truck into traffic.

"Your friend?" Sarah asked.

"He knew my dad. It's a small island."

Sarah watched Matsui's truck shoot through a yellow light. "He doesn't look healthy."

"Too many hostess bars."

"How do you know?"

"Believe me. I know."

At eleven, an ancient professor in blue slacks and a faded aloha shirt offered Sarah a spam musubi wrapped in cellophane.

"Professor Chun," he said. "One of my students works at Iliaha Bakery. You like musubi, Ms Costa?"

Sarah nodded and unwrapped the double-thick slice of Spam sandwiched between white rice and wrapped in seaweed.

"Did your father work for the county?" he asked. "I knew a Costa."

"Twenty-five years," Sarah said, covering her mouth while she chewed. "We ate plenty of these."

Her father would take her with him to work, and she would watch him cut grass and empty rubbish before they sat at a picnic table and ate musubi for lunch. The memory led to pancakes in the mornings and roasted chicken for dinner. She wiped sticky rice off her fingers with a paper napkin.

Professor Chun handed her a steel thermos. "You'll need this."

Sarah felt a soft ocean breeze. She twisted the cap off the thermos and smelled dark coffee and something stronger.

"I like scrambled eggs layered in with the Spam," Celeste said, standing behind Sarah. "My father made musubi with Korean chicken."

Ten students, all women, all dressed in shorts and t-shirts, walked up carrying a blue-and-white cooler big enough to be a footlocker. "Professor Blake, you go, girl," one shouted. "Fight the power." One raised a fist. And Celeste hugged each of them, then sat with them around the cooler in the shade.

Professor Chun led Sarah away from them, saying that Ms Blake was one of the good ones. A fighter. "Not like her parents."

Sarah sipped coffee from the thermos's steel cap. It was hot, sweet, and spiked with rum. "Nice thermos. Good coffee."

"Your father was Portuguese, Ms Costa?"

Sarah waited for what would come next. Her high school? Cousins, uncles? Born and raised? How many generations back? But Professor Chun surprised her.

"I apologize if I offended you. I forget it's different here. Not like the mainland."

"Never mind." She drank more coffee.

The old professor wiped sweat off his forehead. Most of the picketers had moved into the shade, leaving behind a thin line of shuffling sign wavers. Under the Banyan tree, a stack of picket signs rested on the grass. Hilo was a rainforest, but when the sun came out, Sarah remembered, it could melt steel. "What's next, professor?" she asked.

"I'm supposed to take you to the upper campus. Show you around. Talk story with the trades folks."

As they drove by the high school, Professor Chun waved to the teachers on the picket lines. Most of them wore aloha shirts and slacks and looked as if they worked in a bank or law office. Across the street, a sprinkling of university pickets wore costumes and Halloween masks. A pirate and a drag queen walked arm in arm with a pair of women in white tennis outfits. Folding tables offered pitchers of lemonade and plates of donuts. Music blared from boom-boxes. And when a car challenged the picket line, the strikers gave way, opening a space and waving the driver through.

Professor Chun shook his head, made a quick left, and squeezed by pickup trucks parked next to classroom buildings that looked like workshops. He told Ms Costa they belonged to Auto Repair, Electrical, Welding, and Diesel Repair. Pointing at a wooden building in the shade of tall eucalyptus trees, he said, “Over there, behind the theater and the old gym, is where I teach. That’s where the community college started.” He paused a second, then asked, “Why did you leave Hilo?”

Ready for it, Sarah had a simple answer he’d understand. “I promised my dad I’d go to college on the mainland.”

A heavyset striker had stepped into the road, waving his sign: “Construction Workers 4 Students!” Professor Chun hit the brakes, and when he stuck his head out the window, the striker stepped aside and pointed his sign at a space behind a semi-truck. “This is Diesel Repair,” Professor Chun said. “You’ll like them. Drink more coffee.”

The trade guys wore work boots, jeans, and polo shirts. Their department names were stitched above their shirt pockets, where most of them kept their cigarettes. They walked the line as Auto-Body, Diesel Repair, Welding or Carpentry, determined to block all traffic from entering their campus. A delivery truck pulled up, shouts were exchanged, and the truck driver backed up, reversing to the main gate.

“Union men,” Professor Chun said proudly.

Sarah couldn’t help smiling. She had seen the union files and knew many of these men were the highest-paid faculty on campus. Some made twice as much as their union brothers and sisters who taught liberal arts classes. They had hired in at salaries intended to lure them away from work in the private sector, and they could offer their students a path to high-paying jobs. Math and history teachers could offer only a path to more classes.

As Sarah opened her door, two hefty faculty members jumped into the back seat of the Nissan sedan and told Professor Chun to back up, turn around, and drive.

"So, you're the new union advisor?" the man behind her said, reaching over her shoulder to shake hands. "Good to meet you. Bobbie's my name. This is Leo."

They exchanged quick grips while Professor Chun kept his hands on the steering wheel. The men smelled of coffee and cigarettes and something stronger. In the rearview mirror, Sarah saw polo shirts and Union baseball caps. The man behind her was "Auto Repair." The one behind Chun was "Carpentry."

Auto Repair said, "We get one problem..."

Carpentry stepped on his union brother's sentence, "You like being back in Hilo?"

"It's a job," she said.

The two men looked at each other. They asked her if she would stay on the island now and if she still ate rice?

"No," Sarah said. "And yes, to the rice."

"I can't live without rice."

Maybe it was Auto. Or was it Carpentry? Sarah wasn't sure because both were nodding their agreement. Gotta have rice, Sarah silently agreed. She shifted in her seat so she could face them. Carpentry was stocky and long-armed, with obvious biceps and thick black hair greased back and combed in 50s style, not a single hair out of place. Her father's style. He poked Professor Chun's shoulder and said, "Go to… you know where."

Auto-Body was short and thin, his head shaved bald, and he was reaching for his cigarettes.

Sarah rolled down the window to make up for the old car's lack of air-conditioning. A few minutes later, after the carpenter had given up trying to light his cigarette and the auto mechanic had named his relatives back to the overthrow of the monarchy, both men said, "We get one problem."

"Tell me."

Professor Chun parked in the YWCA lot, in the shadows of a Banyan tree, across the street from the old administration building.

"Watch there," Auto-Body said, pointing across the street at a covered walkway, its tin roof supported by pillars of varnished ohia.

"That asshole is coming here to screw the strike," Carpentry said, checking his watch. "Any minute now."

"Who?"

"Look there."

The dark blue pickup truck eased through the loose line of strikers. "Those UH guys are worthless," AutoBody said.

"Never mind dah scrubs," Carpentry said, "Matsui said he'd flunk his students if they didn't come to class during the strike."

Sarah waited, letting them work up to it.

"We have to do something," one of the voices from the back said.

When Matsui stepped out of the truck, his aluminum briefcase looked like it belonged in a spy movie.

"He crosses the line every day."

"He wants to be an administrator."

They were quiet as Matsui unlocked his classroom. Sarah turned to the men in the back and said, "You want to do something? Go ahead. Just don't let it come back on the Union."

The two men looked at each other. Sarah waited for one of them to accept responsibility. Finally, she said, "You want me to talk to him?"

Professor Chun said, "He won't listen."

"Not him."

"Not him."

Sarah motioned for Professor Chun to drive. As they turned onto the street, she kept her eyes on the road and said, "I'll take care of it."

13.RED DOG MEMORIES

Time: April 2001
Location: Hilo

Saturday morning, Sarah watched Celeste grind the stick into third, let out the clutch, and step hard on the gas. Sarah rolled down the window and reached for the seatbelt.

"Never mind that," Celeste said. "It's rotted out. I mean, you can buckle up if you want, in case we get stopped. Lots of rust on your side. Sorry, no one ever sits there."

Sarah buckled in.

"I'll take it easy. Don't worry, the brakes are good, the radio works, and we got gas." She down-shifted, cut into the left lane to dodge potholes, and sped past the House of Pancakes.

"I used to work there," Sarah said.

"I eat there all the time." On the radio, the Rolling Stones were crying about their search for satisfaction. "Jagger," Celeste said. "He's never satisfied."

"I need to talk to your friend Matsui."

"He's not a good listener."

"I'm not surprised."

The Stones gave up their search, and Creedence took over,

claiming not to be fortunate sons. With both hands on the wheel and foot on the gas, Celeste turned to Sarah. “Matsui’s okay. Just stubborn. Like the music on this radio, he never changes. Like this town never changes. Maybe a little at a time. A drop of change. Is that why you left?”

“Better watch the road.”

“It can be frustrating.” She pressed down hard on the gas.

Sarah used her foot to cover a hole in the floorboard. “Where can I find Matsui? Someplace quiet. Not close to school.”

“Like in The Godfather?” Celeste laughed. “Let me think.” Fat raindrops splashed against the cracked windshield. “Talk about never changing. It’s raining in Mountain View. Surprise.”

“Country,” Sarah said. “Open space.”

“Did you grow up here?” Celeste asked.

“In town.”

“Where?”

“Back there.”

“An old house? Plantation style?”

“Old enough to have collapsed by now.”

“On the Hilo side, houses never die. Like old soldiers, they just fade away.”

“You are, indeed, a history teacher.”

Celeste downshifted and said, “We’ll be at the starting line in a few miles.”

The Toyota surged uphill, the sun broke through the clouds, and Sarah tried to remember what it was like being Celeste’s age. In her twenties, early thirties, with time to train for a triathlon. “What made you enter the Ironman?”

“I didn’t enter.”

“What?”

Celeste rolled down her window. “They can’t keep people out of the ocean and off the public streets. They don’t own this island.” Her hands gripped the steering wheel as if holding the truck together. “It’s a matter of principle.”

“Oh, one of those.”

"Sports should be for keeping people healthy, not for entry fees."

Thick walls of bamboo lined both sides of the road.

"I'll be extra happy if I beat Matsui."

"What? Who?"

"Matsui."

Sarah gave Celeste a hard look. She was at least 30 years younger than Matsui. She didn't drink or smoke. "Matsui?" she said. "He looks like a physical wreck. If he's in the race, there'd better be an ambulance close."

"He has friends."

What did that mean? She checked the back of the truck, shook her head, and said, "You need a new bike."

Celeste's Schwinn Varsity was a steel tank. It had to be 40 years old and weigh at least 50 pounds. Sarah hadn't seen one on the road since she was a kid. "Even at pre-strike levels," she said, "you make enough money to buy a lighter bike."

"It doesn't matter."

The bamboo wall broke open, and Celeste pointed at the first building they had seen in miles. "Hirono Store. Best hot dogs anywhere. Red dogs. You know the place?"

"Who doesn't?" Sarah remembered her father stopping here for red dogs smothered in relish, ketchup and mustard. He could eat three of them. She had never managed more than one. "In my day," she said, "the red dog was king."

"Still is." Celeste turned into the muddy, rutted asphalt parking lot, parked next to a commercial-size propane tank, and said, "Lucky for me, it's close to home."

Paradise, Sarah thought, if not for the earthquakes, lava flows, freezing winters, freezing rain, and brutal winds tainted with sulfur smog. But at least it was close to the best hot dogs on the island.

Celeste set the parking brake and turned to Sarah. "Tell you what, I'll race you to Volcano, the park entrance, and back."

"What's that? Twenty miles?"

"Close."

"Before or after red dogs?"

"After."

"Let me think."

"And if I win, you show me the house where you grew up. If you win, I'll show you where to find Matsui."

"Deal."

Celeste ran into the store while Sarah kicked at a gang of stray chickens and studied the bulletin board. Roommates Wanted. Lawn Service offered. Tree Cutters for Hire. Cars 4 Sale. Plumbing Repair. Fencing Installation. Lost Dogs. Lost Cats. Goats 4 Sale. Corrugated tin for sale, no kine rust. Smoked Meat. She saw her father standing there, reading each word as morning clouds drifted by, heavy and slow.

"Wake up," Celeste said, carrying a flimsy box with five red dogs to a weather-beaten picnic table.

"A toast," she said and raised a red dog. "To protein."

"To grease."

"Red lightening."

While Celeste ate, Sarah searched the table for initials carved in wood and found her father's.

"Perfect." Celeste used a paper napkin to wipe mustard off her lips. "One down, two to go. You have to eat at least one."

"Who said?"

"It's part of the bet."

Sarah picked up a dog by its white bun, smelled mustard and onions, and remembered hot dogs and chocolate ice cream in San Francisco. "They look smaller now," she said.

"No way. They never change. That's what's good about them."

"Ever tried an It's It?"

Celeste shook her head and picked up a second dog. "What?"

"Cookie and ice cream sandwich."

"Sounds like an energy bar. I make my own." Celeste bit off a chunk of dog and bun, chewed, and swallowed. "Red dog. One of my secret weapons."

"You have more?"

"My power Cookies. Standard Oreos dipped in 90-proof dark

chocolate. They're better than any commercial crud sold as protein bars, and mine cost almost nothing. I have better things to do with my money."

Sarah watched a poi dog, some kine Pit Bull mix, wander out of the bamboo and sit at Celeste's feet. "Who's this?" she asked.

"Brisket."

Sarah tried feeding it a red dog, but Brisket refused until Celeste tossed a piece in the air. As the fatty red morsel reached its peak, Brisket leaped. Snapped. Swallowed. And landed, before walking proudly back into the bamboo.

"Let's ride," Celeste said.

At the back of the truck, Sarah lifted out her rental, a 21-speed Fuji aluminum, while Celeste found room in her frayed nylon backpack for the last red dog. "After thirty minutes," the young woman said, "I have to refuel."

Even though Celeste claimed she could do it herself, Sarah helped her lift the Varsity out of the truck. Instead of quick-release levers on the wheels, it had nuts and bolts. If Celeste had a flat, a good possibility with the bike's bald tires, she'd need a wrench to free the wheel and change the tire. A big wrench and a can of WD-40.

"Got it," Celeste said. "Out of respect for Kona's roads, I carry a pump and patch kit in my backpack."

"You need a bike bag," Sarah said.

"Waste of money. A student abandoned this one in my office on her way to the mainland."

"A water bottle?"

"No need." She held up a 32-ounce plastic bottle. "Used to be soda. Now it's water. There's room in the backpack."

"You'll have to stop every time you need a drink."

"My times are always better when I take rest stops. They help me enjoy the experience."

Sarah looked down at Celeste's rubber sandals. "Shoes?"

"I can run barefoot."

Apparently, along with a misunderstanding of nutrition, bicycle weight, and entry fees, her young friend had a problem with shoes.

“Hawaiians ran barefoot,” Celeste said. “I have Hawaiian feet.”

No. They weren’t Hawaiian feet. Sarah remembered how she had learned to play soccer in rubber slippers and had hardened her soles into thick human leather by climbing barefoot over rocks and dead coral to reach the ocean. In those days, she could run three miles barefoot on asphalt along Kalanianaole, avoiding the spots where drunks had tossed empties as they sped toward police roadblocks. In those days, her feet were wide and flat, like snowshoes, but they weren’t Hawaiian. Never could be.

“Country strong,” Celeste said.

“The Hawaiians didn’t have to deal with hot asphalt.”

“Only lava. But I know what you mean.” She dug a ratty pair of Chuck Taylors out of the pack. “High Tops. Thick rubber on these suckers. Plenty good for the bike and the run. Out of respect to Kona.”

Sarah shook her head. Was it possible? Could Matsui beat her? Yes, if he didn't have a heart attack.

Celeste climbed on her Varsity. “Let’s race.”

14.REUNIONS

Time: April 2001
Location: Hilo, Hawaii

Near midnight, Sarah parked in a vacant lot across from Auntie Kim's Place. The street between the harbor and the airport was dimly lit, but she knew the neighborhood and had dressed for the occasion. Two trucks passed before she hurried across wet asphalt in cowboy boots, black Levis, a silk blouse, and her black leather jacket.

She was not surprised Auntie Kim's had survived thirty years. Restaurants struggled, and churches lost parishioners, but hostess bars embraced their loyal congregations, despite their lack of spiritual guidance. Sarah stopped at the door, inhaled fresh air, with only a hint of dumpster, then stepped into the neon glow of beer signs. Coors and Budweiser, Heineken and Hamms. The booths along the walls were hidden in shadows and cigarette smoke. The music was turned down low, and the bar was in the back, a lifeguard station in a neon pool. Sarah walked toward the light, telling herself she had good luck with bartenders.

"What can I do for you, auntie?" The bartender was thin and young, with blue eyes and blond hair, the curly ends protruding from under a Giants baseball cap. His white dress shirt and black tie were a nice touch. “Old Grand-Dad with a water chaser.” Sarah draped her jacket on the stool. There was a pool table to the right and a door marked “Exit.” She glanced at the bartender, at the mirror behind him, and stopped at a Ferris-wheel rotisserie glowing with red dogs. “You know anyone who can eat three red dogs,” she said, “then ride a bike fifteen miles?”

“Sounds like a bar joke.” He set the Old Grand-Dad in front of her. “Or is that your way of ordering a red dog?”

“No way. They cost me big today.” Sipping sweet rye, she checked the mirror and saw Matsui sitting in a booth near the door. A heavy dose of patchouli caught her as the bartender leaned across the bar and said, “I’m David.”

“What?

He held out his hand. He had a gentle grip, and when he let go, Sarah heard him say, “Only my sister calls me Kawika.” He rested his forearms on the bar. “She lives on red dogs. Professor Blake is my sister. The red dog eater.”

Sarah sipped her Grand-Dad. She wanted the right words.

“And you’re the union lady. Sarah Costa.”

“That’s me.”

“I hope the strike ends soon. I don’t want to lose six credits.”

“No worries.”

“Good. I’m tired of being a student.”

“There are worse jobs.”

In the mirror, a grey-haired woman sat next to Matsui. Where had she come from? In the next booth, a bald man with his sleeves rolled up glanced at Sarah.

The bartender said, “My sister thinks I work too hard at going in the wrong direction. She wants to stay. I want to go.”

“I know the feeling.” Sarah was trying to place the bolo head. She looked again. Now he was wearing a baseball cap. “Mind if I call you Kawika?” she asked.

“I’m not Hawaiian, but sure. I just don’t want you to think I’m trying to be someone I’m not. I was born here, but I’m not Hawaiian.”

"And your sister, she was born here?"

"No way."

Sarah thought she was beginning to sound like Professor Chun. "Sounds reasonable. Maybe you can help."

"She doesn't listen to me."

"No. See the guy who just put his hat on? You know him?"

"Him? I think he comes for the food."

"Red dogs?"

"Sad, right?" He nodded. "Or the chili. But he's a big tipper. The girls like him."

"And who's the mama-san with Matsui?"

"That's Auntie Kim. She owns the place. Nice lady."

The music switched to country music, George Strait crossing his heart, his love unconditional, drifting down from box speakers hanging from the ceiling.

"You running a tab?" David asked.

Sarah slid a twenty across the bar. "You know Matsui?"

"Sure do. He's one of my teachers." When the bartender turned around to work the register, Sarah noticed he was wearing board shorts and rubber slippers. When he turned back, she looked up as he said, "I mean one of my professors." He set two bills on the bar. "It's college. I keep forgetting."

"Is he any good?"

Kawika rolled his eyes. "He's okay. If you do the work and smile at his old jokes."

"Sounds like college. Are you going to class during the strike?"

"It's required."

"By him?"

"Unless I want to retake the class next semester." Kawika poured another Grand-Dad, leaned over the bar, and smiled. "He's a regular. Every night. For an old guy he can drink. I don't know how he does it. Auntie told me she knew him back in high school, said he smoked too much pakalolo. Now he's all Mr Straight. Except for beer and cigarettes."

Sarah checked the other booths. Older men sat with younger

women, casual and relaxed, drinking, smoking, and leaning into each other. Some were chatting, some staring into the smoke. All of them looking familiar, like characters in a painting, even the bolo head.

When Auntie Kim stood up, the young women perked up, and Kawika drifted to the other end of the bar. Sarah sipped her Grand-Dad, enjoying the slow burn while Auntie Kim made the rounds, pausing at each booth to chat with the customers. When she passed the bar, she left a stack of drink orders for the bartender and stopped to say, "Nice to see you, Ms Costa." Then she disappeared around the corner.

Sarah left a $20 tip on the bar.

"Coming back?" the bartender called.

"Keep it for your tuition. Thanks for the help."

At Matsui's booth, a young woman in a red dress had replaced Auntie Kim. When Sarah sat down across from him, the woman left, and Sarah said, "I thought you were in training."

"What else did the history teacher tell you?"

"Not much."

"How about the bartender?"

"He said you were a good teacher."

"Did he tell you about his sister?"

"Tell me what?"

"About her parents?"

"You know," Sarah said. "In this neon, you almost look human." His frayed green polo shirt had his department's name above the pocket: Administration of Justice. One hand on his cell phone, the other on an empty longneck next to an ashtray full of cigarette butts. He flipped open his cell phone, snapped it shut, and said, "Well, if you don't want to know."

Auntie Kim came back with a Grand-Dad and water for Sarah, a beer for Matsui. "Ms Costa," she said, "I knew your father."

"Oh?"

"He was a good friend."

Sarah tried to imagine her father sitting in one of the shadowy booths. Did he sit close to her and rest her hand on his knee? She must've been a beauty back in the day. Still was. Even in the neon, her eyes were clear and sharp, her skin free of makeup.

"Be careful of this one," Auntie Kim said. "Malcolm is still growing." She patted his head as if he were a child. "Do you have any children, Ms Costa?"

Sarah shook her head, and Matsui offered a thin smile. Aunite Kim picked up the trays and said, "Tell him not to smoke. Bad for the lungs."

When she was gone, Matsui asked, "Why no kids?"

Sarah sipped her rye.

"Me too." He lit a Camel, no filter. "Time for business."

"Sounds good."

"That's why the trades guys sent you, right? To make me understand? How did you find me? Oh, right, the history teacher and her…brother."

Sarah reached across the table, and pushed the Camels out of his reach.

"Right," he said. "An interrogation. No smokes."

The door swung open, and a long hair wearing a black muscle shirt and black Levis walked in, saw Matsui, nodded, saw Sarah, and stopped. Tattoos covered his arms and shoulders. Chunks of turquoise embedded in silver hung from his tattooed neck. Three tiny loops of silver pierced each ear. His thick grey hair was tied in a ponytail and matched his salt-and-pepper goatee.

"Just in time to meet someone important," Matsui said. He stood up and hugged the man. "This is Ms Costa. Sarah Costa."

"Vincent," the man said, offering his hand to Sarah, each finger studded with silver rings. The rings pressed gently into her skin and held her for a moment too long.

"She's from Frisco," Matsui said.

"The City," Vincent said.

They were still standing. "He's a policeman," Matsui said. "Do you believe it?"

"I do." She stood up, hugged her old friend, and kissed him on both cheeks. "Nice to meet you."

"Vinnie," Kawika called from the bar, "Vinnie, come here, my man."

Sarah watched him go.

"That was friendly," Matsui said.

"I liked his look."

"He's married."

Sarah shrugged.

"Three times. To a woman, then a man, now a woman."

"Smart to test the field."

"Funny." Matsui sucked on his cigarette and blew a cloud of smoke to emphasize the point. "He's a Buddhist."

"Good for him."

"At peace with the universe. Forgive and forget."

"I like him even more."

"Really? He's planning to testify at a parole hearing for the man who shot him twice. Going to plead for an early release." Matsui inhaled, held his breath. "Can you believe it?"

Sarah glanced at the bar where Kawika and Vincent were laughing together. "What's he doing here?"

"What's it look like," Matsui said. "Who cares, right? How about you? Can you forgive and forget?"

"About what?"

"About me."

Sarah watched the bald man stand up and head for the pool table. He was wearing a baseball cap now. She stood up, and Matsui grabbed her elbow. "Hey, wait, where you going? What about me? Aren't you going to play union hard ass?"

Sarah jerked her arm free, pinned Matsui's hand to the table. "Take my advice. Go home, take a bath, use plenty of soap. And leave your students out of this mess."

Sarah ran out the back door and stopped. Waiting for her eyes to adjust, she heard a car engine turn over but refuse to start. She felt her way through the dark, past a dumpster over-stuffed with fish scraps and topped with cats. A pickup truck passed in the red glow of a streetlight.

The front door to the bar door swung open, and Matsui walked out, shouting, “Hey, you!” He drained his longneck. “Where you going?”

Sarah ran across the wet asphalt, heard an engine kick over, and saw the headlights blink on.

“I got something to tell you,” Matsui shouted. "Wait right there." He tossed his bottle at the street, shattering the glass.

As he stepped into the street, headlights lit him up.

15.MISTAKEN IDENTITY

Time: May 2001
Location: Hilo, Hawaii

Three days later, the Hilo Medical Center released Professor Matsui with a week's supply of painkillers and a recommendation to rest. Sensing an opportunity to use a backlog of sick leave, Matsui requested a substitute to cover his classes. Professor Chun selected his replacement. And three weeks later, after the strike ended, Professor Matsui returned in time to see his students graduate.

To celebrate, Sarah rode with Celeste to the edge of Hilo.

In rubber slippers, nylon shorts, and baggy t-shirts, they studied a single-story house wedged in between its neighbors.

"Comfy," Celeste said.

The wood house seemed to sag under the weight of its metal roof. But the paint was new, the windows clean, and the small yard neatly trimmed inside a chain-link fence.

Celeste looked up and down the street. "Too many neighbors," she said. "I'm not a fan of neighbors."

Sarah rested her hands on the fence. It had failed to keep out a mother hen and her four chicks, now busy pecking and scratching at the grass near a For-Sale sign. Sarah smiled to herself. Her father would've liked fresh eggs to go with his pancakes.

Celeste reached for the gate. "Let's go inside. A bet is a bet."

"So I've heard."

The real estate agent had given Sarah the key, explaining that the house had been on the market for nearly a year. If she was interested, she could rent it by the month, but only if she could move out on a month's notice if it sold. The woman's card was sitting in the union office under Sarah's ticket to the Mainland. Her flight was scheduled to leave the next morning.

"It's your home," Celeste said.

Sarah pointed at an old man pushing an ancient lawnmower through ankle-high grass in the morning light. With a cigarette dangling from his mouth, he stopped at the fence and let the mower rattle.

"He's staring at us," Celeste said. "You know him?"

"I think so."

"He must be a hundred."

Sarah nodded, waved, and said, "Mr Tanaka?"

The mower died, and the old man said, "Where you been?"

"Mainland."

"You get old."

Sarah nodded.

"How many keiki you get now? That your daughter?"

"Yes, sir."

"She more pretty." He sucked on his cigarette.

"Yes, sir."

"More like her father."

Both women smiled.

From a cloud of smoke, Mr Tanaka said, "Your mother one hero. She tell you?" The old man let the cigarette rest between two crooked fingers. "I seen her. Seen lots of things. Right down there." He pointed his cigarette down the road at a moss-covered bridge. "I saw it. I tell you. Hero, your mother. Saved that boy and baby Jesus from the flood."

The old man smiled, bent over the lawnmower, and pulled its starter cord three times. When it sputtered and coughed, Celeste jumped the fence, jerked the cord, then stood back with the old man in a cloud of gasoline exhaust.

"Like her mother," the old man said. "She one angel."

Fighting off memories, Sarah watched the old man shove the mower along the fence line. Celeste pointed down the street at a bridge over a thick patch of banana trees.

"Tell me." Celeste said.

"That was thirty years ago."

"History."

"Who remembers that stuff?"

"Speak it, mom."

Sarah felt herself running downhill, Celeste chasing her, reaching the bridge, and bending over the concrete railing. Together, they looked down at a ditch overgrown with weeds and banana trees.

"Where's the water?"

"It was the worst rain in years. Days and nights of it," Sarah said. "I thought he was going to drown."

"Jesus?"

"A drunk soldier in a jeep." Sarah laughed. "In his underwear."

"That's history."

Sarah remembered the water rushing over her. "He stole a plastic baby from a nativity scene up there. Mr Tanaka's church."

"I know the place. Big neon sign. Jesus is Coming."

"Still waiting."

"Better late than never," Celeste said.

"I nearly busted my butt jumping down there. I could've drowned."

"You've been baptized."

"What?"

"The driver?" Celeste said. "What happened to him?"

"He was just a kid. A young lieutenant trying to stay out of Vietnam. His men caught up with us and dragged him out of the gulch.

"More drunks?"

“I don’t think so. There was a corporal from here. Local boy. He said he would take care of everything. They had been training up on the mountain, were supposed to leave for Vietnam, and they were taking him with them. No matter what.”

“Local boy? From Hilo?”

“That’s what he said.” Sarah was thinking now. “Hilo High.”

“Did you call the police?”

“No.” A few years older than her. What was his name? She looked up the street, then down at the gulch. She tried to see the lieutenant’s face. Remembered a newspaper clipping and a photograph on a magazine cover. Then she ran uphill.

When Celeste caught her, she was lifting Celeste’s Varsity out of the truck.

“Where are you going?”

“To see an old friend.”

Sarah waved goodbye as she pedaled the bike uphill, aiming for the university.

In the afternoon, Sarah found Matsui in a booth at the Pancake House. She sat across from him, his beer and giant saimin bowl.

A waitress from the old days stopped to say hello and catch up. Like Sarah, she was grey around the edges and seemed tired, end-of-her-shift tired, but happy to see an old friend. “Stay away from this one,” she said with her hand on Matsui’s shoulder. “JJ’s trouble.”

Matsui rubbed his sore ribs. “Trouble, yes. That’s me.” The waitress scribbled Sarah’s order, and when she left, Matsui said, “What now? Want me to thank you again for knocking me on my ass?”

“Not me. That Volvo…"

“I know. I know. I’ll find it. Don’t you worry. That scrub could’ve killed me.”

"Not him," Sarah slid a black-and-white photocopy across the table and tapped it with her middle finger. “Him. You recognize him?”

The December 8, 1969 Newsweek cover featured a shoulder-up shot of Lt. William Calley Jr in uniform. Against a dark background, the headline shouted, "The Killings at Song My."

"What a surprise," Matsui said. "I must've made a big impression. It took you long enough."

"Was it him? It says he trained here." She flipped the photocopy over as the waitress dropped off another beer. When she was gone, Sarah asked. "Is that him? The one I saved?"

"The plastic-baby kidnapper?"

She poked his chest. "Was it Calley?"

"Easy." Matsui stared at the photo.

"Were you with him?" she asked. "At Me Lai."

"You mean when he murdered 22 people?" He tapped the photocopy. "Why blame him? A stupid second louie? Dropped out of junior college with F's and Ds and one C? Why not blame Medina, his captain? Or Westmoreland. He's still alive, isn't he? Or McNamara? He's the one responsible. We were soldiers."

"Following orders."

"We weren't all murderers." Matsui shook his head. "Damn lucky for me that I wasn't there. At that village. I don't know what I would have done. I never had to decide."

"Tell me." Sarah waited, digging her fingers into her thigh. She showed him another photocopy, this one of the bodies, a Vietnamese woman and her children piled in a ditch.

Matsui fingered his phone, flipped it open, snapped it shut. "Here's the truth. Our louie, your louie, he got hit the first day in country. Spent a month in the hospital, never got back to our unit. He was killed three months later. Stepped on a landmine, his first day in the field. Just another second louie, a scared young kid. So, if you want to feel guilty, you can have a piece of that."

Sarah leaned back, gazed up at the ceiling. There was no air conditioning, and the ceiling fans struggled to beat the heat. The air smelled of car exhaust, grilling burgers, and Matsui's Old Spice.

"Beer," Matsui shouted at the waitress hiding behind the ancient cash register. "Beer."

The waitress put a finger to her lips.

He turned to Sarah. “Thanks for the memories, Ms Costa. You’re innocent. If you called the police, they would’ve done the same thing, no matter what you said. He was going with us.” He looked away. “Beer!”

A family crowded into the booth next to them, a mother, father, and three children old enough to sit up straight, a fourth cradled in her mother’s arms, all there to celebrate a pancake treat.

Sarah stuffed the photocopies in her pocket before the children could see them. “Sorry,” she said and left Matsui there.

That night, she couldn’t sleep, so she sat in the recliner in a room with a view. She blamed the union for sending her, she remembered the 30-year-old telegram she had read a hundred times, each time trying to change the words.

Footsteps rushed up the stairs, then a hard knock on the door. “Sarah, you in there?”

She opened the door to find Matsui in black jeans and a field jacket. Something in his face made her want to shove him down the stairs. But he stepped back first. “Come with me,” he said, heading down the stairs. “I want to show you something.”

Sarah grabbed her Orchidland hoodie and locked the door.

Matsui was sitting behind the wheel of his pickup. She sat shotgun, and he drove onto the main road, saying it would take a while. “Relax.”

“Early flight out,” she said.

“Drink.” He pointed at his glove compartment.

She closed her eyes.

When she woke up, they were parked on a narrow road. She heard waves breaking and smelled rotting jungle. In the dark, Janis Joplin was singing about Bobbie McGee. Waves were breaking on the rocks. “Where are we?” she asked.

“Check the glove compartment. It’ll help you wake up.”

Sarah found a half-pint of Grand-Dad. “Where are we?”

“Puna.” Matsui rolled down his window, and they heard a dog bark.

“Over there.” Matsui pointed across the narrow road at a porch light almost hidden in the dark. “That’s where he lives. Auntie Kim found him.”

Sarah screwed the cap off the Old Grand-Dad.

"He’s there now?”

“No, he’s a snowbird. But he’ll be back. A few weeks. A month. Maybe sooner. Maybe later. Auntie Kim will tell us if he shows up at the bar. Who is he?”

“I’m not sure.”

PART III

BABIES AND RUNAWAYS

And this young guy gets Mac outside, grabs him from behind. Lifts him up by the belt and collar and charges him at the water. But Big Mac latches onto the railing. His legs fly up and his glasses fly off. And he's gripping steel, frigid, frozen, refusing to let go.

Just like in the war.

That's right. Waiting for the cavalry to arrive.

Counting the dead. And you?

Half of me wanted to toss him over the side. Teach him a lesson.

Good lesson. That buggah deserved it. And the other half?

Believe me, I was reaching for him.

16.SNOW IN SAN FRANCISCO

Time: January 1974
Location: Fleishhacker Pool

Bottle of Korbel in hand, Sarah Costa forced herself to wait for the FBI agent to stop talking. His sudden appearance at Fleishhacker Pool had sent Ms Jane running down the stairs, through the men's locker room, and out the side door. Now, as the wind blew through Agent Smith's red hair, Sarah remembered the advice given to her at the Korbel winery. Hold the cork steady while turning the bottle. Not the other way around.

The special agent pointed his pen and notebook at Sarah. "It's a little early to be drinking."

"Late, really. My 24th birthday was a month ago."

"Funny."

She had not meant it to be funny.

"Can you put the bottle down, Miss Costa? Heavy as it is, it could be considered a dangerous weapon."

Sarah held the bottle by the neck, felt the weight, and tried a short, hammer swing.

"Miss Costa."

"Sorry." She set the heavy bottle next to her foot. "Thank you. I hadn't thought of that. Good to remember."

He smiled, and she wondered if he was too young to be an FBI agent. And where had he learned to wear white socks with a black suit? Was this a good time to ask? And what would a Korbel-bottle wound look like? How dark the contusion?

"I'm looking for Private Terrence Costa," he said. "This pool is listed as his last place of employment."

When she told him she hadn't seen Terrence since he had enlisted in the army more than a year ago, the agent acted surprised, then concerned. "That could make things difficult for his parents. Lying to the FBI is a criminal offense."

"They've never lied about anything."

"They told me they saw him before the holidays."

It hurt Sarah to hear that Mr and Mrs had been dragged into this, hurt even more to say, "They're confused. Worried. They lost their oldest son in Vietnam, that war, and now their youngest boy has run off to Mexico."

The agent checked his watch, then glanced at the pool. Sarah thought he looked tired, in a suit too thin for San Francisco's dark clouds and cold wind. "Did you notice the snow on Mount Tamalpais?" she asked. "This is San Francisco, not LA, agent John…."

"Jonathan Smith."

"A likely story."

"Your boyfriend should do everyone a favor and turn himself in."

"He's not my boyfriend."

The special agent flipped open a stainless Zippo, tried three times to light a fire, gave up, and said, "The war's over. Secretary Kissinger signed the peace agreement a year ago, and there's no danger of your cousin being sent overseas."

"Is that a guarantee?"

"So, you have seen him?"

Sarah shook her head.

Was it her imagination, or did she actually feel sorry for him?

The longer he stayed, the stronger the wind blew, making him look fragile and helpless like everyone else in the city, shivering in the cold and afraid of the dark. Sarah wanted to turn him around, point him at the city, and warn him to go home and lock the door. Instead, she said, “You should stop smoking. It’s bad for your health.”

The agent handed her a business card. “I'm sorry for your loss."

"What?"

He shouted into the wind. "I hear David was a fine soldier. Call me when you want to do the right thing.”

“What would that be?”

“Save Terrence.” He turned to go, stopped, and pointed at the Korbel bottle. “And stop drinking alone. It’s bad for your health.”

As the special agent’s car disappeared toward the ocean, a black-and-white Ford Galaxy appeared at the pumping station and drove along the pool. She stuffed the card into her shirt pocket and wiped her hands on the back of her jeans.

The Galaxy stopped in the FBI’s space, and the driver, a uniformed patrolman, stepped out, opened the back door, and waved at her to get in.

“A second,” she said and reached inside for her field jacket and watch cap, telling herself there was no use asking why. Seven years in the city had taught her that the San Francisco Police Department was like the weather. Good or bad, it did whatever it wanted to do, whenever it wanted to do it, so worrying whether it would rain or shine, good or bad, wasn’t worth the trouble. She thought about picking up the bottle of Korbel, said goodbye instead, and walked to the police cruiser.

The uniform holding the door was a stranger. The suit in the front seat looked familiar, in the same clothes he wore when he talked to the press on TV. A funky plaid suit that almost hid his shoulder holster and a bow tie that looked like it belonged to Soupy Sales. His curly black hair added to the wild effect. “Nice tie,” she said as she tried to remember his name, but could only think of Dirty Harry and something to do with the Zodiac.

"Get in," he said, pointing his thumb at the back seat.

"If you're looking for my cousin, he's not here. The FBI guy was just here asking for him."

"They couldn't find their own TV show if they knew the channel. Get in."

The suit in the back patted the seat, saying, "Please, sit here, Ms Costa."

"Sarah," she said, climbing in, relaxed. She couldn't remember his name either, but she recognized him and thought about thanking him for getting Terrence out of jail. Was it three or four times? But she saw Harry watching her in the rearview mirror. So instead, she said that she liked the younger man's "threads," a word she had picked up from Ms Jane and Terrence. His tan corduroy sport coat, dress shirt with a green tie, and pressed slacks made him look like an old-school college professor, except this professor was carrying an inspector's gold badge. Maybe the times were changing because he wasn't Irish. She could see that.

"How are the Costas?" he asked. "Losing David must have been tough on them. He was a good man."

"Thanks."

The driver eased the Galaxy onto the main road while Dirty Harry talked at him about the Niners and how he wished they were still playing at Kezar instead of Candlestick. The car stunk of cigarettes, coffee, and sweat. The two men in front reeked of Old Spice and red wine with a splash of Irish Spring. Luckily, her gold inspector was a good neighbor, offering a hint of citrus and minty fresh breath as he assured her, "This won't take long."

Sarah glanced at the shotgun racked to the dashboard. The north wind was whipping huge winter swells into snowy avalanches. When the uniform tried the wipers, they smeared salt and dirt into the glass, and he had to hunch over the steering wheel, trying to see through a narrow slit in the dirty mess.

Harry said, "Drop these two at the diner."

They made a quick U-turn and drove under the fiberglass Dachshund stuck at the top of a red pole. "He's got a tie like yours," Sarah said.

Harry didn't look back.

"Sophisticated," Sarah added.

The uniform smiled in the rearview mirror and swung the patrol car into the parking lot.

"We're dropping you and the Inspector here," Harry said. The car stopped in front of the diner's glass doors. "I've got somebody else to see."

Sarah and the gold inspector stepped into the wind and watched the police car head toward the ocean. The detective held the diner's door open, letting the smell of burning hamburger escape as he said, "Now that he's gone, you can call me Hitch."

"Shut the goddam door!" a waitress shouted behind the counter.

Sarah stopped at the cash register and searched her memory until she tied the waitress's foul mouth and dirty blond hair to Terrence's half-finished docudrama about a waitress in love with a female impersonator. "Linda, right?"

"Who else." She blew strands of yellow hair off her eye and nodded at Hitch. "Where did you pick him up?"

"Other way around."

"Nice." Linda turned to yell at the cook. "Hot dog and chili with mayo for the girl from Hawaii." When she turned back to the counter, the same strands of blonde hair had fallen over her eye. She blew them back and said, "You should bring that one to Winterland. He's bitchin. In the Fillmore, right, honey?"

"He's police."

"Nobody's perfect."

Over Sarah's shoulder, Hitch said, "I know where Winterland is." He stepped by Sarah to order.

While the Inspector and the counter girl chatted like old friends, Sarah sat at her favorite table next to the window, telling herself she liked the way he moved, smooth and cool for a big man with a solid body.

The Inspector settled onto the stool across from her, and Sarah guessed he was in his late thirties. Too good-looking to be a cop. She glanced under the table, saw brown wingtips, brown socks, and tapered slacks. “I hope those aren’t Wrights,” she said.

“Roos Brothers.”

“What’s that?”

“Clothing for men. A store.” He glanced past her. “Nice gal, the waitress.”

“Too young for you. Why aren’t we with the other guy, the man with the outspoken tie?”

“He’s on a different case. I avoid bodies if I can.”

“What kind of body?”

“The dead kind too hard to identify. On the beach. Close to here.”

“If you’re going to San Francisco,” she said, “be sure to wear a flower in your hair.”

“Young lady, you’re not old enough to be so cynical.”

“How old do I have to be?”

“Order up,” the blonde shouted. “For San Francisco’s finest.”

Sarah stood up, but the Inspector stood up faster and came back with their orders.

They talked between mouthfuls of chili, hot dogs, coleslaw, and crispy fries. He drank Coke. She drank water, and when he asked when she started eating mayo with chili, she told him that she grew up in Hilo, a small town in a rainforest in the middle of the ocean, where mayo was considered a staple.

He wiped his lips with a paper napkin, told her he was born in Texas and raised in San Francisco, graduated, like her, from SF State, and was a bus driver before a cop. "Even worked in a toll booth at the Golden Gate Bridge," he said. “I’ve been lucky."

Then they ate with purpose, without talking, until he nudged his leftover fries at Sarah and said, “David used to help us. Terrence, too. Not for money.”

Sarah looked down at her leftover fries.

“You knew?”

“I guessed.”

He poked his straw at the ice in his cup. "If Terrence were still in the city, he could help us. You could ask."

"He's a fugitive in Mexico." Sarah wrapped the leftover fries in a napkin and headed for the door. Hitch followed her, and they stood together in the wind.

"You could help."

"I'm a nurse."

"I'm on a case." They were both looking at the ocean when he said, "These people won't talk to me."

"What people?"

"Gay people."

"You think I'm gay?"

"You have friends."

"More reason to keep my mouth shut." Sarah looked up at the diner's Dachshund. He was still up there with a smile and a wink.

"Maybe you could ask Ms Jane," Hitch said. "Tell her this is about saving lives. We think we've got a serial killer working the gay bars."

Later, after Hitch left with Dirty Harry, Sarah waved goodbye to the fiberglass doggie, crossed the street, and climbed over the zoo's fence. Ms Jane was waiting in front of the monkey cage.

"What did Lois Lane's friend want?"

"Who?" Sarah asked.

"The FBI."

"Looking for Terrence."

"And the other one?"

"He's working on a murder," Sarah said. "You know him?"

"We've met. I've said hello."

"He wants me to help. Or you. Or Terrence."

"Terrence? He can barely help himself."

A seagull landed near Sarah's foot. She dug into her pocket, found the wad of fries, and tossed one to the gull. From his cage, a monkey held his long fingers through the bars. “Not good for you,” Sarah said and turned to the lion cages, where a tall attendant in worn overalls was fire-hosing blood off the floor.

Three seagulls landed in front of her.

Sarah tossed another fry.

“Go away,” Ms Jane said. “Crazy birds. What the hell are you doing here?”

“Hunger.” Sarah tossed the last fry and watched the birds fly off with it toward the ocean. Behind her, the monkeys climbed the bars, turned upside down, and screeched.

17.A RAISED FIST

Time: January 28, 1974
Location: San Francisco

Ms Jane's VW Van had a new CB radio and an optimistic gas gauge. It read empty today, but Ms Jane wasn't worried. She assured Sarah that she had driven from Fleishhacker Pool to San Quentin on empty.

"San Quentin?"

"The gas shortage is sucking the heart out of the city."

In one month, gas prices had jumped from 39 to 59 cents. Now, the gas stations were drying up. The first station they passed featured a line of cars stretched around the block. Ms Jane eased her foot off the gas. "No worries. We coast down Geary, check your cousin's favorite dives. If Terrence is out and about, we'll find him."

"Before we run out of gas?"

"Maybe." Ms Jane was wearing her "athletic" outfit: faded black jeans, black leather jacket, and black hoodie, with a new pair of bright red Converse high-tops. "He's a fast runner," she said, tapping the gas pedal. "Slippery and paranoid, but I'm ready for him."

"I'm not worried about him." Sarah had swapped her nursing uniform for a striped rugby shirt, jeans, and combat boots, topped with a blue watch cap. Even with the gas crunch, cars jammed the streets out of the City. The Zebras were nighttime killers, and it would be dark soon.

Near Winterland, people were lining up for the screening of the Ali-Frasier fight. Ms Jane's new CB caught the police chattering about Black Panthers trying to sell their propaganda rag to fight fans. "Muhammad Speaks," the dispatcher laughed. "Good luck with that."

Ms Jane checked the gas gauge, said, "Still empty!" And coasted onto Scott and circled Alamo Park until she spotted an opening between a panel truck and a Cadillac. Across the street, three-story Victorians, stacked like giant speakers, blasted shouts, cheers, and television gunshots. "Terrence's favorites," Ms Jane said.

"The Painted Ladies."

"Prostitutes," Ms Jane said. As the streetlights blinked, she reached behind the seat and fished out her gear bag. "Hold this," she said, handing the canvas bag to Sarah. She reached again, deeper this time, and hauled out a loop of garden hose and an empty jug of Red Mountain. "I'll be back."

Sarah stuffed the gear bag between her feet, leaned out the window, and watched Ms Jane check the panel truck, and hurry back to the Cadillac. She was tugging at the license plate when a window flew open across the street and a man's head popped out, shouting, "Hey you, dick-heads. Whitey. What're you doing?"

Three kids on bikes, dragging a reluctant dog by a rope leash, sang, "Stealing gas. Stealing gas!" A long hair in sagging bell bottoms and a crusty orange sweater stepped out of the shadows, shaking his head, saying gently, "Peace, man. Not cool."

Ms Jane waved a beauty-queen salute to the neighborhood and climbed back into her van. "Damn," she said, "Where the hell did that mob come from?" She swung the van into a tight U-turn and let it coast down Golden Gate. "We'd better wait until it's darker." She kept her foot on the clutch. "Where the hell do Cadillacs hide their gas caps?"

Sarah punched her friend's shoulder. "I won't steal gas."

"It's not stealing. It's appropriating for the cause. I passed on the working man's panel and went for the Cadillac."

"Don't be stupid."

"Fascist insect."

The VW coasted to Finocchio's on fumes. The drag bar was packed tight but with no sign of Terrence. Ms Jane, with Sarah in tow, shoved her way through the crowd to the bartender, an ex-heavyweight that Ms Jane knew from way back. "Hey, Bubba," she said. "We're looking for a friend." She pointed at her chest. "About this tall. Beatnik-looking skinny guy? Talks jazz."

"Terrence? I heard he was working for the pigs."

"Not anymore. He's on the run."

"From?"

"The Feds."

"Karma. Righteous. Haven't seen him. Who's the sister?"

"A friend. From Berkeley."

"You can check the back. But leave your friend here. It's a tight squeeze."

Ms Jane flashed him a peace sign, told Sarah to wait, and disappeared through the door marked "Off Limits: Dressing Rooms."

Sarah stood at the bar watching a young man sketch a charcoal caricature of what she guessed was a cross-dressing shadow. "Would you like one?" he asked. "I'm not very good, but I'm learning." He told her the performers were his favorite subjects because no one could tell if he was making a mistake or a stylish interpretation. He smiled and patted the stool next to him. "Sit."

When she did, he handed her his leather portfolio and flipped his sketch pad to a new page. "I'd like to try. You're not exactly my type. You're too…normal. I'm sorry. I meant that as a compliment. I meant you're not a performer."

"I'm a nurse."

"Exciting." He went to work. "I'm not good with faces. Have a drink on me. This will only take a minute." Still slashing the page with charcoal, he ordered two red wines.

As he worked, she flipped through his portfolio, rough drawings of what she guessed were men dressed as women, most in costumes with oversized hats. There was one nude. And one wearing what appeared to be a newsboy cap and dark glasses with a splash of goatee. “Who’s this?” she asked.

In the smoke-filled light, he squinted at his drawing. “Let me see. I didn’t get far with it. Lucky for me, I heard he was a cop.” He checked the entrance. “These boys don’t need more cops. It’s dangerous enough without more cops.”

When Sarah leaned in for a close look at the murky drawing, the artist’s aftershave made her see Joe Namath on television, the Jets quarterback claiming Brut was “For men who go all the way.” Terrence claimed it burned like gasoline and smelled worse, but he kept a green bottle in the Falcon’s glove compartment. “For emergencies. A disinfectant.”

“Here you are,” the artist said. "Just like you."

Holding her breath, Sarah saw a cloudy woman wearing what might have been a nurse's cap and a Red Cross armband in black and white. A charcoal smudge at the bottom of the page had the correct year: 1974.

“Where are they going?" The artist grabbed the sketch pad and glanced at the club’s entrance, where a line of customers was bogged down at the exit. “The cops have been in every night,” he said. “You know how that is.”

“Not really.”

“Oh, sorry. I forgot. You’re a nurse. And your girlfriend?”

“Who?”

"Her." The artist pointed behind at the stage door, where Ms Jane was watching a slight performer in a sequined gown with a fruit-basket headpiece step gallantly onto the small stage

“She’s a lifeguard.”

“That makes sense.”

“It does?”

“Your friend. He was here, maybe thirty minutes ago. I thought he was crazy because he said he was going for a swim.”

On the road, Ms Jane stopped for two Brew 102s, both tall-boys, and a bag of peanuts. She finished one on Columbus and number two as they reached Aquatic Park. She parked in Terrence's secret space and hurried through the Dirty Harry tunnel to the Maritime Museum.

"Your painter friend is a narc," Ms Jane said. "Lucky for us."

They walked along the beach, smelled dark water, and sat in the bleachers, watching an old man toss donut chunks to seagulls. He caught them staring and said, "Beautiful night, young ladies. Beautiful day. My birthday."

"There's two of us," Ms Jane said.

He stepped closer, squinting into the shadows. "They'll eat anything," he said. "Gotta love em."

"Or hate them," Ms Jane said. "How long have you been here?"

The old guy pushed his shoulders back, offered a salute, and declared, "Mams, I've been on this earth for 69 years. Today's my birthday." He had dressed for the occasion in baggy jeans, a thick sweater, two raincoats, and a blue watch cap.

"Have you seen anyone swimming?" Sarah asked.

He buttoned up both raincoats. "Swimming? Here? No way. I'd know." He pointed at a Coast Guard patch on his shoulder. "Retired. 30 years. How do I look for 69, ladies?"

"Out of sight."

"Perfect," Sarah said.

"Thank you, ladies." He offered a nod, almost a bow. "But I must go."

They watched him walk toward Van Ness, and when he faded into the dark, they chased handfuls of peanuts with gulps of Brew 102. "Terrence Costa," Ms Jane said.

"Where is he?"

"He's not good on his own."

"Or with people."

The City was alive with lights. A cold wind brushed against Sarah's face.

Ms Jane shook her head. “It’s getting late.”

“Always.”

“Let’s go.”

“Afraid of the Zebras?”

“Not me,” Ms Jane said. “They only kill white people.”

They were on Van Ness when they heard the sirens. Ms Jane turned on the AM-FM, and they heard an excited sportscaster shouting that Muhammed Ali had won a 12-round unanimous decision. Ms Jane raised a fist in salute. Sarah threw a practice jab at the front window.

Switching to CB, they heard a calm voice calling for an ambulance to respond to a shooting.

“Oh, so usual, right?” Ms Jane said. They passed a gas station with a hand-painted sign offering grim news: “No gas! Closed!” Ms Jane used her Zippo to throw light on the gas gauge. “We’re a fingernail off empty.”

“Still?”

“I told you.” Ms Jane sat up straight. “We can check Scott Street. Bet it’s quiet now. And it’s close.”

“I’m not stealing.”

“Stealing gas is not stealing. It’s appropriating for the cause.” She turned off Geary onto Divisadero, then stopped. In a circle of streetlight, a man was kneeling over a body. A woman watched with both hands over her mouth.

Sarah jumped out and ran. The man looked up, yelling, “I was on my way for cigarettes. I was on my way for cigarettes.”

Sarah knelt over the body.

The man shouted, “Can you believe that? Can you? I ran all the way. The hospital, they wouldn’t…”

Sarah saw the blood on the sidewalk, and when she tried to turn the body over, she heard a woman’s voice cry, “Please, no, don’t touch me.”

A policeman stepped between Sarah and the body. “Out of the way. Let the ambulance guys handle this.”

From across the street, a man shouted, “It was a white man done the shooting!”

Sarah backed away, watching the ambulance crew work on the woman. Inside the van, she heard the dispatcher’s voice, excited now, worried and in a hurry, sending patrol cars and an ambulance to a second shooting, on Scott Street.

“That’s right around the block,” Ms Jane said and stepped on the gas.

Sarah slammed her hand against the dashboard. “I didn’t do crap to help her.”

“There!” Ms Jane shouted, pointing at more police cars, two ambulances, and another body.

As Sarah jumped out, she heard an attendant shout, “Get back! He’s still alive. We’ll move him.” A policeman turned to Sarah and waved her back, shouting something Sarah didn’t hear. As the attendants lifted the body onto a gurney, Sarah recognized the raincoat, the Coast Guard patch on the shoulder, and the blue watch cap.

“Get in,” Ms Jane shouted.

“It was him,” Sarah said.

“Who?”

The VW started, sputtered, coasted in the dark, and stopped at Alamo Park. The Cadillac was gone, the panel truck still there. The street was quiet, and Ms Jane turned the CB down low as the night pressed in on them.

Ms Jane reached behind the seat and dug out a gallon jug of wine and a body-length of garden hose. “I’ll get the gas."

"Not good. Look."

Both women read the lettering on the panel truck. "Black Self-Help Moving and Storage.”

“I’ll leave a five on the windshield," Ms Jane said.

While Ms Jane worked on the truck, the dispatcher reported three more shootings. An old man in an alley. A woman in a laundromat. And a woman on her doorstep. Sarah unzipped the gear bag between her feet and found Lois Lane's gun wrapped in an SF-State hoodie. She was tucking it in her waistband when Ms Jane came back spitting gasoline.

"Horrible," Ms Jane said, turning away to spit again. "But it tastes better than Red Mountain."

"You left the money?"

"Sure did."

Ms Jane drove into the night as a man's voice shouted, "Screw you!"

18.WALKING THE PLANK

Time: April 15, 1974
Location: San Francisco

It was April, Easter dead and gone. And Sarah Costa was tossing her polyester uniform in the nurse's laundry bin.

The Zebras had murdered two more people, raising their total to twelve. Not to be outdone, the Symbionese Liberation Army had emerged from its fog of kidnapping and Maoist rhetoric to try its luck at bank robbery. Their captive heiress was now a gun-pointing comrade. Not to be outdone, the mayor had promised to implement a series of Zebra Checks. The newspapers warned people to expect a heavy police presence on the streets. The Chronicle's headlines were predicting "Extreme Zebra Checks."

Searching for something stronger than soap, Sarah skipped a shower and changed into what she called civies; Levis, palaka shirt, and jungle boots. She left her transfer request at the nurse's station. And in return, the nurse working the phones handed her a message pad. "Ms Jane sounds like a doll."

"Do I need to read this? Or can you fill me in?"

"She's waiting for you at..." He shifted to a whisper, "At the People's Temple."

"Why are you whispering?"

"I don't know. It happens whenever I mention church. Even that one. It's going to be a mess down there. You need an escort?"

Was he kidding? Sarah tried to remember his name. Something to do with the sea. He had a pleasant smile and a devil-dog tattoo on his forearm. Her supervisor had warned her that he was living in the Castro. Could she believe it? Did she know what that meant?

Sarah did, and she didn't care. Now she watched him turning the dial of a small transistor radio. He had long fingers, almost delicate, like a musician's, but his shoulders and tight-fitting uniform hinted something more physical. A swimmer's body?

"I like your tattoo," she said.

"Marines."

"I know."

"Not really me. I'm navy. Don't ask. I'm a student now."

She leaned into his hint of cinnamon. "Sorry, I forgot your name."

"Around here, they call me Cappy."

Sarah was surprised at how dark green his eyes were, and she wondered why he still cut his hair short, like he was still in the service, shaved on the sides and flat on top. His gentle voice deserved something softer.

He stepped from behind the desk, was about to hug her, stopped, and said, "I'll be off in a minute. You need a drink. I know a place that's always open."

"I'm on my way to church."

He spread his arms wide. "That's what I mean. The Gangway is the best spot in town for $1 shots before church."

"Maybe next time." She stopped at the stairs, looked at the phone message, and saw Lois Lane's name. She turned back to Cappy. "The Gangway?" she said. "Where is it?"

"You've never been there? I'm surprised they let you take care of babies."

Sarah managed a smile. "One drink."

"Far out."

While Cappy changed, Sarah looked down at her new boots. She had found them at Ms Jane's pool, abandoned there by Terrence after he had used them to escape from basic training in San Diego. The boots had worked like magic for him, boosting him over a fence and into a VW bus that carried him back to San Francisco. If she wore thick socks, the boots fit her perfectly, but she was still waiting for their magic. She closed her eyes and tapped the heels together three times, and Cappy appeared in tight jeans, a loose-fitting plaid shirt, heavy hiking boots, and a puffy green down jacket.

"That was quick," she said.

"Lots of practice at my night job. You should see me change between acts."

In his old Galaxie, they drove deep into the city, Sarah thinking he would make a super bus driver, fast as a speeding bullet and able to leap over the city's passive-aggressive traffic in a single bound. "How's Terrence?" he asked.

"Who?"

"The nurses told me the FBI came to the hospital asking about your cousin, Terrence."

"We haven't heard from him in months."

"They said he was a deserter."

"That's Terrence."

"Good for him."

"I thought you were a vet."

"Corpsman. Two years in the boonies. Not a shot fired. That's me. No war stories."

Cappy made a hard left and parked near the Hotel Heartland. Sarah thought it looked like it had lost its heart long ago, but she stepped into misty sunshine, eager for a drink. Cappy hurried her past a liquor store and stopped at the bar, a ship's bow protruding from a brick wall.

How did I miss this before, Sarah wondered, and then, without thinking, asked, "A sailor's bar?"

"Sailors always welcome."

A covered gangway led past a wall of purple handprints to a

heavy door with a brass porthole. They had to squeeze sideways between tangles of men to reach the bar.

"Is it okay for me to be here?" Sarah asked.

"Why not?"

"Looks like men only."

"We're learning," he said. "Wait here, order me a whisky. I have to say hello. Fans, you know. I'll ask around about your cousin." He stopped. "Do you have a picture? Maybe someone has seen him. We're all friends here. Some of us."

She showed him a 1x1 from her wallet.

"I like him already," Cappy said. He took it from her and pushed through the crowded room, stopping to talk to men at tables and a few singles along the bar. Sarah sat at the end of the bar and asked for a whiskey. "Make that two whiskies with water chasers and the phone."

The bartender reached under the bar and set the phone in front of her. "Calling your lawyer?"

"Do I need one?"

"The cops been showing up regular."

She shrugged. "I can handle."

"Really? You from around here?"

"Close."

"A working girl?"

He was a good-looking young man with a beginner's beer belly and pale skin. Too much night work and bar food, offering a polite cloud of patchouli. She said, "I'm a nurse."

"Jack fine?" He poured two shots.

"I'm looking for a friend."

He nodded. "Me too." He mopped the bar with a clean towel. "You know why women want gay men? Because they can't have them. Makes sense. Why want something you already have, right?"

"Good to know. Not my problem."

He checked behind her. "When they come, you can hide behind the bar. Don't worry. It's the boys they're after. They don't know how to handle girls, not yet."

"Who?"

"The pigs. And keep the queen quiet. He can be uppity."

"Who?"

"Cappy."

"Oh."

"I've seen him work the stage at Finocchio's. Outstanding."

"They won't hurt him. He's a vet."

The bartender shook his head. "Where you from?"

"Berkeley."

"No way. You'd know better."

He walked to the other end of the bar, and Sarah saw a familiar face in the corner, near a sign for The Head. The artist, in black slacks and t-shirt, was working on a large sketch pad. His model looked distinguished, much older, in a suit and tie. Sarah was headed their way when a blast of sunlight hit the room, and three uniformed cops crashed in, shouting, "Police! Shut the fuck up and get on your feet."

"Fuck you, pigs," voices shouted back.

"No, fuck you, homos."

Cappy appeared, shouting, "Everyone be cool."

"Up against the wall, sucker."

A cop grabbed the artist and tossed his portfolio. Sarah picked it up, and the cop shoved her out of the way. The suit disappeared into the chaos of cops working their way down the bar, grabbing men, cuffing them, shoving them against the wall, shouting, "Faggots against the wall. Now! Bitches."

The artist grabbed Sarah. Sarah grabbed Cappy. And the three of them shoved and tugged and crashed their way out the door, along the gangplank, and into the street.

"Run," Cappy shouted. "Time for church."

Before they reached the car, somewhere along the way, the artist disappeared into the night with his portfolio.

Still shaken, Sarah and Cappy found Ms Jane three blocks from The People's Temple.

"Who's this?" she asked.

"Cappy. You talked to him on the phone."

"Oh.

"We can trust him."

"What the hell happened to you two? Is that blood?"

"A scratch," Cappy said.

"Walk with me. Stay close. It's crazy out here. Frickin mayor.

"No need to tell us," Cappy said. "We just got a taste."

"We'll be okay if we keep moving. This is special for black people." Walking fast and talking faster, blending into the flow, Ms Jane told them Lois Lane was working on a story about Rev Jones when she found a woman who ran the nursery for him at the Temple. "Val's her name. When she finishes work, she goes home to more kids in an old Victorian not far from here. Like the old lady in the shoe. Fifteen or twenty of them ent there by Jones. He likes to separate parents from their kids. Vinny's one of those parents. Jones sent his kid there."

Sarah grabbed her friend's shoulder and tugged her off the sidewalk, out of the flow. "Stop. What the hell? Jane, we're looking for Terrence."

"That's what I'm trying to tell you. Terrence has been hiding out at the Temple. Vinny and Terrence are like this." Ms Jane crossed her heart. "They're at the Temple now helping Val."

"Let's go."

The sidewalk was jammed so tight with people they had to lock arms and let Cappy drag them toward the Temple.

"Today of all days," Ms Jane said. "Lois calls me today of all days."

"I don't trust her," Sarah shouted.

"You don't know her. Valerie was the Roman goddess of childbirth."

"That was Diana," Cappy shouted.

"Are you sure?"

"Prince Valiant," Cappy said. "Brave and strong."

"That's even better."

"Keep moving," Sarah said.

They passed a row of police cars and a television reporter interviewing a bearded prophet in a rainbow-colored robe that looked like a hand-painted graduation gown. Bits and pieces of his prophecy shouted at the reporter survived the crowd noise. "The madness that drives men… to kill innocent people…" he cried out as he struggled to stay on his feet after a violent shove to his back. "It's a sickness," he whimpered. "An American sickness."

A woman in a dark dress and high heels blocked their way, and shouted, "What are you doing here, girls? You all better get off the street. The Death Angels are coming out tonight. You go home."

"Pardon me," Cappy said, and they slipped by her and into a line of men waiting to enter Muhammad's Temple. Uniformed police officers were blocking the entrance, stopping to check every man's ID, demanding they fill out a Zebra-check card.

"You folks don't belong here," a cop said. The cop, a young fellow with a hint of blond mustache, showed them a flier with an artist's drawing of two Zebra suspects. Both black. "Have you seen them?" he asked.

One suspect was wearing a watch cap. Sarah thought they were the same man.

"We're looking for the People's Temple, officer," Cappy said.

The cop jumped an octave, "We're looking for a god dammed serial killer!"

A swirl of people caught Sarah and spun her into the street. Police radios blared staticky commands. Cars braked, honked, and sped up. She dodged a Ghirardelli delivery truck before Cappy caught her arm and tugged her back onto the sidewalk. In front of the Peoples Temple, at the top of the steps, Jim Jones stood in his white suit and aviator sunglasses. Surrounded by six black bodyguards in black berets, suits, and ties, he raised his hands to heaven.

Sarah saw his lips moving, his bodyguards holding back the crowd. She tried to run up the steps, but a bodyguard shoved her back. The Reverend Jim Jones retreated. The Temple doors swung open, and the rising tide swept Jones and his guards inside. The crowd jabbed Sarah in the ribs, punched Cappy in the kidneys, and kicked Ms Jane as it pressed them through the doorway. Behind them, the doors slammed shut.

The Reverend Jim Jones had climbed to an elevated pulpit and was preaching to the congregation through a microphone, warning them in a deep, almost singing voice. “I told you. This is why we have to pray. This is what’s coming. We have to prepare for this. Revolutionary suicide.”

They found a quiet spot against the back wall.

“I don’t see Terrence,” Sarah said.

“Revolutionary suicide?” Cappy said. “Jones sounds crazy.”

Ms Jane held his hand and pulled him close. “Back when Jones was only half crazy,” she said in his ear. “Vinny needed a preacher for his wedding. Jones is the only preacher who would do the service, so Vinny thinks he’s the real thing. Sad story. Vinny’s wife nearly dies giving birth. Now, she’s in a coma and Jones had the kid.”

“That’s enough,” Cappy said.

“I thought you were a Marine.”

“There!” Sarah said. A sturdy woman in jeans and a sweatshirt was waving to them from a doorway.

“Val,” she said, leading them down a dark hallway into an explosion of light and chattering kids, screeching, laughing and shouting, spilling in and out of playpens, throwing toys, and chasing each other in circles, squealing, “You’re it. Tag. You’re it!”

They waded through children, stepped over them, around them, through them. Ms Jane picked one up. Sarah made her put it down. And Val pointed at the back door. Squeals and laughter followed them outside, where they saw Terrence’s and his newsboy cap swept away by a river of Zebra-Check refugees.

19.UPSTAIRS NEIGHBORS

Time: May-Sept., 1974
Location: San Francisco

On May 1, acting on a tip from one of the killers, the SF Police raided two apartments on Grove Street, a block from Alamo Square Park. By the end of the day, seven suspects had been arrested. Four were held for trial. And the Zebra killings were over.

On May 17, acting on a tip from Ms Jane, Sarah knocked on the door of an apartment on Golden Gate Avenue, a few blocks from Alamo Square. Terrence answered in his newsboy cap, t-shirt, and blue boxers. Said, long time no see. Hugged her, stepped back, and waved her inside. "Hurry. You gotta see this. Hurry."

Sarah saw a beanbag aimed at a black-and-white TV balanced on a packing crate. While Terrence fiddled with the rabbit ears, a tiny black Buddha wrapped her in sandalwood clouds.

"Where have you been?"

"There!" Pointing at the TV, he sank into the beanbag. "Look."

In the TV, a woman was peeking around a corner then ducking back to provide commentary into a handheld microphone. In her thirties, with blond hair, frightened eyes, and a steady voice, she called the siege the biggest shootout in history. The Los Angeles Police

Department had surrounded a rundown single-story house at East 54th and Compton Ave. They had asked the SLA members to surrender, the revolutionaries had opened fire, and now the authorities were pouring bullets and tear gas into the house. The reporter confirmed that Field Marshall Cinque and his followers were trapped inside. She couldn't confirm that Patty Hearst was one of them.

Over what seemed to be continuous shots fired, she informed Sarah and Terrence that it was 5:30. This was a live broadcast, the first of its kind.

The cameras cut to helicopters circling overhead, shifted down to police running across the street, and shooting from behind parked cars. From the smoking house, a woman walked out with her hands in the air. The police dragged her to the ground. More shots were fired into and from the house. Policemen lobbed gas grenades. Detectives in suits shouted for more ammunition, more firepower.

Sarah heard screams as the house caught fire. Two women crawled out from under the house, and when they stood up, they were shot, both on the ground, one dragged back under the house by her feet.

The flames spread as Terrence said, "If they were looking for a place to die, they found it."

A policeman behind a patrol car reloaded his handgun. The TV flickered, filled with snow. Terrence jumped up to adjust the rabbit ears, and the TV came back to life. While the fire burned, the woman's voice off-camera reported that thousands of shots had been fired.

"Who's counting?" Terrence asked. "You want something to drink?"

"Stay here. I've seen enough." The kitchen was in the living room. Sarah opened the refrigerator and found a dead light bulb, an empty ice tray, white bread in a cellophane bag, and bologna slices on a plastic plate. "How about water?" she asked. "Is it drinkable?"

In the TV, the house had burned to the ground. "How long have you been living here?" she asked.

Terrence closed his eyes and pressed his fingers to his temples.

"Let me see." He rubbed his eyes. "Three or four months. Did Ms Jane tell you about the apartment upstairs?"

The television voice reported that no policemen had been injured.

"Up there." Terrence pointed at the ceiling. "That's where they were hiding."

A knock at the door. Two more. Then Ms Jane walked in carrying a brown bag of groceries, saying, "Jeez, lock the door."

"It's safer this way. No one gets hurt when they have to bust it down."

Ms Jane twirled in her bright yellow summer dress and black pumps.

"A dress?" Sarah said. "First time?"

"Have to look respectable." She flipped her ponytail off her shoulder and handed the groceries to Terrence. Kissed him on the cheek and tossed her leather jacket at the TV, knocking off its rabbit ears. "Turn that off. Television is driving me crazy."

"How long have you known?" Sarah said. "He should be in Canada."

"I'm not leaving," Terrence said. "This city is my home. Besides, no one cares about me. The war is over. Almost." He lifted a bottle of plum wine from the grocery bag. "I've been meaning to try this stuff." He twisted off the cap and swallowed three times before spitting plum wine into the sink. "Man, I can't drink that. I can drink Ripple, not that."

Ms Jane took the bottle. Sipped the dark wine, swished it side to side, and spit into the sink. "Revolutionary. The Field Marshal's favorite, with a horrible front end and even nastier finish." She spit again. "I can't get rid of the taste." When she tried emptying the bottle into the sink, Terrence grabbed it, screwed the cap tight, and set it in the refrigerator. "Waste not. Want not."

"I was sending it back to the Field Marshall." Ms Jane dug a jar of peanut butter and a loaf of SF sourdough out of her grocery bag. "There's enough violence in this world without that wine adding to it."

Sarah looked inside the bag. A carton of eggs, a bag of carrots, and a paperback book by Dr. Spock. "Spock, really?"

"He was against the war," Ms Jane said.

"It's about caring for babies," Sarah said.

Ms Jane shrugged. "I have to read something. I might volunteer to help Val." She ripped off a chunk of sourdough and dipped it in the jar of peanut butter. "It's spring and I don't want to think about killers. Not Nixon or the Zebras or the Zodiac. Not anybody with a gun. I've had enough. Babies are good. Guns bad." She bit into bread and peanut butter, chewed, and tried to swallow. "That's… my…advice."

Sarah handed her a coffee cup filled with tap water. "Drink up. That's my advice."

Ms Jane gulped half of it, bit off another chunk, and said with her mouth full, "You'll see."

"See what?" Sarah asked.

"That even dogs know you can't chew peanut butter," Terrence said. He had rescued the rabbit ears, and flickering TV jumped from the streets of LA to the broadcast studio in LA, where an excited talking head reported that the Ulster Volunteer Force had detonated bombs in Dublin, killing 33. India's government announced it would detonate a nuclear device in a defense program named Smiling Buddha.

"What Buddha would smile about that?" Ms Jane asked, then patted the brass incense burner. "Not mine."

The TV's talking head interrupted her. "We have unofficial confirmation that Field Marshall Cinque is dead. Burned to death or suicide, one of the six SLA members dead. No confirmation yet that Patty Hearst was one of them."

Ms Jane turned off the television, sank into the beanbag, and opened her book. "Fascist insects with guns," she said. "I'm going to a better world."

"Come with me," Terrence said to Sarah. He opened one of the studio apartment's two windows, climbed out, and motioned for her to follow. "This way. I don't trust the neighbors."

"You still have neighbors?" Ms Jane said, not bothering to look up from her book. "You better go, Sarah, and keep him from getting lost. That place gives me the creeps."

Sarah climbed one flight up, watching Terrence pry open an apartment window with a butter knife sticky with peanut butter.

"It stinks," she said. "Something, many things, died in here."

"No kidding." Terrence led her through two small bedrooms, a bathroom, and a kitchen. Roaches crawled along the floors, over mattresses, and up the walls. The toilet was plugged full of human waste and newspaper. In the kitchen, Sarah found three empty bottles of plum wine on the floor. In the living room, the walls were covered with hand-scrawled political messages. Sarah read one: "*Patria O Muerte, Venceremos!*" Signed by *Tania.*

"Fatherland or death, we shall triumph!" Terrence said. "I looked it up. It's from Cuba." He touched the name. "I wonder where she is."

"Poor little rich girl." Sarah inhaled the stink of rotting garbage. "Probably dead by now. When were they here?"

"I heard them doing calisthenics, stomping around, but what was I supposed to think? In an old Victorian with wood floors, who doesn't hear their neighbors stomping through the ceiling?"

Sarah rubbed her nose.

"Our city is like a Disneyland of crime," Terrence said. "The FBI headquarters is less than a mile from here, and the Zebra's apartment was over there, on the other side of the Alamo. Victims and killers, that's what we are. Hell, I wouldn't be surprised if the Weather Underground has a bomb factory in the neighborhood."

Terrence stopped at a small closet next to the bathroom and said, "This was Tania's room."

Sarah stepped inside, sat down, tried to stretch her legs, gave up, and closed her eyes. Tried to imagine what it would feel like to be locked in this space. To make love? To be raped?

Behind her, Terrence was doing jumping jacks on the filthy floor. "This is where they counted the money after the bank robbery," he said. "Right here in the living room."

"How do you know that?"

"I didn't realize until later what was going on, but before that, I heard them up here partying. The one time they turned up the music, playing something about money."

"Money, money, money."

"That's it. Over and over."

"The O'Jays."

"I knew that." Terrence stopped at the window. "I hope they didn't suffer in that fire. No one deserves to suffer."

Sarah didn't argue, but she wasn't sure. She followed him down the fire escape, wondering what he would do now. There had to be a better place to hide, a better way, starting with a locked door. Did he want to hide? With Terrence, there was no telling.

Ms Jane had news. "Three of them weren't in the house. No Hearst. No Emily or William."

"I thought you turned off the TV," Terrence said.

"I did. But I couldn't stop myself. It's addiction."

A talking head in the black-and-white TV reported: "It is estimated that six thousand shots were fired by the police, ten thousand by the SLA."

"Who drives around with ten thousand rounds of ammo?" Terrence said and slammed the window shut. Sarah turned off the TV.

In June, Sarah and Cappy wanted to see the buffalo in Golden Gate Park. Instead, they saw three police cars parked alongside Spreckels Lake. Lois Lane was there with Inspector Hitchens. Two uniforms blocked the path to the body. From where they were standing, Cappy and Sarah could see the bloody face, the stab wounds to his chest.

"You don't want to go any farther," Lois said.

Sarah zipped up her leather jacket and squared her shoulders.

"We found a car parked up the road," Hitchens said. "Registered to Joseph Stevens."

"Maybe. There's too much blood."

"Jae."

Hitchens took Cappy by the elbow and led him away from the two uniforms. "You knew him," he said.

Cappy hesitated, saw Sarah nod, then said, "Jae was his stage name. I worked with him at Finocchio's. Smart. Had a comedy schtick, a good one. I think he was working at the Cabaret Club, too."

"You certain?"

Cappy nodded. "A good man."

"Any idea what he was doing out here?"

"What do you think, detective? A quiet place where no one will see them."

Sarah stepped between them and led her friend away.

"No worries," Cappy said. "I've seen worse. Much worse."

On June 29, Sarah heard that Walt Disney had opened a new ride in Anaheim: America Sings.

To clear her mind, Sarah tried walking the beach along the Great Highway, enjoying the ocean on one side, the sand dunes on the other.

On July 7, Sarah heard a report that a woman walking her dog had found a body at the west end of Lincoln Way, at Ocean Beach, off the Great Highway. Claus A. Christmann's had been stabbed fifteen times and his throat cut. Inspector Hitchens called to say he was certain there would be more.

On July 8, Sarah turned on the radio to hear that an 18-year-old worker at Disneyland had died after falling into the mechanical works at a ride called "America Sings."

On July 15, Sarah switched from radio to television in time to see a news anchor point a gun at her own head.

20.A NEW YEAR

Time: February April-May 1975
Location: San Francisco, California

It took Sarah three months to swear off wine. Twenty-five years later, she could still remember every step, starting with a visit to Union Square. It was February, cold and windy, and Cappy was still wearing his blue scrubs. When they walked past the Dewey Monument, he pointed at the Goddess of Victoria perched on her 100-foot column. "That girl should know better," he said. "Her and her silly pitchfork."

"It's a trident," Sarah said.

"It's a war monument, and she should know better."

Sarah preferred to think of her as a woman doing her job, but she kept following him, zipping up her field jacket, eyeing a thin line of sign wavers. "How long will this take?" she asked. "You promised a swim."

"If the Doggie Diner dachshund were up there, we'd live in a better world."

"Be serious."

"Only a minute or two. Maybe three. Promise. This is serious."

Sarah didn't like the looks of the sign wavers. They reminded her of wasted efforts. As for Union Square, in the last seven years, she had been there once, on the back of Jane's motorcycle, dodging tourists and city buses as Jane pointed out buildings that she had seen in the opening sequence of *The Conversation,* her favorite movie. Later, they had sat together in the Balboa Theater and watched Gene Hackman cruising the Square's sidewalk while Jane elbowed her, whispering, "This is how it happens. This is where the U.S. is headed. Big Brother is coming. He hears everything. Sees everything."

Sarah had given up arguing. She knew Big Brother had bigger problems. He might be able to see and hear everything, but he couldn't find the Zodiac or the remains of the SLA. A spoiled heiress in a Che beret and the Vietnamese in black pajamas were kicking his ass. He couldn't find Terrence, and he had lost David. And now he was shooting in all directions, hoping to hit a thousand moving targets.

"We should get in the water," she said. Wait it out. Keep our heads down. But she let Cappy lead her to the speaker's platform while she searched for signs of Big Brother, the sniper armed with a shotgun.

She saw people smiling. She saw hotels, department stores, and bars. Thick green grass, shade trees, and tourists wrapped in new jackets. Two old women sat next to each other on an iron bench, feeding pigeons and eyeing the shoppers who rushed across the street to the City of Paris. Tourists wandered out of the St. Francis Hotel, cars swirled by on Stockton, Geary, Powell, and Post, startling pedestrians balanced at the edge of crosswalks.

At the speaker's platform, the reporters outnumbered the sign wavers, but the protesters shouted their approval when a balding speaker hidden behind aviator sunglasses and a scraggly beard appeared in red sweatpants, a paisley shirt and jogging shoes. At the microphone, he introduced himself as Jack Scott, representing Bill Walton, and said he was there to pledge his support for the boycott of Gallo.

Cappy gazed up at the speaker.

"He's against wine?" Sarah asked.

"Don't be silly. Who would be that stupid?"

"I was joking."

"This is serious." Cappy held her shoulders and looked into her eyes. "This is against Gallo wines. That guy Jack Scott supported Tommie Smith and John Carlos after they raised their fists at the 68 Olympics. Now he's writing a book about the SLA."

Since the shootout last year, Tania and her gang of murdering misfits had disappeared. Jane said they had fled to the East Coast. Terrence said Las Vegas. Sarah had no idea. She heard Cappy shout at the platform, "Avery Brundage was a nazi!" In response, the speaker leaned into the microphone and reminded the growing crowd they would rally again in every city on the way to Modesto. "In Oakland, Hayward, Pleasanton, Livermore, Tracy, and Manteca." When he paused for a breath, the crowd, still growing, shouted their agreement and waved red flags, black eagles in circles of white.

Cappy stood behind Sarah, shouting in her ear, "This is for a good cause. The United Farm Workers. The poor bastards."

"No need to tell me." Sarah knew about farm work. She had seen the men and women working the fields in Cali and Hawaii. Why had Cappy brought her here? She was about to ask him when Ms Jane appeared and kissed her cheek.

Sarah kissed back, then stepped back, eyeing Jane's battle fatigues, a thick Christmas sweater with Santa Claus, and a black beret. The Bota bad hanging from her shoulder didn't fit with a wine boycott. The jungle boots looked familiar.

"What are you doing here? You're supposed to be helping Terrence find Canada."

"Soon. I'm helping Lois."

"Here?"

"For the moment."

The crowd erupted as the speaker raised his fist in a black glove. The protestors set the sky on fire with red flags splashed with black eagles, sending Cappy zig-zagging through the crowd to a table where organizers handed out signs and straw hats.

"I'm here for Dolores Huerta," Ms Jane said. "Chavez is our man. No lie. But this is for Dolores. For women. No table grapes, no lettuce, and no wine!"

"You're giving up wine?"

"Just Gallo. Gallo wine."

"No more Mountain Red?"

"That's Gallo?"

"Yes. And no more Thunderbird."

Jane glanced up at the Goddess of Victory for inspiration. "What about Mad Dog 2020?"

"Gallo owns the dog."

"Gallo's not even a man," Jane said. "Gallo is just a model standing in front of a camera. Are you sure about Thunderbird? How about Ripple?"

"Ripple too."

In silence, the two women pondered the insidious intent of big business, sportswriters, and cheap wine. Cappy returned wearing a straw hat and carrying a union sign with thick red lettering against a white background: "Si Se Puede!"

"Can what?" Sarah asked.

"Yes, we can walk a hundred miles. That's how far we're marching."

"We?"

"They need a nurse," Cappy said.

"You're going in scrubs? What about swimming? And lunch?"

"Next time. Okay? They said they'd take care of me. Food and lodging. Friends of the movement are putting us up. I'm being swept away."

"What about work?"

"This is work," Jane said. "There's only a couple hundred people now, but we'll have five thousand by the time we reach Modesto."

"I'll call in sick," Cappy said. "This is more important. We'll be back in a week. Promise. Even better, come with us. Be swept away with us and forget Lady Victory."

Jane held up her Bota bag. "Si, Se Peude!" she shouted and

uncorked the stopper, tipped her head back, and squeezed a shot of clear liquid into her mouth.

"Is that wine?" Sarah asked.

"Water." Ms Jane patted the imitation leather. "With a splash of tequila. For endurance. Come with us," she shouted as the crowd carried them away, a peacenik in fatigues and a decorated vet in blue scrubs, dreaming of Modesto.

Sarah waved to them. She didn't want to be swept away. She had work to do.

A week passed without a word from either of them, but Ms Jane had been right about the numbers. By the time the march reached Modesto, the television news reported as many as 10,000, needed most of them farm workers, had joined the dreamers.

Sarah worked through an endless series of night shifts filled with babies. She slept during the day, and while she ate, she searched for war news. The North Vietnamese were sweeping south from the central highlands. The experts said the South's million-man army would defend Saigon, the U.S. Embassy would never be evacuated and promised a new B-52 bombing campaign.

Finally, near the end of March, near midnight, Terrence appeared at the hospital in polished shoes, Wright slacks, a clean white shirt, and a close shave. Jane stood beside him in her bright yellow summer dress, black pumps, and green sweater.

Before Sarah could say anything, the night supervisor caught them standing at the baby-viewing window.

"Friends of yours?" she asked Sarah. "It's a bit late for visiting."

"So sorry, we know. We apologize." She offered her hand. "I'm Ms Jane Hathaway. And this is my husband, Terrence Hathaway. We're here to volunteer."

"For?"

"We heard the hospital needs help."

"The mercy flights from Vietnam," Jane said. "Operation Baby Lift."

The head nurse smiled, nodded, shook her hand, and said, "Oh yes. Wonderful, but you're at the wrong hospital."

"As usual," Sarah said, but the head nurse smiled, patted her shoulder, and kept talking.

"Our hospital has been put on alert, but the emergency hospital on the Presidio needs help with Operation Baby Lift. You're not with the newspapers? Good." She told them that the evacuation of Saigon had started and every available bed and volunteer was needed. "If you really want to help, trucks are loading downstairs. We're sending over emergency supplies. You could follow them to the temporary medical center. You won't find it on your own. It used to be an armory or a gym. No signs, somewhere on the Presidio."

"Too bad you're not qualified," Sarah said.

"We're lifeguards at Fleishhacker," Terrence said. "We've taken so many first-aid courses, I've lost count."

"Can you change diapers?" the supervisor asked. "Hold a baby? Carry boxes?"

"Of course."

"That's us."

The supervisor checked her watch. "There's a flight expected from Saigon tonight. An unofficial plane. Any time now. With a hundred orphans. I just got off the phone with their head nurse. They do need help. Lots of it."

"Where did you say those trucks were loading?" Terrence asked.

The supervisor led them away, down the hall. Sarah walked in the other direction, where she found her bottle of Zinfandel on her locker's top shelf. She left Lois Lane's .38 behind her Chuck Taylors, took the wine, and dropped it in the trash. No matter what happened, the world was moving too fast for wine.

21.BABIES AND RUNAWAYS

Time: April 1-21, 1975
Location: Harmon Hall, SF

Sarah worked ten days before Jane called to report a miracle. She had been stacking diapers when the first flight of orphans arrived from Vietnam. Arranged by a businessman who feared the advance of North Vietnamese troops, he had been stripped out the insides of a DC-8 World Airways jet, covered the floor with mattresses, lined the walls with cargo netting, and filled the space with volunteer nurses and sixty orphans. The plane had taken off from Saigon and landed in San Francisco.

"They're safe," Jane said. "Every one of them."

The next time Jane called, she was crying. The first government-sponsored flight, a cargo plane loaded with orphans, had crashed on take-off. "78 dead," she managed before hanging up.

Sarah studied the city's two major newspapers. Thanks to heroic efforts by the crew, more than half of those on board had survived. Captain Mary Klinker, the eighth nurse to die in Vietnam, was one of the casualties.

An editorial suggested sabotage. What else could be the cause of so much suffering? Who else but the enemy would want to stop such a noble effort? Later, the facts trickled into print. The C-5A cargo plane had a record of structural problems. No further flights were scheduled in that type of aircraft.

The next time Ms Jane called the hospital, Sarah heard the joy in her voice as her friend described the inside of Harmon Hall. "Laps, that's us, because we're the laps for the babies. Get it? At first, they had me helping at registration, you know, keeping track of where they're from, how old, and their relatives, if any. It's crazy, me organizing things. They aren't all babies. Some are children. Older, you know. Some have no records or crazy records. Newborns that weigh thirty pounds, girls when they're supposed to be boys. Or the other way around. All kinds of mix-ups in the rush to help children escape. Good kind mistakes."

Sarah said, "The newspapers say people are waiting in lines for those babies."

"What people? Never mind them. You should see the little girl I'm caring for, not even a year old. She loves me. She knows me. When I pick her up, she squeezes my finger, even smiles. All the nurses think I'm a miracle worker because none of them can make her smile."

"Have you seen Cappy?"

Ms Jane kept talking too fast for Sarah to interrupt. "Terrence has a job unloading supplies from the trucks. Diapers, medicine and food. You should see him. He has muscles again. Can you believe it? I don't. Ha ha. We're helping. Doing good things. My baby…"

"My baby?"

"Peace."

Sarah grabbed her field jacket and caught a taxi in her blue scrubs. At the Presidio gate, an MP looked inside, nodded to her, and gave her driver directions. "Go by Crissy Field. Keep the bay on your left. Harmon's a wood building, a big one. You'll see trucks parked all around it. Doctors, nurses, and reporters packed inside. Thanks for helping the orphans, and good luck."

At Harmon Hall, Sarah stepped out of the taxi into a criss-crossing of chaos and fog. At the building's main entrance, a woman with a Red Cross armband on a down jacket stood in the back of a pickup truck, shouting into a hand-held megaphone aimed at a group of volunteers huddled together in the cold.

When the megaphone failed, the speaker jumped from the pickup and motioned for the volunteers to close around her. She expected the next flight after midnight. The babies who didn't need hospital care would be bused here.

The volunteers nodded and glanced at the double doors that promised entry inside the Hall. Some of them, including Sarah, edged closer to the door while the woman in charge explained that the army had added new plumbing and telephone lines. The phones were only for official business. She paused before saying, with a smile, "The new plumbing is for everyone." A ripple of laughter followed, and she thanked them again for volunteering and invited all of them to the officer's club for Hawaiian Night next Friday.

The volunteers shuffled their feet, rubbed their legs, and inhaled deep breaths like runners in a chute waiting for the start of a race. As a plane passed overhead, Sarah looked up, half expecting to see babies parachuting from the sky.

The woman in charge pointed a long finger at her. Why me? Sarah wondered. "Remember this," the woman warned. "It's very important. This is a triage station. The babies will be here three or four days, then leave for adoption services or continued medical treatment. Do not become attached to your patients, or this experience will change from challenging and rewarding to depressing and painful."

Sarah wondered if they had given Jane the same advice.

"Listen, after we register the children, volunteers will give them a sponge bath and a snack. After that, your job is to support the medical staff and keep the children calm. It's been a long trip, and the orphans need to rest."

As the group broke for the door, she thanked Sarah for coming and handed her a name tag: SPOVO 133. "That's our official name. *Support for Vietnamese Orphans.* You're 133." She offered a pen. "Write your name in and wear your badge at all times. We've had problems with people trying to sneak in to see the children. And take their pick. Can you believe it?"

"I can believe anything."

"Good for you."

"Where do the supplies come in?" Sarah asked. "My friend works there."

"Who?"

"Terrence, a short fellow…"

The woman broke into a smile. "Oh, Terrence, sure, he's awesome, out of sight. A good worker. He's around back at the loading dock."

A woman in white scrubs rushed out of the building, looked left and right, and disappeared around the corner and into the fog. Sarah thought of the white rabbit in the Jefferson Airplane song but hurried after her. At the back of the building, the woman in white was shouting up at the open doors of a semi-trailer. Terrence appeared, pushing a handcart piled high with boxes.

"You ask and Terrence provides. Go forth and diaper." He tossed her a box and jumped down in jeans, a t-shirt, and a newsboy cap. "Terrence, the Teamster," he said and hugged Sarah. "Sorry for the smell. Been working all day. No time to waste. Have you been inside yet? Did you bring your earplugs?"

"What for?"

He stuffed toilet paper into his ears while she said, "Funny how everyone wants to help orphans from Vietnam. We create them, then we save them. Don't we have plenty of our own orphans?"

Terrence shrugged. "Help or talk?"

Sarah picked up a box of diapers and carried it on her shoulder as she followed Terrence to the back door. "You look good," she said. "Dedicated, not at all worried about being arrested. You're on a military base, you know."

He smiled, showing coffee-stained teeth. "If at first you screw-up, try again."

"Maybe you should try something bad and see if it turns good."

"I'm thinking about it."

"Has anyone been asking about you? The MPs? The Feds?"

"Sure, lots of people. They asked me to haul more diapers, blankets, clothes, and food. Diapers from Walgreens. Baby clothes from Sears. Even leftover food from the SLA giveaway."

They stepped through double doors into a basketball court, its wood floor covered with mattresses laid in rows, twenty by twenty, with enough space to walk sideways. There were three babies on each mattress. Boxes of supplies were stacked against the walls, while doctors in white lab coats and nurses in blue or white scrubs mixed with volunteers in civies, all on the move, stopping for quick consultations, examinations, and confrontations before moving on to more of the same.

"Ladies and gentlemen," Terrence said to Sarah, "welcome to Harmon Hall, 33,000 square feet of noise."

Industrial lights hung from the ceiling, and in the balconies, observers leaned over the rails to look down at the chaos as children ran through the aisles, screaming, laughing, crying, and crashing into doctors, nurses, and startled volunteers.

Sarah helped Terrence stack the boxes along the wall, then searched the aisles for Jane. She heard a woman in a business suit speaking to a young boy. Was it Vietnamese? As Sarah edged closer, she watched tears form in the young boy's eyes. The woman waved to a tall man in a white lab coat.

The lab coat spoke English. The woman raised her hand to stop him and said, "I am certain some of these orphans have parents in Vietnam." When he shook his head, she raised her voice. "This boy is not an orphan. He doesn't understand why he left Vietnam. I know there are more like him."

The doctor listened, nodded, and waited for her to stop talking. When she reached down to calm the child, he said, without raising his voice, "I don't doubt you, but it's not my concern now. We're trying to save these children."

"You should determine the status of their parents in Vietnam before you turn them over to adoption agencies."

"Please, miss, not now. We're dealing with hepatitis, measles, chicken pox, diseases that we thought we had under control. Add pneumonia, dehydration, diarrhea, and malnutrition. The usual. Someone down the line will have to help you."

Sarah stared at row after row of crying babies a thousand light years from home. The doctors and nurses were here to help them survive, but maybe.... She looked for Terrance. The noise made Sarah feel as if she were underwater. She checked outside. The truck was there, but Terrence was gone.

Two nurses walked from the building. They lit cigarettes, and Sarah heard one say, "That poor woman."

Another poor woman, Sarah thought. The world was full of them.

"I heard she was a nurse," one said.

They both drew deep on their cigarettes.

"With kids."

Before she could stop herself, Sarah asked, "What happened?"

The nurses exhaled clouds of smoke and shook their heads. The one closer to Sarah said, "The SLA. They're back robbing banks."

"Killed a woman."

"With a shotgun."

"She had kids."

"Two of them."

"Was it Hearst?" Sarah.

The nurse shrugged. "Who knows?"

"Probably. I bet it was."

The nurses tossed their half-smoked cigarettes into the dirt. "No one is safe in this damned world."

"No one."

Not even babies, Sarah told herself.

22.FASCIST INSECTS

Time: April 1975
Location: San Francisco

Sarah stared at the chaos inside the auditorium. Men in dark suits stood at regular intervals along the balcony rails. Still no Ms Jane.

Sarah stepped into the light. At the registration table, she ran her finger down the list of volunteers. Ms Jane had checked in at ten that morning. It was six now, but she had not checked out. She asked the volunteer behind the registration table, a sleepy girl wearing an over-sized letterman's jacket from Galileo High School, if she had seen Jane Hathaway.

The volunteer flicked her ponytail. "Oh, Ms Jane?"

"That's her."

"A real trip. Kinda far out, man, if you know what I mean? I like her. She was just here. She's taking care of a baby girl."

"Where?"

"Here. Standing right where you're standing."

"Did she have a baby with her?"

"That's funny. You're funny."

The phone rang, and the girl told the caller to wait a moment, covered the receiver with her hand, and said. "Everybody here has a baby. I can't get away from them. I used to think I wanted a baby, but they're so noisy. Wait." The young woman winked at her, then spoke into the phone. "Have you applied through an agency, sir? No, it doesn't work that way." She slammed the phone down. "Like we're a retail store?" She looked up. "Sorry, not you. You should ask Terrence. Ms Jane and him are like this." She touched her heart. "He's usually back there." She pointed at the back entrance. "See where that man, the real cute one, is standing?"

Sarah turned to see Cappy waving to her with his imitation beauty-queen wave. Sarah said, "Cute?"

"Like Paul Newman."

"Did Ms Jane leave an address?" Sarah asked. "Contact information?"

The young woman dug through the pile of clipboards, scratched her head, and checked again before she found a yellow legal pad. "Here it is."

Sarah recognized the street address and phone number for Fleishhacker Pool. She ran into the fog, into Cappy standing by the truck.

"Have you seen Ms Jane?" she asked. "Or Terrence?"

"Nice to see you."

"Tell me, quick." Sarah grabbed his arms and shook him. "Tell me."

"She left a few minutes ago with Terrence."

"You saw her?"

"I just said that."

"She stole a baby."

"You're crazy. They wouldn't do that."

She ran to the front of the building and watched red lights fade into the fog. Cappy caught up to her. "I know where they're going."

In the Salvation Army delivery van, Sarah rode shotgun, into a neighborhood of houses stuck together at the hip. "Where are they going?" she asked.

Cappy eased the brake to a stop. "What difference does it make? From what they told me, we stole all these babies."

"Is this the right place?"

Cappy parked in front of a three-story. “It’s the address Ms Jane gave me.” He screwed the cap off a metal thermos and sniffed. “Want a drink?”

“What is it?”

“Coffee?” He sniffed again. “Terrence left it.” He sniffed again. “Brandy?”

“Brandy is made from grapes.”

“No grapes for me.”

“Viva La Raza.”

Sarah strained to see through the fog. A narrow street made even narrower by cars parallel-parked under fading lights. The outer Mission. Garages on the first floor, concrete steps that led to front doors.

“Who’s this?” she whispered as three figures appeared from the fog.

Two women and a man walked by the van, talking about a movie, something with a girl’s head spinning and a devil puking. When they turned into the driveway, Sarah heard the man in Levi’s and a rain jacket mention something about a long day painting houses. One woman wore a down jacket and jeans, with long black hair and dark bangs. The woman holding her hand hid under a bulky sweater and jeans that clung to her like hand-me-downs waiting for her to grow. Her puffy brown wig tilted right, making her head look too big for her skinny body.

“Have you seen them before?” Sarah whispered.

“I can’t see them now.” Cappy scratched his chin, and shrugged. “Is that their van over there? Neighbors? Terrence said he was living in a garage apartment.”

Sarah slipped out of the van and slammed the door.

"What the hell?" The painter turned with his hand in his jacket pocket, pointing something at her. “What the hell?"

“Sorry,” Sarah said, holding up her hands. “I’m looking for my friends. Two of them. A man and a woman. They live downstairs.”

The man looked at the Salvation Army van while the two women backed away toward the house.

"Do you folks know Terrence?" Sarah asked. "Short guy who looks like a beatnik? The woman goes by Ms Jane."

"Like in the Hillie Billies?" the man asked. "Or Tarzan?"

"The first one," Sarah said. "I never thought about Tarzan. She might like that better. They have a baby with them."

"Nope. No one like that around here." The man kept his hand in his pocket.

Cappy climbed out of the truck, waving his thermo. "Sorry to bother you, folks. We've been drinking."

"They kidnapped a baby," Sarah said, taking one step at him.

"I think we got the wrong address," Cappy said. "It's been a long day. She's had a little too much, you know?"

The two women retreated up the steps. The man gave Cappy a close look and smiled. "I know what you mean." He mumbled something about a scary movie. "Priests and devil. You spooked us." His hand was still in his pocket.

"Sorry," Cappy said, waving the thermos.

"Not me," Sarah said. "You should be ashamed, mister. Whoever you are. They're kidnappers."

"Go away, sober up."

Shaking his head, he followed the women up the stairs to the front door.

Sarah wondered if she was wrong. The 70s were making her paranoid? Until the woman in the wig turned to her and waved. "Do you know her?" Sarah asked Cappy.

"Maybe. It's a small world." He waved to the woman, and she ran back, straightening her wig. "Did they really…take a baby?" she asked.

"Yes," Sarah said.

"We don't know that," Cappy said. "Not for certain."

"They did," Sarah said.

The woman took Sarah's hand and whispered, "Check downstairs. The door's behind the stairs. Goodnight." She dropped Sarah's hand, turned, and ran up the steps into the house. The door slammed shut.

"Come with me," Sarah asked.

Cappy swallowed twice from the thermos and wiped his mouth with the back of his hand. "I still don't know what's happening, but this wine is choking me."

"Stay here," Sarah said and disappeared into the fog at the side of the house. A tie-dye sheet covered the apartment's only window. Sarah heard the baby crying. She knocked on the door, and when it swung open, Terrence stood in the light. Sarah looked behind him, saw Ms Jane lying on the couch, hugging a bundle of blue blanket to her chest. Two duffel bags were waiting next to the door.

"The police are outside," Sarah said, stepping by Terrence into the tiny studio. "Inspector Hitchens is right behind us. Is that the baby?"

"None of your business," Ms Jane said.

"I'm taking her back."

"No, you're not. We're taking her."

"Where to?"

"To Vietnam," Terrence said.

"You can't even find Canada. How are you going to make it to Vietnam? And what are you going to do when you get there? Drop her on the dock? Leave her in a locker at the airport?"

"We'll find her a home," Ms Jane said.

"No you won't."

"We will. The two of us."

"You already playing daddy?"

Ms Jane pressed the bundle to her chest and said, "Go away. We don't need rescuing."

"If you give me the baby, I'll take her back for you. You and Terrence can leave town tonight and make it to Canada."

Ms Jane shook her head. "No way. Go back and hide."

Sarah felt Cappy behind her.

"Terrence, hello. You too, Ms Jane." He squeezed by Sarah and opened his arms to Ms Jane. "Give me the baby."

"No way." She stood up, holding the bundle in one arm, straight-arming Cappy with the other. Terrence moved to her side.

"The baby," Cappy said softly. "Give her to me."

"What's going on here?"

Sarah turned to see the upstairs neighbor. Paint-stained and smelling of popcorn, he said, "Can you guys keep the noise down?"

Sarah said, "Give me the baby."

"No."

"The police are coming," Sarah said. "I called them. Do you understand? It's not yours."

"You called the pigs?" the painter said.

Cappy shook his head. "Stay cool, man. She wouldn't call the police."

Terrence said, "They created orphans. Now they're stealing them."

"They're only pretending to care," Ms Jane said.

"They're not pretending," Sarah said.

"Did you call the police?" the painter asked, trying to get by Sarah.

"They stole that baby," Sarah said.

"She didn't call the police," Cappy said.

"She said she called the police." He slipped by Sarah and pushed Cappy out of the way.

The baby was crying, and Sarah could smell its diaper. "It doesn't belong to you," Sarah said. "Please." She saw the man reach into his pocket, thought he said something about a fast insect, then felt the back of her head explode.

When she woke up, she smelled disinfectant and Old Spice. A hospital orderly was bushing a mop through the emergency room. "How did I get here?" she mumbled.

"You're awake," the orderly said.

"Almost." She recognized him from the supply room, where he had worked before being assigned to the ER. "How?" she asked, rubbing the back of her head.

"Nurse Frederick dropped you off."

"Cappy?"

"He said you slipped in the fog."

"And the baby?"

"What baby? Wait, I'll get the doctor."

"Never mind." Sarah pointed at the elevators. "Give me a hand, will you?"

"No, you stay there. I'll get the doctor."

When he left, Sarah sat up, waited for the dizzy feeling to pass, and stumbled out of bed. Instead of the elevator, she climbed the stairs, stopping at each floor to catch her breath and stop her head spinning. Found it behind her Chuck Taylors, sat on the floor, back against the wall, holding the .38 close, waiting for the feeling to pass.

PART IV

NEW FACE, OLD HOSPITAL

So there I was, and I started thinking.

Not good.

Thinking, nasty water and Big Mac is about to go swimming. Will his hair finally get screwed up? Thinking, no one can swim with their clothes on. Not me. Not in that water. Not in any water.

Only in the movies.

That's right. Funny thing. That's what Big Mac said after we pried that guy off him and stood McNamara on his feet. He said he would've drowned. Told us how strong a swimmer he was, used to swim with JFK in the White House pool, but he couldn't swim with his clothes on. That only happens in the movies.

PT 109.

That's JFK. He could do it. Not Big Mac. Three or four strokes. Then under. Too bad it wasn't Kissinger. He'd go down like a rock.

He was a rock. What about the other guy?

23.ENTER SIERACKI

Time: Sept 18, 2001
Location: Lompoc, California

A week after 9.11, Special Agent Peter Sieracki caught a military flight to Vandenberg Air Force Base, drove six miles to the Federal Correctional Institution at Lompoc, and ran into a prison guard who couldn't stop talking.

"No problem," the old guard said. "I'll show you the way. Follow me. I'm on my way to the admin building. What about the hijacking? Why the hell are you here instead of New York? You should be hunting those Arab sons-za-bitches."

Agent Sieracki had no experience dealing with local authorities, no experience at all, so he tried to explain. The guard cut him off. "Why do they waste your time and our money on a parole hearing? Leave Layton right where he is now. In a cell."

Agent Sieracki tried, "You know how it is…"

"I do, but do you?" he laughed, said he was joking, and asked again. "Why you?"

Still a rookie, Agent Sieracki chose the truth. "I was the only one left."

The guard adjusted his gun belt and said through his thick

mustache, “Hey, this place is no joke. We have our share of hard asses. That summer camp stuff ended a long time ago. This is serious. No place for a rookie.”

Sieracki pointed past him. “Is that the admin building over there?

“We have important prisoners here. Back in the day, Nixon’s chief of staff was here. Remember him? Haldeman? Lots of Watergate guys were here. And Nixon’s lawyer. Clambake, we called him.” The guard laughed, turned, and started walking, then stopped. “Then we got the Wall Street guys, plenty of them. Even spies. You bet.”

“I bet.”

“The druggies were a step-down, but them and the illegals blew our numbers through the roof in the Nineties.”

At last, Agent Sieracki felt a tiny piece of solid ground. He had studied the numbers at the Academy. Federal inmates had doubled in the 80s, in the 90s, and in 2,000 had climbed to 130,000 prisoners behind federal bars. The Lompoc facility was doing its share by housing 2,000 of them. Agent Sieracki, who now considered himself as number 2001, said, “We should keep walking.”

“The towel-heads are next,” the guard said. “They’re our job security.”

Special Agent Sieracki smiled.

“What’s so funny? In business, you’re either growing or dying.”

Agent Sieracki saw “Administration Building” above the double doors. “Is that it?” he said, picking up speed.

“People think Cali is a tropical paradise,” the guard said, blocking his way, wiping sweat off his forehead and rubbing it into his pants. “It isn’t. It’s a friggin desert. A dry hell hole. Why do you think there are so many prisons? That’s right. Because it’s California. What else can you do with a state like this?”

“Not much.”

The guard smiled and offered his hand to the young agent. “You got it.”

“You bet.” Agent Sieracki gripped the guard’s damp hand,

thankful he had said nothing about being born and raised in Santa Barbara, fifty miles south of the prison.

"And your guy, Layton," the guard said, still holding the young agent's hand. "He doesn't deserve parole. Killing those kids."

"He didn't kill any…"

"They should keep him here until he's a dried-up raisin." The guard let go of the agent's hand. "I'd like to see that."

To Agent Sieracki, the front door, within his reach, seemed miles away, so he kept his mouth shut and said, "It could happen."

"Yep, this is the right place for Lawrence Layton," the guard said, holding the door open for the young agent. "Parole hearings on the second floor. Third door on the left. Tell Officer Bennsal I sent you."

Sieracki took the stairs two at a time.

24.LOIS LANE IS ALIVE

Time: September 2001
Location: Lompoc, California

Lois Lane was lucky the correction officer at the hearing-room door was a friend from the old days. He leaned into her and said, "Have you been smoking weed?"

Lois straightened her back. It wasn't easy. She was 52, still at her fighting weight, but six hours behind the wheel of her VW bug had twisted her into knots. Stepping back, she tucked her tie-dyed silk blouse into her Levis, zipped up her leather jacket, and tried to wish away the ketchup stain on her blouse. "Burgers," she said. "Could be burgers. Burnt cow flesh smells a lot like weed. Blame three stops at In & Out."

"You're making me hungry."

"I like a hungry man. I'd fix you a TV dinner if we were at my place. Too bad there's no time. I'm looking for an FBI agent."

He checked his list. Pointed at the back row.

"The young guy?" she asked. "Are you sure?"

"Special Agent Peter Something."

"Something?"

"Something like that."

"What about Layton?"

"Next up."

"Officer Hart?"

"You're too late. He testified early. Didn't want to miss his plane to paradise."

"Lucky man."

"Living the life."

"Did you hear his testimony?"

"Can you believe it," the correction officer said, shaking his head. "Told the commissioner that Layton deserved an early release."

"What's a couple bullets between friends, right?" Lois checked the room and noticed the parole commissioner sitting at a long table facing the scattered audience. Lois had seen him in action, a middle-aged man in a dark suit and tie. He was one of the good ones, except for his taste in clothes. She waited for him to look down at his papers, slipped by the guard, and sat beside the young FBI agent. "Lois Lane," she whispered, holding out her hand. "Journalist."

It took a moment before he managed a quick smile and a whisper, "Special Agent Peter Sieracki."

"Sorry. Say it again. The last part."

"Sier-racky." Still a whisper. "Like SirRocky. It's Polish. Call me Peter."

Lois liked his looks, but he was too soft to be a Fed. Right out of college, a ginger with rosy cheeks and freckles. She hoped he was smarter and more dangerous than he looked. She slipped a recorder from her jacket pocket and set it on her lap.

"That's not allowed in the hearing room," he said.

"Oh."

When the recorder stayed on her lap, he glanced at the guard by the door.

"Oh, don't bother him," Lois said. "He'll only confuse things. He's a nice enough fellow, but he doesn't like Feds."

The parole commissioner asked for quiet.

"Sorry," Lois whispered, hiding the recorder in her jacket. "Force of habit." She took a deep breath and asked, "How's Special Agent Jonathan Smith these days?"

The Commissioner cautioned those present to remain seated and quiet.

Peter whispered, "Supervisor Smith is in charge of Victim Services."

"Really? Victim Services?" Lois rested her hand on the young agent's knee. "Is it a cover? A way to hide the budget for something nasty?"

"Serious?"

"Always. Who are you victim-servicing today?"

"Quiet, please," the Commissioner said.

"Vincent Hart," Peter whispered.

"You helped him?" Waiting for an answer, Lois wondered how this minty child with rosy cheeks planned to help a grown man, especially one like Hart? Patch the bullet holes? Bring back his son? Cure his addictions, understand his love for men and women? End the day-to-day torture of being a cop?

"I did."

"How?"

"Excuse me, mam…"

"Sorry, I'm working."

"What about Layton?" she asked. "Can you assist him?"

"Are you really a journalist?"

"Quiet, the movie's starting."

On cue, the prisoner's lawyer stood up, introduced himself, and pointed at a middle-aged man swimming in prison khakis.

"That's Layton," Lois whispered.

"Go away."

According to his lawyer, who considered the petitioner a friend, Layton had been a model prisoner for 18 years. The judge in his trial for conspiracy had recommended parole after five years. That was thirteen years ago. Why? Mr Layton was not involved in the planning to kill Congressman Leo Ryan. He was a cult member, a follower, one of the thousand that fell under the influence of Jones, a virulent cult leader who had isolated his followers in the jungle and worn them down until they were convinced that there was no way to escape except revolutionary suicide.

The lawyer paused for a breath. The Commissioner looked up from his paperwork. And Agent Sieracki turned to see Lois Lane picking at the ketchup stain on her knee.

The lawyer continued. Jones' security team murdered anyone who refused to drink the poison. The same security team killed the congressman and died later in a suicidal cyanide frenzy. Here are the facts. Mr Layton was ordered to board a plane with Vincent and the other cult members attempting to flee. Jones ordered him to bring the traitors down in a fiery crash. Did Layton follow those orders? No. He wounded two passengers, but one of his victims, a man who lost his son at Jonestown, was here today to plead for Mr Layton's early release. As Officer Hart said, it's time to heal.

Lois looked at Layton and saw him standing with Vincent Hart and his son, the son never to be more than knee-high, waiting in front of a sagging Victorian. Waiting for her and Special Agent Jonathan Smith to save them.

25.A PRISON, A BURGER, AND THE 101

Time: September 2001
Location: Lompoc, California

Lois Lane stood up, walked to the takeout counter, and carried away two cokes and a bag of burgers. On her way back, she stopped at the side counter for straws and ketchup. While she worked, she turned her back to the young agent, wishing he was older, more experienced. She checked the lids.

"What's next?" she asked, dropping the bag on the table, keeping the extra-large Coke for herself, and handing him the small.

"I have a plane to catch. And you?" Agent Sieracki asked, poking the greasy bag toward her. "Do you have enough to eat?"

"Long trip. Like to eat while I drive." He didn't look the type, so she didn't tell him about the Jim Beam in her glove compartment, the perfect complement to caffeine, corn syrup, and food coloring. Thick and sweet with a relaxing kick in the ass.

Special Agent Sieracki sipped his Coke, then slid an envelope across the plastic table. "Special Agent Smith wanted you to have this."

She glanced down but didn't touch it.

"What did he tell you about me?"

"He said you had…financial problems."

"He's feeling guilty."

"He said you were an informant."

"We were friends." She gulped her Coke, looked inside the bag, picked out a fry, and said, "Johnny was a good guy, not a good agent, but a good guy. Did he tell you how long it took him and his buddies to find the Hearst girl?"

"Before my time."

"The Rev Jones?"

Peter sipped the Coke, didn't tell her that he had read about both cases at the Academy, didn't care, just wanted to get back on the plane to DC. He watched the journalist sip her drink.

"At least he was honest back in the day."

"We're all honest."

She tried to hold back but couldn't stop her mouth. "You're too young to be honest."

"The Bureau has changed."

She picked a fry, smothered it in ketchup, and said, "Drink your Coke. Let's get out of here. I got a long way to go."

"There's money in the envelope."

"You peeked?"

"Guessed."

"You smarter than you look. Come to think of it, you don't look so good."

"Tired."

"Finish your drink."

On their way out, Peter tossed his empty. While Lois unlocked the driver's side of her bug, he leaned against the government-issue SUV and searched his pockets.

"Can't find your keys?" She set the burgers on the VW's roof. "Let me help."

"What?"

"Help."

"Wait. Is your hand in my pocket?"

"It is. Found the keys. Doors open, get in." She pushed him into the SUV. "Relax, man. Watch your head. Ooops. Sorry."

He closed his eyes and let his head rest on the steering wheel.

"You've got some strong points," she said.

"Thank you."

"Bulk."

"Thanks."

"Sturdy and polite."

"Thanks."

"And you smell good. I mean, you don't smell bad." She leaned into the SUV. "Really? What is that smell? Government issue? That's it. Government sweat, air-conditioning, and man soap."

"I'm…"

She caught him as he planted his face into the steering

"I'm sorry about this." She searched his pockets, kept his badge and Glock, wrote a phone number on a faded business card, locked the door, and took his keys inside.

She introduced herself to the counter girl, and discovered her name was Isabella, three months out of high school and missing her boyfriend, who had fled Lompoc in the night. Ending the sad story, Lois asked if the SUV would be safe in the parking lot overnight.

"In this town?" Isabella said. "Absolutely. Most everyone is asleep by now."

Lois checked her watch. "It's only 8."

"Lompoc."

Lois smiled and said, "My boyfriend had a little too much to drink."

"That guy is your boyfriend?"

"Was."

"He looks too…"

"Young?"

Isabella nodded. "I don't care about that. I like older men. Not too old. He's different, not like you. Super straight. Is he a cop? Or a prison guard? We get lots of those. He doesn't look like a prison guard."

"Just a kid looking for his mother," Lois said. "Needs someone to take care of him. So I had to let him go. One must be firm."

"Sure." The waitress nodded, "Believe me, I know."

Lois Lane brushed a hand through her hair and gave the girl a second look. Clear skin, blue eyes, and pink lipstick with a tiny gold cross hanging from her neck. The cross could mean anything. A good sign? "Can you make sure he gets his keys and this business card in the morning?"

"I'll leave a note for the early shift. They come in at 6."

Lois Lane slipped a twenty across the counter. "Could you do it yourself?"

"No problemo. I live around the corner."

"Thank you, dear." Lois Lane turned to the door, then looked back to say, "I wouldn't want anything to happen to him."

"I'll take care of him. No problem."

On the way north, on the 101, Lois Lane bit into a cold wedge of burger, sweet onion, and sloppy red tomato. "A little dry," she managed to say and reached into the glove compartment, where she found the Beam and the agent's Glock. Washed the burger down with a shot. Pressed the bottle between her thighs and left the Glock in the glove compartment, disappointed it was a model 23 with finger grooves too big for her.

She pressed her back against the seat and let her mind drift, changing subjects with each bump in the road. The old bug, a 67, was the last of the short seats. It was fun having a boyfriend for a few minutes. A few minutes was best, and she wondered how Johnny Smith looked these days?

She took another swig of Beam, and held it in her mouth, enjoying the taste before she swallowed. The bug climbed uphill, slow and unsteady. She bit off a hunk of burger and, with her mouth full, said to the car, "Sorry, lover. You and me need help."

She remembered the first time she had seen Johnny, a rosy young agent standing across the street from the People's Temple trying to look inconspicuous in heavy hiking boots, new jeans, a flannel shirt, and a puffy down jacket. His red watch cap was a cherry on top.

Lois had crossed herself twice. A year attached to the Marines in Vietnam had napalmed her belief in god and converted her to a religion based on nicotine, caffeine, alcohol, and superstition. But she still knew the moves. And from the looks of this young Johnny, she would need all the help she could steal.

She had plucked a stray feather from his down jacket and asked him for a light. He had told her he didn't smoke. So she snapped open her zippo and torched the end of a fat joint, blew smoke at him, and said, "Where'd you get the puffy jacket?"

"That's illegal."

"Your jacket?"

"The pot."

"Part of my disguise." She spread her arms wide, showing off her Sunday best, doubling her drinking attire and tripling as her work disguise: cowboy boots, bellbottom jeans, and a worn leather jacket. "Lois Lane," she said.

"That's a silly code name for a journalist."

"It's my name. My father's a famous lawyer. Look it up. How about you?"

"Jonathan Smith."

"Okay, if you want to play that game. Agent Smith."

"It's my name."

She blew more smoke, this time at a young woman who had turned to smile at her young agent. Lois slipped her arm through his and led him to a neighborhood bar. "How about a drink? Where we won't look so federal."

She pinched off the joint, and they sat by a window table where they could watch the street. She ordered a dark beer. He ordered coffee. And they sat in silence, Lois thinking he was a fine-looking redhead, a few years younger than her and not as bright, but better looking. "Where'd you get the costume?" she asked.

"My college clothes."

Lois nodded. "Where?"

"UCSB."

"Santa Barbara. That explains it. Me, Berkeley."

“That explains it. What have you got for me?”

She told him she was following a lead from a reporter at the Examiner who had been warned off a story about Reverend Jim Jones. Death threats every night. Politicos calling to complain until his editor had killed the story.

“We’re not interested.”

“My source works for Jones.”

Special Agent Smith waited a second before saying, “We’re watching the Muslims. Can you help with them? Checking ties to the Panthers.”

“Nothing wrong with the Panthers.”

“We’re watching them.”

“The Zebras are dead. But Jones is alive and well. Claims he can bring back the dead and cure cancer. Threatens members who want to leave. Has his own security force. Sucking up drugs like Hoovers. The vacuum cleaner, not your Hoover. Drugs are all over the place. My source says they tried to kill her husband.”

“My supervisor’s not interested. As far as the Bureau’s concerned, Jones’s only crime is having Black Muslims for neighbors. You know anything about Patty Hearst?”

“Crazy preacher or crazy heiress,” Lois said. “Pick your poison. Want to bet which one kills more people?”

“Not funny.”

She wanted to tell him that being funny kept her from killing someone, but he wouldn’t understand.

“Tell me about the SLA,” he said. “We’re lost.”

“At least you’re honest. How about the Doodler?”

“Who? Not interested.”

“Didn’t Hoover die in 72? Still against gay people?”

“We want Hearst. Or Panthers.”

She checked her watch. “I might have something. You help me, I’ll help you.”

“Give me a name.”

“Relax, big man.”

“A name.”

"A minute." Lois sipped her beer. Wished she could light up the joint. "Vincent Hart."

"Reliable?"

"A druggie who lives in the People's Temple."

"Forget it. No Jones."

"Hart used to be married to a Panther. She told me she saw Jones talking to Angela Davis and a group of Panthers."

"When can we talk to her?"

Lois didn't tell him that Vincent's wife had nearly died on the operating table. The baby had survived, but the mother was in a coma. She'd never be talking. Instead, Lois said, "Sure." And finished her beer.

"What else?"

"Hart did some day work with a house painter out in Pacifica. One of the crew claimed he knew Hearst. Bragged about dating Tania."

"Where's Hart now?"

"I'm going to meet him." She checked her watch. "Now."

"I'll go with you."

Her VW bug was parked around the corner. She dug a heavy canvas gear bag from the back seat and gave him two Nikon 35mm SLRs to hang around his neck. "Maybe you can pass for a photog if you keep your mouth shut. Take any pictures. Look like you know what you're doing. Pretend."

Now, too many years older, Lois Lane rolled down the VW's window, tossed the empty bottle a road sign and followed the white line to San Francisco.

26.STRANGE BREWING

Time: September 2001
Location: The road to San Francisco

If she had known, Lois Lane would have been vaguely disappointed and extremely proud of Isabella. When the eager young woman arrived the next morning, she had left her gold cross at home. After serving Special Agent Sieracki enough coffee to keep his eyes open for two days, she handed him his keys and offered him a proposition, a deal. If he would give her a ride to San Simeon, she would help him find his girlfriend.

Peter told her that he was an FBI agent, that she was interfering with an ongoing investigation, and she could be charged with obstruction of justice. And he didn't have a girlfriend. Only a suspect.

Isabella told him her boyfriend worked at the castle near Big Sur. She was an adult now and could go wherever she wanted. They had to leave right away. She was in a hurry and in love.

Confused and energized by a heavy dose of caffeine, Peter called his supervisor, reached his assistant, and was told that Special Agent Smith had been called to New York. Agent Sieracki was to report to the Bureau's office in San Francisco. Supervisor Smith would contact him with further instructions.

When he hung up, Isabella held up a greasy bag of burgers. "I packed us breakfast and lunch."

Ten miles later, Peter realized he had made two mistakes: Not reporting his stolen gun and taking Isabella's offer. She was, at best, a confused romantic, at worst, a danger to herself and him. Mildly, slightly, possibly mentally challenged. Since leaving Lompoc, she had been talking about a movie from the Sixties called "Harold and Maude." She had assured him it was "almost a documentary." The main character, Harold, was a "slightly suicidal youth" who lived in a mansion, "almost a castle," and fell in love with an older woman.

"I think she was 80 or 90 or maybe a hundred," Isabella told him as she clutched her backpack to her chest. "But she was spunky, happy, a real hippie, who lived in an abandoned railroad car that she had fixed up super nice. They made a cute couple. Like you and your girlfriend."

"What girlfriend?"

"Cats Stevens did the music. It was beautiful." She closed her eyes to the morning light. Was that a tear on her cheek? "Beautiful."

Hoping to derail her, he asked, "How did it end?"

"It was all very romantic. When he was about to propose to her, she told him she had promised to live life to the fullest and then commit suicide on her 80th birthday. I think it was 80. It could have been 70 or 80 or 90."

"Sounds interesting," he lied. "And did she?"

She sniffled, rubbed her nose, and nodded. "Yes."

"And him?"

"He drove his Jaguar off a cliff."

"Like in Thelma and Louise?"

"Oh, no. He wasn't in the car. That would be crazy. He was too young. At the last second, off camera, he rolled out of the car. That was the message."

Remember that, roll out of the car, Peter said to himself.

"He had learned to love life, to seize the day and enjoy it. He was dancing along the cliff's edge to a Cat Stevens song. I can't remember the title."

At San Luis Obispo, he turned left, heading for the coast. Isabella sighed, closed her eyes, and fell asleep, still clinging to her backpack and the bag of burgers.

Two hours later, in the parking lot for buses carrying tourists up the foothills to Hearst Castle, Isabella's blue eyes and pink lips popped open. "We're here," she said and handed Peter the bag of burgers. "She loves you."

Peter nodded as if he knew what she was talking about, and she handed him the faded business card. And by the time he finished reading both sides, she was gone, running toward a double-decker bus, where a slender woman with flowing grey hair welcomed a line of tourists.

"Just like that." Peter shook his head and headed north on narrowing asphalt, leaning into sweeping s-turns and sudden twists that led to burned-out redwoods and steep drops to stretches of beach lined with kelp beds rolling on glassy swells. A breakfast burrito in Monterey led to pizza slices in Santa Cruz. Then a trash can for the leftover burgers and pizza in Pacifica. And by sunset, he was cruising the Great Highway in San Francisco, passing the zoo, the sand dunes, and Golden Gate Park.

He had surfed this break on a weekend escape from college. There was another good spot at the fort under the bridge, but this was his favorite. He sat on a cement wall near the Cliff House and studied the business card. There was a name and phone number on one side, a handwritten message on the other: "See you in The City, fascist insect."

He made the call while watching the seals on the rocky point. A man's voice answered with a bark. "Talk."

Peter managed "Special Agent…" before the gravel voice interrupted. "Where you at?"

"Cliff House."

"Good. You're close. Come to me." The voice turned softer. "I don't get around so good these days. Look across the highway. See

Balboa? Good. Take it up six blocks and look for a two-story on the right corner. It's over a two-car garage. Take the glass door on the left. I'll buzz you in. Got it?"

"The address is on the card."

"I know that. You coming?" The man hung up.

Peter wasn't surprised. Growing up, he had learned his lesson. The closer to San Francisco, the more likely an encounter with odd behavior. Not rough and aggressive like a visit to New York City or slippery and condescending like LA, but strange, subterranean, dark, and mildly disturbing. That was San Francisco. Underground. And Isabella was only the beginning.

He parked across the street from the two-story and shouted his name three times into the intercom before he heard the buzz-in. At the top of the stairs, he ran into a stocky old man in bedroom slippers, grey slacks, and a white dress shirt buttoned at his neck. Seventy at least, 190 to 200 pounds, 6 feet with white hair trimmed short, brown eyes, and no distinguishing scars.

"Looking for tattoos?"

"Sorry."

"Never mind. I saw the look. You're doing the cop thing. Sizing me. Good habit." He checked the stairs and held his ground. "You're Johnny's boy? Johnny Smith's boy?"

"He's my supervisor," Peter said.

"Didn't I say that?" The old-timer stepped back into a dimly lit room, pointed at an overstuffed leather couch facing a bay window. "Sit."

"I'm looking for Lois Lane."

"Got my card? Give it to me." He took it, tore it up, and stuck the pieces in his pocket. "I'm Caesar Jeffery Hitchens. Used to be Detective Jeffery Hitchens."

"It's on the…"

"Take my hand."

Peter returned a gentle shake, said his name, said it was Polish, and was about to explain how to pronounce it when the ex-cop said, "Sure. Sieracki. I'm not deaf yet, believe me. Call me Hitch. Sit. I don't like Caesar or Jeffery" He disappeared around a corner into the smell of brewing coffee. "Lois never pays her phone bills. I'm her answering service."

Peter sank into the leather couch and studied the room. On the walls, a huge oil painting with thick swirls of agitated color competed with black-and-white photographs of policemen in uniforms. At the other end of the long room, a dark oak cabinet with glass doors protected an amplifier, turntable, and bookend speakers. The shelves were packed tight with LPs. A deep blue rug covered most of the hardwood floor. The coffee table was made of smoked glass resting on two steamer-trunk pedestals.

"Nice place," he said.

"Victim Services?" Mr. Hitchens called from the kitchen. "I like that. I like that. Good idea!" He appeared with two large mugs, set them on leather coasters, left, and came back with two blue-and-white plates, each with a croissant and slices of banana. He handed Peter a paper napkin. "You sure you're not Johnny's kid? You look a lot like him. When he was younger. No offense."

"I understand."

"You do?"

Peter didn't know where to start. He sipped his black coffee, wondering if he had mentioned Victim Services. It had been a long day.

"Good man, your Johnny. I'm surprised he's still working. I knew him back in the day when he was just a kid. Me and him. All you Feds look alike." He laughed. "Kidding, man. Johnny was smart. Not smart enough to understand he was in The City. If you know what I mean?"

Peter didn't, but he nodded yes.

"Too nice, your boss." He shrugged. "What are you working on, Pete? "

"I'm looking for Lois Lane."

"Sure, I know that, man."

Peter told him he had met her at a parole hearing.

"For Layton?"

"You knew him?"

"I heard they're keeping him inside." Hitch headed for the kitchen. "They blew that one. Johnny and Lois. And me."

Peter rubbed his eyes. Sipped his coffee and said, "She stole my badge."

Hitch returned with a dusty bottle of Meyers rum, broke the seal and twisted off the cap, then poured a long shot in his coffee. "And your gun?"

"She told you?"

"That woman always had a thing for guns. Picked up the habit in Vietnam. Can't blame her." He offered Peter the bottle. "You want a Dirty Harry?"

"No. I'm working."

"I guess you could say that." Hitch spiked Peter's cup. "A lot of the Jones people are buried across the bay." He spiked his coffee. "People had to work hard to find a place for them." The old cop shook his head and sipped his coffee. "Too many bodies. Jesus, that man Jones. What a fricken disaster."

Peter wanted to ask what Lois Lane and Supervisor Smith had to do with Jones, but the old man was quicker.

"We should've done better. All of us, we were busy. Bullshit, I know, but those were some crazy times. Me and your boss, we had to follow orders. People didn't realize how crazy that freak was. I shouldn't say freak. It's too nice. There were plenty of freaks in town. Know what I mean? He was freak gone bad."

Peter tried not to picture a thousand corpses, including three hundred children. Hitch saved him by saying, "Your boss did better on the SLA."

Peter managed, "Lois Lane…"

"The LA cops started the job. Overkilled it. But it took us to finish it. A year and a half to find the scraps, the Hearst girl, and that was after the Opsahl killing. Too late. Not good, but like I said, we were busy. Poor woman." Hitchens rubbed his chin, then his forehead. "What's it been? Twenty-five years? And we're still working the Opsahl murder."

A Muni bus groaned as it struggled uphill toward the city. When the noise cleared, Hitch said, "You tell Johnny about your badge and gun."

"Not yet."

"Not yet? Hmmmm. First time in the field? Hoping for the best? Think you can catch Lois before Johnny finds out?"

Petter nodded.

"Not a good start."

"You're telling me." Peter sipped his coffee, shook his head. "This is strong stuff."

"You shouldn't be drinking on the job."

"But…"

"You need to find Lois."

"Where is she?"

"Who knows? Lois always was a little crazy. Still is." He pushed away his empty cup. "Serial killers and revolutionaries. That's what was her specialty. Me, I was just a grunt. Sanders and Gilford were the smart guys, the brains. Lois is a wooden shoe stuck in the works. A saboteur."

"You know where she is?"

Hitch smiled with coffee-stained teeth. "Sure do." He stomped on the wood floor and leaned over as if listening for a response. When none came, he stomped on the hardwood again, gave up, and said, "Your boss should've shot her when he had the chance."

Peter noticed the old cop's slight limp as he went to the stereo and searched the albums.

An electric sax filled the room, smooth and smokey. "Eddie Harris," Hitchens said. "1972."

Peter tried again. "Lois Lane? Can you help me? She can't get away with drugging a federal agent."

"Why not? It's better than shooting one. It's more like you let her drug you. You're supposed to be FBI."

"I didn't let her…"

"Wait here a minute, Pete. Can I call you Pete?"

Peter heard him shuffling through drawers in the kitchen,

mumbling something about jazz and where the hell is it, until he came back. “She left this for you,” Hitchens said, tossing a badge at Peter. "It's yours."

“My Glock?”

“Say thank you.”

“Thank you. And my Glock?”

“Said she might need it.”

“Where is she?”

“Not sure. But I know where to start looking.” He pointed at the floor. “She lives downstairs.”

27.HOME

Time: September 2001
Place: The City, California

The door was locked.

"I have a key," Hitchens said. "In case of emergencies."

Agent Sieracki stepped into Lois Lane's apartment. A narrow path led through stacks of books and piles of clothes to a futon couch next to a dorm-room refrigerator topped with a toaster and hotplate. In the corner, a metal TV tray sagged under the weight of a war-surplus typewriter. Next to it, a folding chair was leaning against a file cabinet overstuffed with manila folders. A hefty grey cat was sleeping on a narrow windowsill, its head resting on a tiny alarm clock.

"I think her place used to be a hallway," Hitchens said.

"Is there another room?"

"The bathroom."

Peter tried, "Lois Lane."

"There's a Fed to see you," Hitchens added at normal volume.

The cat woke up, blinked twice, arched its back, and stretched its legs before closing its green eyes and falling back to sleep. "That's Ms Jane," Hitchens said, stopping at the window. "Good cat." He rubbed the cat's belly while Peter scanned the file cabinet, reading the masking-tape labels on the manila folders: Alcatraz. Sarah Costa. Terrence Costa. Ms. Jane. Bill Harris, Emily Harris, Sara Jane Olson. SLA. The Doodler, Dan White.

Hitchens found a stickie note on the cat's food bowl and handed it to Peter. "Feed the cat. Take care of the Fed. I found the Doodler."

"Doodler?" Peter asked.

"An old case. Nasty stuff."

"The file is empty."

"We never had much," Hitchens said. "Two confirmed killings in 74, two more in 75. All gay men. Never found the killer. Had a few leads, a few suspects but no luck, and no one willing to talk. But Lois kept looking. She was always chasing someone."

Peter searched the apartment. It took seconds. The bathroom gave up three wet towels, a toothbrush, and a bar of soap. A tiny closet offered a raincoat, a pair of alligator-skin cowboy boots, a pair of jeans, a hoodie, and a baseball bat.

"I'm worried," Hitchens said. "Last time she asked me to feed the cat, Lois disappeared for a month."

"How can we find her?" Peter eyed the files. "Who's Costa? Sarah Costa?"

"Never mind her. I might have an idea." Hitchens said. "Lois has a friend. Used to be a friend. But you'll need me. She won't talk to you."

"Of course not."

"Sarcasm?" Hitchens picked up the cat, cradling it like a baby. "I'm old. I get tired quick these days. Maybe I need encouragement."

The cat opened its eyes, purring, seeming to say to Peter, "Trust him. I do."

"I need you," Peter said.

"That's it."

"Can't do it without you."

Hitchens set the cat down. Stood tall, thin, and solid. "No one trusts a Fed, even one as harmless as you. And since you're Johnny's boy..."

Peter was opening his mouth when Hitchens cut him off, saying, "This city is tricky. Fifty square miles of shifting sand on a major fault line and surrounded by water."

Peter wanted to say the city wasn't an island. It's a peninsula. Instead, he opted to keep moving. "Where do we start?"

Hitchens picked up a legal pad, the cat's mattress, from the windowsill and said, "I'll change. You stay here." He handed Peter the legal pad. "Evidence. "

While Hitchens went upstairs to find a jacket and tie, Peter leafed through the tablet's yellow pages. They were blank except for the top page. Brushed off the cat fur and saw "Valerie Fur" next to a note in brackets: [BRING WINE!]

Peter turned on Lois Lane's tiny clock radio in time to hear it shout a staticky appeal to bomb Iran, Afghanistan, and Iraq, one of them or preferably all three. "Back to the stone age," the radio demanded, solemnly but emphatically adding that the 9-11 death toll was the worst loss of American life since Jonestown, almost 25 years ago.

For a long moment, Peter stood by the window with the cat, both of them staring at the fog drifting in from the ocean. Peter remembered a class at Quantico discussing the difficulty of dealing with 10,000 pages of interviews with Jonestown survivors. The instructor had identified the bureau's first African-American female agent as one of the agents assigned to that duty, then quickly gone on to the difficulty of sorting the remains of a thousand bodies.

Detective Hitchens had returned wearing black slacks, a mid-thigh black leather jacket, and a pink silk shirt with a yellow tie. His shoes were polished to a reflective black. His white hair half hidden by a black leather beret. All of him wrapped in hints of citrus, mildew, and burned toast. "How do I look?"

"Respectable."

"Listen," Hitchens said, holding up a bottle of red wine. "I got the juice for a bribe. You should clean up. You look like you've been sleeping in those clothes."

"I have."

"Shave, brush your teeth, comb that hair."

"I'm in a hurry."

"We're going to meet people."

"It's San Francisco. Who cares?"

"What does that mean? This isn't the sixties, my friend. We dress for work. If you want to deal with Val, you'd better look the part."

Peter felt better after a shower and even better after Hitchens handed him a clean shirt. "One of my old ones," he said. "From back in the day when I was heavier. Pink will make you look less like a Fed."

Outside, Hitchens pointed into the fog. "The Haight is up that way. Go right until you hit the park, then left."

Peter eased the heavy SUV through narrow streets.

"Val used to have a place on the Great Highway. Talk about fog. Nearly got myself killed one night, crossing that street." Hitchens tapped the side of his head with a gnarly finger that looked like it had been broken three times and fixed twice. "Keep your eyes open and your head on tight."

Peter slowed down to let a motorcycle squeeze by on the right.

"Her and Lois didn't always get along. They met back when Lois was snooping around, tracking a lead complaint about Jones kidnapping kids. Val had a bunch of them in her home, some of them orphans."

"Some?"

"Lots of heart that Val." He unbuttoned his leather jacket. "But we have to be careful."

Peter dodged an incoming truck.

"Don't get her talking about those kids. She can go on forever. Nice lady. Just don't talk about kids." Hitchens pointed at a blue three-story Victorian. "There. Park there."

"I thought you said she lived by the Great Highway."

"Too many bodies on the beach. Moved back to the Haight."

Peter didn't ask. He set the parking brake as Hitchens slipped a palm-size Colt into the glove compartment. "Where'd that come from?"

"From here." Hitchens patted his coat pocket. "Colt Junior .25 caliber. It won't do much damage. But if I keep pulling the trigger, it makes plenty of noise. Don't forget to lock the car." He picked up the bottle of wine. "Val doesn't like guns."

They stopped on the sidewalk to let a neatly dressed couple, bundled up for the cold, walk by looking prosperous and fit.

"I don't see Lane's VW." Hitchens stopped at the door to the Victorian. "This used to be a funky neighborhood."

"Funky?"

"The SLA and Patti Tania Hearst were hiding a few streets over. The Zebra killers had a safe house around the corner." He knocked on the freshly painted door. "Val fit right in."

At the window, curtains pulled back long enough for a woman's face to appear, then disappear. Hitchens knocked again. "Remember what I said about kids." He stepped back, a deadbolt clicked, and an open door revealed a thin woman in baggy sweatpants and a t-shirt. She hugged Hitchens, called him Hitch, and kissed him on both cheeks. Hugged him again before asking, "Who's the handsome young man?"

"A friend. Special Agent Peter Sieracki."

"Really?" She offered Peter a smile.

"He's Johnny's boy in D.C."

"He's my supervisor."

"Same thing," Val said, offering another smile. "It's always tough to see what's right in front of you."

Orwell? Peter tried to make the link while he sized Val, in her fifties, five-four, a hundred and twenty pounds, narrow face, dark eyes, and thick black hair tied in a ponytail.

"Orwell," Hitchens said.

"Close." Val took Peter's hand. "Sieracki? Polish? My first husband was Polish." She led him to the couch. Did he want anything to drink? Coffee? Juice, tea? Something harder?

Hitchens handed her the wine.

"Perhaps a nice pinot from Oregon?" she asked. "It just arrived."

"That's for you," Hitchens said.

"We're on a case."

"That never stopped you. Sit."

The couch was oversized, deep, and comfortable. The floors were hardwood, the rug oriental. "Baluch," Val said. "From my Peace Corps days."

"We're looking for Lois Lane," Hitch said.

"Peace Corp. Like in "corporation"? A business. We were in the business of selling peace while some of us bought and sold rugs."

Peter nodded.

"Did Johnny send you?"

"No way. He's on his own. Lois stole his badge."

"Only your badge?"

Peter pointed at photos on the fireplace mantel, a horizontal procession of babies, toddlers in diapers, kids, bigger kids, and even bigger kids in jeans and graduation gowns.

"Those are my children," Val said, sitting cross-legged on the hardwood floor. "Were my children. They're all out and about in the world now."

She lit a joint, inhaled, held her breath, and offered the joint to Hitchens, then Peter. Peter waved it off and pointed at the driftwood frame at the end of the mantel. It was a faded black-and-white of four adults huddled together in a rowboat. "Who are they?" he asked.

"More of my kids." Val blew a cloud of smoke at him. "That's David Costa. And the smaller one, the geeky-looking guy, is Terrence, his little brother. Then Sarah and Ms Jane. Lois Lane," she pretended to spit, "took that picture."

"That's who we're looking for," Hitchens said. "Have you seen her?"

Val closed her eyes and dragged on the joint. "Do you have children, Peter?"

"Lois?" Hitchens said.

"Of course not. You're too young." She pinched off the end of the joint, checked the Mickey Mouse clock on the mantel, and said with a straight face, "I was like the old lady in the shoe. I had so many kids I always knew what to do."

“Lois,” Hitchens said. “Have you seen her?”

“I was a nurse back then, working hard hours.”

“It must have been difficult,” Peter said.

“No way. I loved those kids. And I saved a few. It was wonderful. I saved a few. It’s not a secret.”

“Let’s not get into that.” Hitchens cleared his throat, checked his stainless Rolex, and said. “We should stay on Lois Lane.”

“Do you believe in forgiveness, Special Agent Sieracki?”

“Sometimes.”

“Are you carrying a gun?”

“Not me,” Hitchens said.

She placed her hands on Peter’s knees. “And you, young man?”

“Ms Lane stole my service weapon.”

“Maybe that’s for the best,” she said.

“I could lose my job.”

“All the better.” She squeezed his knees, stared into his eyes, and said, “You look like a big Huckleberry Finney.”

“Finn,” Hitchens said

“Tell me, Peter, what will you do to her when you find her?”

Peter wanted to say he’d lock her up for life, would shoot her if necessary, but opted for, “She drugged me.”

“She could’ve done worse.”

Hitchens said, “Come on, Val, he’s a kid. Give him a break.”

Val leaned back and sighed, staring at Peter. “Just a kid. Well, yes, that’s a different story.” She handed Peter the bottle of wine. "You might need this. Lois was here, we talked about the old days, old friends, and old enemies." She pointed at the door. "She's looking for the Doodler.”

"How long ago?" Peter asked, still sitting, but Hitchens was already at the front door when Val said, “She’s at Tanya’s place. On the Great Highway. My old place, near where they found Cappy.”

28.HIDDEN FILES

Time: September 2001
Location: The City, Cali

"Go that way," Hitchens said, pointing toward the ocean. The fog was patchy, thick and thicker. On their way, they passed an abandoned hospital, a U-shaped concrete block protected by a chainlink fence. "That's where Sarah used to work."

Peter was trying to think. He followed the Great Highway until he felt a hand on his knee. "Park across the street from that two-story. The railroad-car house. When Val moved out, Tanya moved in. I'll be back in a second." He took his Colt Junior with him.

From the SUV, Peter watched him cross the street, hand in his jacket pocket, and disappear into the fog. Peter stepped out, flipped open his phone, and dialed D.C.

The connection was sketchy. The woman's voice in a hurry, telling him that the Opsahl trial had been delayed. Prosecutors were waiting to see the outcome of Olson's trial in Los Angeles before pressing charges against the remaining SLA members. Special Agent Smith had left instructions. The SF office needed help surveilling William Harris. Check in ASAP.

Peter was about to ask about Smith when Hitchens waved at him from the fog, and the phone connection went dead.

"This fog is Sam Spade stuff," Hitchens said.

"Who?"

"Never mind." They stopped at a redwood gate, where Hitchens said, "If her boyfriend-husband comes back, we leave. He's not a fan of the Feds. Or me."

"I can handle."

"No, you can't." Hitchens pointed at his head. "He used to play football at City College, with OJ, before he did two years in Vietnam. Then two years in prison. Lucky for him, once he got out, Tanya found him." Hitchens opened the gate. "Now he drives a cab and plays at being a minister. Calls himself Ernesto. When he shows up, we leave."

When Hitchens opened the door, a woman shouted, "Come in!" And they stepped into a long room with low ceilings. The hardwood floors creaked, the leather couch was cracked, and in the far corner, a stained-glass window flooded the room with foggy light. Three easels rested on a canvas drop cloth. Red and yellow paint stains crisscrossed the drop cloth to a hatch-cover table crowded with jars of paint and long-stem brushes.

"Sit," the voice shouted from somewhere in the back, down a long hallway. Peter checked the easels. One caught his eye: An ocean sunset with shimmering sand and what looked like a hunched-backed woman with a dog standing over a man's naked body face down in the sand.

"Been there," Hitchens whispered.

"Where?"

"Never mind. Remember, she's a friend, so be nice."

A door swung open, and a heavyset woman in painter's overalls stepped from the hallway, glanced at Hitchens, then stared at Peter before asking, "Who's this?"

Peter guessed she was five-ten, 160 pounds, in her fifties. Saw wild hair, green eyes, high cheekbones, full lips, and no visible tattoos.

"This is Agent Peter Sieracki. We're looking for Lois."

She pointed at the couch. "You sit there, Mr Fed. Hitchens, you watch the door."

"For what?"

"You know who." She sat on a footstool, barefoot, legs spread wide, with her back to the easels. "What are you looking at, Agent Sieracki?"

He pointed at the easels. "Your work."

"I try to keep things positive, you know, seascapes and bridges. For the tourists."

"The woman on the beach?"

"I try my best. It doesn't always work." She covered the canvas with a paint-stained rag. "Ernest will be home soon. Not good for him to see anything dark. Hitchens, lock the door."

"Won't stop him."

"Will give us a few seconds." She jabbed a finger at Peter's face. "Don't get any ideas. Ernesto is a good man. Gentle, you know?"

Peter leaned back, out of range, and nodded.

Tanya sighed. "Lois is the one you should worry about."

"We know that," Hitchens said.

"Oh, you know. He knows? You're the one who screwed this up in the first place, you tell him." She pointed the same finger at Hitchens. "Tell him, Hitch. Keep it simple, so the Fed can understand."

When Hitchens kept his mouth shut, she kept going. "Back then, me and Sarah were working at the old Seaman's hospital. It's closed now."

"He knows that."

"I don't care. Anyway, Sarah was working babies. I was answering phones in Psychiatric."

"That's how she met Ernest."

"Close your pie hole. The psychiatrist was a good one, back from Vietnam, and he wanted to help the vets. He helped Ernest."

Tanya rested her elbows on her knees, her head in her hands. "Good days. Sometimes."

"Finish it."

"Please."

"Okay, so, one day I hear the Doc on the phone…"

"One day?"

"It gets boring in an office all day. Have to do something to break the monotony. We all make mistakes. Am I right?"

Both men nodded.

"So, one day I hear the good doctor talking to the police, saying he has a patient. He's worried this patient could be dangerous. The police say an investigator will call back. And the doctor warns me to expect an important call, to notify him as soon as the police call back."

"We were busy in those days," Hitchens said.

"All of us. Anyway, a few days later, this little short skinny brother with bug eyes and high cheekbones comes out of the office, and I know it's him. I just know."

"Because she's never one to jump to conclusions."

"Because he's only been in three times and tells me he's cured. Says how nice the doctor has been. Outta sight, he says. And he won't be coming back because the doctor has helped him. Cured him. That's what he said. Cured him, and he's getting married." Tanya dipped a long-stemmed brush in red paint and flicked a thick blob at the drop cloth. "Two weeks later, the doctor gets transferred to prison down south. Am I right? And the police never call back."

"Wait," Hitch said, and the front door flew open. "Hey, Ernesto, how you doin?"

A big man, a bear in fatigues and an aloha shirt, brushed by Hitchens and stopped to stare at Peter. "Who's the Fed?"

"It's nothing, dear. Go to bed, and I'll be up in a minute. Go. The young man is interested in my paintings."

"You are?"

"He is," Hitchens said.

"Bullshit." He hugged Tanya, kissed her on both cheeks, and said, "A few minutes rest, then I gotta go back out. A double shift. Don't sell anything to the Fed. He should be interested, but he isn't."

Peter said to himself, six-two, 250, maybe more. Bigger than he could handle, but at least he recognized a federal agent when he saw one.

"Peter is a friend," Hitchens said.

"Sure he is. What's your name?"

"Special Agent Peter Sieracki."

"Johnny's boy," Hitchens said.

"We're looking for Lois Lane."

"Hope you find her." Ernesto disappeared down the hall. "Before she hurts somebody."

Hitchens waited until he heard a door shut, then whispered to Tanya, "A dead end. That's all we had with the Doodler. We couldn't do anything."

"Poor choice of words," Tanya said. "There were four bodies."

Hitched turned to Peter. "We had an investigator's notes that said a psych called to report a patient with extremely violent tendencies. But the doctor's name was misspelled, and by the time we tracked him down, he had passed, and we could only talk to his wife. The doctor had died in an automobile accident. His wife had some of his files in the garage but nothing from his time at the Seaman's Hospital."

"Until now," Tanya said. "If we can believe Lois."

"I don't."

"Believe what?" Peter asked.

"That's what I'm trying to tell you," Tanya said. "Lois was here, said she talked to a friend from way back, a prison guard at a vacation spot in Lompoc. Told her he had worked with a Doc from San Francisco. Wondered if she knew him. Said it was a sad story."

"Lois Lane," Peter said. "Where is she?"

"Wait, yah? And Lois says, sure I might know him. I've been looking for a doc sounds like that, me and an old cop friend of mine. SFPD."

Peter looked at Hitchens. Tanya kept talking.

"This doc, the guard told Lois, was driving back to San Francisco to check on files he had left in the city, at his old hospital. They were cleaning out the place, storing everything in the basement. And the doc gets killed on the highway. End of long sad story."

They heard a door slam, then Ernesto stomping down the hall. He filled the doorway. "These guys gotta leave," he said. "They're cutting into my sleeping time. Follow me."

Tanya caught Peter's elbow near the door and whispered in his ear. "The old Seaman's Hospital. She's going there after the files. Tonight."

Ernesto hugged her, kissed her on the cheeks, and asked her to go back inside. On the way to the car, the big man handed Peter a scrap of paper with a phone number and said, "Leave Tanya out of this. You need help, call me."

Peter wanted to say he was a federal agent and didn't need help. But he decided it wouldn't make a difference. Instead, he sat behind the steering wheel of the SUV and rolled down the window. Cool air rushed in from the ocean. "Be careful," Ernesto said. "That Lois Lane has a mean streak."

29.ERNESTO'S MAGIC BUS

Time: September 2001
Location: The City

Dark outside, and Hitchens was sitting in the government SUV, waiting for Peter. He had warned the young agent about reporting, told him it would take hours, if not days. Nothing was ever quick in an office.

Now, Hitchens was pressing his phone to his ear, listening to Lois Lane describe her trip to Lompoc, her prison-guard friend, the Doodler's house in Berkeley. "He's meeting me tonight."

"You talked to him?"

"Like I'm talking to you."

"There are no files."

"There's always old files."

"The hospital is trash. The only thing left is concrete and cave paintings."

"It doesn't matter. If he shows up, he's our man."

"Leave that poor man alone."

She hung up.

Hitchens tried calling Peter, gave up, and hurried across the street, careful not to aggravate his bad knee. At the door, he stopped to catch his breath, shook his head, and stepped inside the reception area.

The woman sitting behind bulletproof glass looked up and smiled. For a moment, Hitchens imagined her saying, "My god, young man, how good you look." Anything was possible.

He asked for Special Agent Peter Sieracki, and while she opened the phone directory, he stood at ease, professionally, like he had at his old station in the Mission. He checked the wall clock, and watched the woman run a red fingernail down a page of phone numbers. No rings, no earrings, no jewelry. "Just a moment," she said. "I'm new. Just started a few minutes ago."

"Take your time."

"I'm temporary."

"Aren't we all?"

"You're funny."

"Sieracki," he said. "Special Agent Peter Sieracki. From DC. Talks with an accent. LA type."

"He's not listed."

"New kid. Kinda big, thick, black hair, cut short, kinda pale, six-foot, one-ninety. Talks funny. It's an emergency."

"Wait." She spoke into the phone while she shuffled through a stack of papers. "Sieracki," she said. "From Los Angeles."

"DC."

She covered the mouthpiece. "He's in a meeting." She hushed him with a wave of her red-tipped fingers. "He has a visitor," she said into the phone. "A…"

"Inspector."

"Inspector from the San Francisco Police Department."

"We're working a case."

"He's working a case. Okay." She hung up the phone. "It will be a moment. He's in with the supervisor. The duty officer?"

"Sounds right."

"A do not disturb."

Hitchens checked the clock.

"How long have you been a policeman?" she asked.

"Years."

"Really?"

"Retired. Called me in for 9-11."

"Interesting." After a quick smile, she went back to shuffling papers. "You look too young to be retired."

Hitchens checked the clock. His knee was fine. He was wide awake and in a hurry. His phone rang, and Lois whispered into his good ear. "I'm parked around back by the graveyard. The tennis courts."

"There are no tennis courts."

The phone went dead.

Hitchens counted to ten, took a deep breath, then asked the receptionist for a piece of paper. As he inhaled her Chanel, he scribbled a note. "Could you give this to Agent Peter when he's free? If he ever is?"

"Certainly. Hope to see you again, Inspector Hitchens."

On the way to the door, he turned to wave goodbye, then hobbled to the SUV, thankful he had hidden the Colt Junior in the glove compartment. And pissed off he had forgotten to ask her name.

"How long ago?" Agent Sieracki asked.

"A few minutes." The receptionist handed him the note. "Not long. Such a good looking fellow, for his age. He said he was with a police officer. The SFPD."

"Inspector." Peter read the note twice before asking, "Where is this place? The Public Health Service Hospital? Do you know?"

"Let's see. Wait." She tapped her forehead. "I'm pretty sure I do. I hope he isn't in danger, any kind of trouble."

Peter pointed at the map on the wall behind her. "Can you show me?"

She pointed a red fingernail at a stretch of green. "This is Golden Gate Park." Her finger drifted north. "This is the Golden Gate Bridge. And this is the Sunset."

"And the hospital?"

"Somewhere in here." Her finger came to rest on a tangle of crisscrossing streets.

"I think I've been there. Thanks." Outside, Peter searched the parking lot for the SUV. Tried calling Hitchens three times. Gave up and called Ernesto.

Five minutes later, a Honda sedan pulled into the parking lot. Ernesto rolled down the window. "You called?"

"I need your help," Peter said. "Just a ride. For directions. The streets…"

"Get in. That's my job."

Ernesto looked bigger in the tiny car, a heavy man in Levis and a leather jacket. "The Public Health Service Hospital. Out in the Sunset?" Peter said.

"Presidio."

"You know it?"

"You could say that."

Ernesto drove into the blast of auto horns. "I used to take Tanya there to paint on the walls. She loved the place, called it her concrete easel. I thought it looked like Eastern Europe. Russian modern. A prison."

"We're in a hurry."

Ernesto made a few quick turns, drove down a one-way street. "I'll take a fast route. "Ernesto stuck a cigarette between his lips, lit it with a stainless steel Zippo. "Usually, I don't help the feds."

The car smelled of pachouli and dried beer. "Just drop me there," Peter said. "I'll do the rest."

Ernesto said, "What are you working on now? I mean, when you're not working on Lois, the crazy. You know her father was a big-time lawyer. Radical. Helped Jones. Nearly got himself killed. Didn't help me." Ernesto hit the brakes to let a tour bus squeeze past. "Where the hell are they going?"

"It's a one-way street."

"Inspiring. Stay cool, man."

"What did they tell you at the head-fed office?"

"I'm supposed to help the HPD monitor William Harris."

"General Teko."

"You know him?"

"Sure. Field Marshall Shoplifter. His mistake got his troops in the SLA burned alive, shot dead, and burned again. I was in town when they caught him and his wife. And Hearst. What now? He's still in business? Last I heard, he was working for a lawyer. Researching, investigating."

"You know a lot."

"Facing justice?" Ernesto cut in and out of traffic, ran a yellow light, and kept his foot heavy on the gas.

In between near misses, Peter said, "We're waiting for another trial to finish. Have to make sure he's around for the next one. Maybe January."

"The Opsahl killing." Ernesto looked both ways before running a red light. "I hear his wife was the accidental shooter, a faulty trigger."

"You know a lot."

"I drive a taxi. When I'm not preaching."

Peter didn't ask.

"You don't think I look like a preacher?"

"Not really."

"If I have to, I can pound Jesus into a sinner."

"What would Jesus do?"

"That's right. What would he do? I'm trying to be like him, as long as I don't get crucified." He jerked his thumb at the back seat. "Got everything we need on the floor."

Peter reached over and tried to lift the gear bag by its nylon handle, managed a few inches, and dropped it. "What's in there? Hey, watch the road."

"Frickin Lois Lane," Ernesto shouted. He stuck his head out the window, gunned the Honda down a side street lined with parked cars, spit the cigarette, and pulled his head inside. "I'm a peaceful man. Remember that. A religious man. I'm not killing anyone, especially not because Lois says so."

"Who said anything about killing?"

"We're all killers," Ernesto said.

"Not me."

"Not yet."

"If I have to," Peter said. "I'll do it."

"Whatever we do, we keep Tanya out of this. She's doesn't understand violence."

Peter wondered if Ernesto knew who he had married.

"Check the bag. I got good flashlights and wire cutters. I know all the ways in. Once we're over the fence, it's easy. None of the doors are locked. Me and Tanya worked those walls. Her work is all over the place. On the walls. The floors. Even the roof. You gotta see her stuff. If it isn't painted over. Great art is ephemeral. It gets painted over by upstarts, insensitive, unthinking copycats. No vision of their own. Or canvas. There are too many of those locusts."

"Tough business, art."

"Not always art. Sometimes, I go there to feed the homeless. Praise Jesus. There's canned food in the bag. Heavy stuff. A canvas sack of cans makes a wicked weapon if someone interrupts a man working for peace. You ever been hit by a bag full of Spam cans?"

"Not that I remember."

"You'd remember."

Peter watched a Christmas tree swinging from the rearview mirror, its evergreen scent long gone. Ernesto sucked on an unlit cigarette, one hand on the wheel, and said, "You ever see a dead body?"

"What?"

"A body. A dead one."

"Two of them," Peter said, hoping that was enough.

"At the academy?"

"Yes. For a class. A man and a woman."

"That doesn't count."

"Why?"

"It's obvious."

They followed a dark road to a chainlink gate. Ernesto said, "Wait here." And slammed the door.

Peter rolled down the window to smell the ocean. Felt the air sticky on his face. Smelled something rotten. Human waste. Ernesto was right. On the other side of the fence, six stories of abandoned concrete and broken windows looked like a rotting prison.

Ernesto came back. The gate was open. "Not locked." He drove by an empty guard shack and found the government's SUV parked next to Lois Lane's VW bug, behind the hospital, between two bulldozers.

While Ernesto struggled with the gear bag, Peter stepped into the moonlight and looked up.

30.OLD HOSPITALS

Time: September 2001
Location: San Francisco

Peter stepped back, looked up at the top floor, saw a light moving from window to window. "There," he shouted and took one step before Ernesto grabbed his elbow.

"Wait." Ernesto dropped the gear bag on the ground, dug out two headband lights, kept one, and handed the other to Peter. Showed him a side button. When Peter pressed it, a dim circle of light landed on the hospital's back door. "Batteries are a little low in yours," Ernesto said. "No worries, it'll last. I think. You can't paint without them. Keeps the hands free."

Looking at the hospital, Peter said, "Hope Hitch remembered his Colt."

"You have a weapon?" Ernesto asked.

"Lois has my Glock."

"She has a thing about guns."

"That's what I hear."

Ernesto opened the Honda's trunk and dug out an aluminum

baseball bat. “Just in case. Sometimes people don’t understand unless you look the part.” He practiced a two-fisted swing, smiled, and handed it to Peter. “Aim for the knees.”

“Better than nothing.”

“This way, we don’t kill anyone.” He reached into the trunk and dug out a wrecking bar.

“Or maybe we do,” Peter said. “The wrecking bar was as long as his bat, with a straight claw at one end and a bent claw at the other. “Let me hold that.” He switched with Ernesto, tested the weight, needed two hands to swing it, and said, “This speaks to me.”

Ernesto switched back. “That’s why it’s with me. You’re too young to have learned the wisdom needed to swing this baby.” Gear bag slung from his shoulder, wrecking bar in hand, he climbed the steps to the hospital. “Follow me.”

Peter aimed his dim light at the door. The padlock was broken. And Ernesto was reaching for the knob when the door swung open, launching a bulky figure in an overcoat at Ernesto and into Peter before stumbling into the night.

“That was the Big Bear,” Ernesto said, helping Peter to his feet. “Never seen him run like that. Used to be slow. Kinda stinky, that man. Hold the bat out in front of you. Didn’t they teach you anything in fed school?”

Ernesto straightened his headlight, caught the door swinging open, and watched the next two escapees, smaller and slower in jeans and hoodies, charge into the light, one swinging a gallon jug of wine, the other pointing a can of spray paint.

Ernesto stepped in their way with the wrecking bar and a two-finger peace sign.

“Ernesto!”

“Ernesto!”

The smaller of the two wrapped her arms around him and tried to kiss him but couldn’t reach his lips. The man with the jug of wine pulled her back, saying, “Come on, baby. Hi, Ernesto. Where’s Tanya?”

“At…”

But they were gone, running for the woods, the jug shattering on asphalt.

"That was quick," Peter said, gripping the bat. "Friends of yours?"

"Painters."

"We have to get through that door.."

"Follow me." Ernesto jerked the door open, jabbed the bar at the dark, and stepped in, saying, "Stay close."

Peter aimed his circle of light on Ernesto's back and ran into him at the stairwell when Ernesto stopped at a young woman, blond, chest high, in jeans and a puffy down jacket rolling up her sleeping bag. "It's like grand central station tonight," she said. "Is that you, Ernesto? Who's the narc?"

"Peter."

"Agent Sieraki, FBI."

"Good for you." She pointed at the stairs. "I heard screams up there. Think I'll pack up for the night."

"Good idea," Ernesto said and emptied his cans of food on the floor. "Peace, sister. Give some to your friends. Up we go."

Peter's circle of light settled on a spray-painted warning: "Watch your step! Uncle Sam is watching." A wrecking bar poked him in the back. "No rubber-necking," Ernesto said. "Keep your light on the stairs."

Ernesto led on the first flight, Peter ran past him on the second and made the mistake of stopping to look at a giant skull spray painted on the wall. The wrecking bar poked him in the back. "Keep going," Ernesto whispered.

Two flights up, they heard a woman scream.

"That settles it."

Ernesto shoved past Peter and charged up the stairs. When Peter reached the top, his headlight stopped at a graffiti warning: "Bug doctors. Plague made here!!!"

"Hurry," Ernesto called. His light zigzagged off the walls and shot down to the marble floor. "What the hell!" A door slammed, glass shattered, and Ernesto shouted, "Get over here."

Baseball bat pointed like a spear, Peter found Ernesto on his hands and knees, bent over Hitchens.

“Stay here,” Ernesto said.

Peter cradled the inspector’s head, wiped the blood off his forehead, and bent close, listening for breathing.

"Crappo!" Ernesto came back, breathing hard. “The fire escape must’ve given way. There’s a body on the ground. How’s Hitch?”

“He’s breathing.” Peter wiped more blood off the inspector’s forehead. “And bleeding."

"I can see that."

"A deep cut.” Peter checked his phone. “No connection. No ambulance.”

“Mine too. Nothing. This cement block is a dead spot.”

“The body at the fire escape. Is it Lois?”

“Maybe. Too dark to tell.”

Hitchens squeezed Peter’s arm.

“What?” Peter held him close.

“I’m…fine,” Hitch said.

“Can you stand?” Peter asked, tried to lift Hitchens, then sagged to the floor with him, his back resting against the wall, Hitch’s head and shoulders in his lap. “He’s heavier than he looks.”

“He’s ain’t heavy, he’s my brother.”

“What?”

“Old song,” Ernesto said. “I’ll take his legs. You take the shoulders. I'll lead, you follow. I know these stairs. We can walk him down. That’s the only way. I got the good light. No soldier left behind. Ready?”

“Stop talking and go.”

“Don’t let him close his eyes.” With his back to Peter and arms around Hitch’s knees, Ernesto shouted, “Lift!”

“Run, baby,” Hitchens whispered.

Peter nodded. “Step on it.”

“Keep him talking.”

“Hitch. Hey, Hitch.”

They were moving now, almost at a run, Ernesto saying, “No

problem. I've carried my share in the Nam. Me and Cappy got plenty of practice."

"He's light."

"Old bones," Hitch managed.

"Don't listen to him, Hitch."

Ernesto kept rambling, talking down the stairs, past stencils of Anne Frank with blacked-out eyes and scrawled pleas for peace. Bold splashes of red. Blue skies with clouds made of "love" printed a zillion blue times.

Arms aching, Peter passed a warning: "Unless you know what you're doing, stay out!" Down a flight to block letters: "DANGER: HIGH VOLTAGE!" A giant red eye with a dagger through it watched a spiky-headed stick figure screaming, "Hate is its own medicine!" Another flight, another official sign: "Report Injuries at Once!" Followed by a graffiti scrawl, "I've fallen & got up!" Then a winged horse, deep blue, chased by a hatchet-wielding scarecrow claiming, "You can, you can, you can go home again."

By the time they reached the main floor, Ernesto was breathing hard and deep, shouting for helicopters and mortar rounds. At the door, Peter saw black lettering on a yellow background: "No Visitors Beyond This Point!"

Outside, they collapsed. Peter on his butt, holding Hitchens in his lap. Ernesto on his knees, checking his phone, saying, "I got bars. Wait here." Then running.

31.NEW HOSPITALS

Time: September 2001
Location: SF, California.

Peter woke up to the gentle voice of a tall young doctor assuring him that Mr. Hitchens would be fine, not to worry. They still had a few tests to do, but if all went well, they could release him after a few days for observation.

The doctor led him to a quiet corner of the waiting room. “Mr Hitchens lost a considerable amount of blood. He was lucky you were there,” she said. “The ambulance crews won’t go there without police backup. It takes forever. I don’t blame them. That old hospital should have been leveled years ago. It manages to send us patients on a regular basis. Mostly kids, graffiti artists, slipping on the stairs or hanging from the fire escape to paint on the walls. Or homeless squatters. No lights. Rusting metal. Accidents.” The doctor wrote something on her clipboard. “He said he tripped. Or slipped. A bad knee, poor balance. He couldn’t say for certain.”

“Just the forehead? Nothing in the back?”

The doctor shook her head. “Nothing. A serious laceration to the forehead. Possible concussion. We'll do a few tests. If all goes well, he should be released in a few days."

Peter nodded.

"Do him a favor. When we release Mr Hitchens , keep him at home. At the very least, far from demolition sites. And be nice, our seniors are often embarrassed by this type of accident. "

"We'll try."

"Good man. Him, not you. I'm not certain about you."

When she left, Peter gulped cold coffee from a styrofoam cup, finished it, and called the San Francisco field office for an update. The local police had found Lois Lane's body at the bottom of the fire escape. They were treating it as an accident. A section of the rotting metal had given way, and she had fallen four stories. They had searched the hospital, found a few stragglers, junkies who had slept through the night and heard nothing. The fresh blood on the top floor belonged to Hitchens. It was at the lab. The SFPD was sending an inspector to the hospital. When would Mr Hitchens be well enough for a visit? Did Agent Sieracki know? Van we contact you at the Bureau's field office?

A nurse came to say, "You can go in now. Not too long, please. Your friend needs rest."

Peter sat next to the bed, and when he touched Hitchens' shoulder, the old detective opened his eyes and said, "My knee gave out."

"Happens."

"Blew that one. Slammed into something in the dark. A wall. Something solid."

"Sit back. Rest."

Hitchens closed his eyes. "I almost caught her. I chased her to the top floor and almost caught her. She can move fast for an old gal. I was reaching for her, yelling for her to stop, and snap, my knee blows out."

"Lois?"

"She kept going."

"Chasing someone?"

Hitchens opened his eyes, blinked twice. "Said so. I didn't see anyone."

"Relax. Take it easy."

"Where is she?"

"The locals found her at the bottom of the fire escape. An accident."

"Nice touch," he said. "One of life's little jokes. I found her rifling through file cabinets, must've been hundreds of them in the basement."

"Did she find anything?"

"Mold." He grimaced as he shifted his legs. "There were no files. Never were. That's what I think."

"Your SFPD is sending out an inspector to talk to you. We should talk, decide what to say."

"I can handle it. Probably take weeks for them to get off their butts." He pointed at the chair where his clothes were piled. "Help me. Give me those."

"You're not going anywhere."

"I need a drink." He let his head sink into the pillow. "It's another of life's jokes," he sighed.

"What's that?"

"The older you get, the more time you spend in the hospital. But the older you get, the less time you have to waste in a hospital." Hitchens closed his eyes. "Too bad Lois is going to miss all the fun."

Peter spent the afternoon passed out on Hitch's couch, with Ms Jane the cat purring on his chest. When the light disappeared, he shifted the cat to the windowsill, walked downstairs, and emptied a can of Kitty Banquet into a teacup. The cat sniffed the banquet, blinked at Peter, and waited at the door.

"Sorry about your owner," Peter said as he let the cat out. He watched her run across the street and stop at a Honda sedan parked under a streetlight. Ernesto, Tanya, and Val stepped out. Val picked up the cat and set her gently in the back seat.

The three friends, each carrying a bottle of red wine, met Peter at the door. Ernesto handed him a 24-count Twinkies box, saying it was Lois Lane's favorite snack. Val said she would care for the cat, an old friend, a good gal, and smart enough not to cry. They sat on the floor, a woman on each side of Peter and Ernesto. They drank wine from paper cups while Ernesto drank from Lois Lane's last bottle of Sauza tequila.

"She was no saint," Ernesto said.

Val said she didn't like talking bad about the dead.

"The dead don't care," Tanya said. "They're dead."

"To Hitchens," Ernesto said, lifting his bottle.

They drank to Hitchens. Then to Lois. Then to old times.

"She was a tough gal," Ernesto said. "But no saint. I never trusted her, not after she started working for you guys."

"You guys?" Peter said, testing a Twinkie, squeezing it with two fingers. "We are the good guys."

"Maybe," Tanya said. "Hitchens for sure."

"To Hitchens."

"With respect."

"With respect."

Val poured another round. "To Peter."

"To Peter."

"To Peter."

"Who's he?" Peter asked.

They sat in silence until Tanya said, "Your boss is a sicko."

"You'd know better than me. I only met him once."

"Don't get her started," Val said. "Johnny must have done something right. Thirty years in, and he ends up in Victim Services.

"That's a demotion," Tanya said.

"She's right," Peter said. "No one wants that job. It's too close to social services, not law enforcement."

"That's good." Val drank her wine. Poured another. "In his case, failure is a success. He's better off and doesn't know it. He'll be out of that job in no time."

"What?" Peter asked.

"Bullshit," Ernesto said.

"What?" Peter drank more wine, trying to follow the talk's trail.

"Bullshit," Ernesto said. "That's a good word. Bullshit."

"I bet," Tanya said.

"What?"

"He's still looking for our two friends."

"Who?" Peter asked.

"Never mind."

"Doesn't make sense," Ernesto said. "He's got the whole FBI to find whoever, so he sends Lois? That's too crazy."

"Crazy enough."

The three old friends laughed, raised their glasses, "To Lois."

"To Lois," Peter said.

"Better than the FBI, that girl."

"Anyone is."

"Exacto mundo."

"Except Peter.

"Hey, this is my first assignment."

"A toast to your last."

They drank and reloaded.

Tanya said, "Lois is dead, but wherever she is, I bet she's still causing trouble."

"Chasing a good cause."

"May she rest in peace," Val said.

Ernesto filled their glasses, and they toasted Hitchens, then Peter. Then Sarah Costa.

"Who?" Peter asked.

"To the union girl."

"Doing union work," Val said. "In Hawaii."

The women drank wine and drank wine again.

"Bullshit," Ernesto said.

They laughed, and Peter didn't know why, but he laughed anyway.

"To friends."

"To enemies."

"Fricken Lois Lane."

"That's her."

Later, at the door, Ernesto stopped Peter and waited for the two women to cross the street, then he reached behind his back, found what he was looking for, and handed Peter his Glock. "While you waited for the ambulance, I went around back. Found it on Lois."

Peter looked down at his service weapon.

"This, too." Ernesto handed him an envelope stained with blood.

Peter opened it and found cash and a plane ticket. "Where's Hilo?"

"On the Big Island with the volcanoes. You get there and you find Sarah Costa. Tell her what happened. She'll know what to do." Ernesto bear-hugged him. "Then forget everything and stay there Don't come back. Forgive and forget. Understand?"

That night, Peter drank until he almost did.

PART V

RESCUE

What guy?

The guy that tried to throw Mac overboard.

That guy. He kinda drifted back into the crowd, and McNamara refused to point him out.

Mac must've been knocked silly. Fog of war, right?

Maybe.

But you saw the other guy?

Sure. At the dock, he was the first guy off the boat.

32.LOOKING FOR YOU

Time: September 2001
Location: Hilo, Hawaii

Special Agent Peter Sieracki watched 300 human beings squeeze into 290 airline seats. He wondered why they were so happy? A new job? A family reunion?

He searched their faces for signs of intent. A desperate hunger for paradise? Religious fervor, a pilgrimage? He detected nothing except a young woman pressing a baby to her breast, a clean-shaven man in a sweatsuit unwrapping a double-decker cheeseburger, and a flight attendant sipping from a mini-bottle as she hid behind her partner pantomiming emergency landing instructions.

Buckle up. Oxygen masks overhead, flotation devices under the seat, and emergency exits to the left and right.

Peter felt the jet vibrating up his backbone. Was he being launched in the wrong direction? Aimed at the end of his career? He heard Hitchens on his hospital bed, promising important advice. As the plane lifted off the ground, he remembered his new friend whispering in his ear. "Don't forget to take off your shoes."

In another time zone, still in a suit and tie, Peter climbed wooden stairs, each step sagging under his weight. Fearing a sudden collapse, he reached the second floor and a door with peeling blue paint, where he knocked twice, stepped back, and heard a woman's voice shout, "It's open."

His reached for the knob, hesitated, and said, "I'm a federal agent."

"It's open."

When he stepped inside, he saw a young woman in a t-shirt and shorts standing on a desk, on her tiptoes, stretching to see out a small window. "Take off your shoes," she said, still eyeing the window.

"I'm sorry. I think I'm in the wrong place."

She gave him a quick look. "Could be."

"Is this an office?"

"It is."

"The teachers' union?"

"Professional Assembly." She jumped down and held out her hand. "Celeste Blake, union rep."

"Special Agent Sieracki." He took her hand, felt a firm grip, then showed her his ID and badge.

"Impressive. Now take off your shoes." She pointed at the door. "Leave them outside, next to my high tops." When he hesitated, she added, "They won't walk off."

His loafers came off easy, but he stopped at the door, and said, "They're new."

She took them, set them outside, and pointed at a sagging recliner. "Have a seat, Agent Sieracki. Don't be afraid. People only steal slippers, no dress shoes"

As he sank into the recliner, he noticed a surfboard standing in a corner, a ten-speed bike leaning against the wall, and a one-piece bathing suit hanging from a nail. Bottoming out, he said, "This is quite an office."

She sat on the desk, bare feet dangling near his shins. "What can I do for you, Special Agent?"

"Peter is fine."

"The new casual FBI?"

"I'm not on duty."

"Pete okay?"

"Peter."

"In a suit?" She added a pleasant smile. "On vacation? What's wrong with you?"

"Long story." He guessed she was his age, a few inches shorter. A solid 120. Shaggy hair, black with red streaks, and hand-combed. Green eyes?

She brushed her hair back. "Why are you looking at me like that? Is it my hair? The red isn't mine. That's Kawamoto Pool. They bleach the heck out of the water. Sun and saltwater finish the damage."

"Sorry. It's the job. Trying to be better at remembering details. I'm not good at it."

"Can you do it without staring?"

"I'm getting better."

"You need a different job." She shook her head. "It's maddening. I've been thinking about shaving it."

"In high school, I tried to peroxide mine to look more like a surfer. The pool turned it green."

"Did you shave it?"

"Yes."

"Poor thing. Where did you grow up? Do this shaving?"

"Santa Barbara."

"All your life?"

"Born and raised?"

"Yes, and you?"

"Me? I'm a mystery." She kicked his shin with a bare foot. "I'm sorry, did that hurt? No? Good. If you came for sun and sand, you came to the wrong side of the island. Kona has the sun and beaches. This is Hilo. We have rain and rocks."

"No matter. I'm looking for a woman. Sarah Costa. She works for the union, your union. Friends of hers told me I might find her here."

"FBI friends?"

"Maybe one of them. I'm working a cold case from the 1970s in San Francisco."

"A serious crime? Is Ms Costa involved?"

"Oh, no, not. But she might be able to identify a suspect. If he is a suspect."

"Sarah's not here. She'll be back in a few days, maybe a week."

"Does she have a phone?"

"She doesn't like phones." She shrugged. "Where are you staying? I can call when I see her."

"I don't have much time."

"You're on vacation. You have all the time in the world. Can you ride a shortboard?"

"If there's nothing else."

"My longboard's at home. It won't fit in the office. That shortie does." She pointed at the board in the corner. "I keep it here for days when there's a nice break by the bridge. Like today. And I've finished grading papers. Like today."

"You're a teacher?"

"Five classes this semester. History."

"Heavy load."

"Not for me. I'm used to it."

He watched her stand up on the desk and look out the window. She had strong legs, a swimmer's legs or a biker's. "Is that a Varsity? he asked.

"All original. It's my race bike."

"That's funny."

"That's what Sarah said."

"She did? How much does it weigh?"

"Never mind." She looked at her watch. "It's been nice, but I'm in a rush. Want to catch a few waves before sunset?" Celeste jumped down and picked up her surfboard. "I know where we can find a board for you."

Peter followed her to the door. He was close enough to see the fine hair on the back of her neck. "I used to ride an Aipa, a swallowtail."

"You're spoiled."

"Rincon and the Ranch."

"Do you have trunks?"

"Boxer shorts."

"Stan's shop is a few blocks away. You can buy trunks and rent a board. You ding it, you pay for the repairs. They're old logs, and you'd have to hit the reef pretty hard to crack through four layers of glass."

"I need a place to lock my badge and service weapon."

"You can leave it here."

He checked the office again. There was a plastic file cabinet in the corner, a black phone on the desk, and an ancient footlocker on the floor. "Can you follow me to the Naniloa?" he asked. "I'll lock it in the hotel safe."

"You don't trust me?"

"Not yet."

"Same here."

33.TEN DAYS TO IRONWOMAN

Time: September 2001
Location: Hilo, Hawaii

"That's the Singing Bridge." Sarah said.

They were drifting off the river mouth, Celeste straddling her shortboard, only the board's nose poking out of the water. Peter was kneeling on a longboard, dry except for his hands, thanks to ten feet of the waterlogged fiberglass.

"It took longer to build than the Golden Gate," she said.

Peter was half listening. The Hilo break was nothing like his favorite spots in California. At home, the waves broke on sandy bottom, the water so cold he needed a full wetsuit. The water in Hilo was warmer, but the waves broke on river rock and dead coral.

Under dark clouds, with no wind, the waves were breaking waist-high, and Celeste had paddled a spot with an easy left for a goofy foot.

"Watch the current, don't drift past the bridge, and don't drop in on anyone," she said.

"That's a lot of don'ts."

"Unless you want to beef."

Peter had no idea what that meant, but he felt the ocean move, saw Celeste swing her board around, point it at the shore, and paddle fast. The wave peaked, and she stood up, dropped in, shot up and off the lip, tracking left along the shoulder before kicking out and paddling back toward him.

She's good, Peter thought, as a turtle periscoped, took a quick breath, glassy-eyed Peter, and dove under, hidden in the murky water.

The ocean lifted Peter up, and he swung the heavy board around, paddled on his belly until the nose dug in, stood up and stepped back, lifting the nose up then swinging the board left, riding the wave old-style, straight along the chest-high face, stepping to the nose, holding it, stepping back, and twisting at the waist to swing the board up and over, to where he could drop to his knees and paddled out.

“You're old school,” Celeste shouted as she paddled with him through the foamy white water. “You’re not that old, are you?”

A small wave slapped his face.

Outside the break, she stopped and pointed at the mountain behind Hilo. "That’s Mauna Kea,” she said. "The tallest mountain on earth."

When he looked, he saw clouds broken by streaks of the setting sun.

“It’s getting late,” she said. “We’d better head in. Keep an eye out for Diego.”

“In a minute.” It felt too good to be in the ocean, to taste its salt in his mouth. He surfed until it was too dark to see, then rode mushy whitewater to a tiny patch of sand and river rock. Careful not to step on sea urchins or broken glass, he stepped between the rocks, climbed a short trail, and found Celeste pouring fresh water over her head. “Did you see Diego?” she asked.

“Bad dude?”

“You could say that. Big Tiger"

He slid the board into her truck’s bed, nose first, and strapped it down with a frayed bungee cord. She handed him a plastic jug of water, and as he poured it over his head, he watched her wrap herself in a towel and step out of her bathing suit. He turned to look at wooden storefronts, the surf shop, the Mexican restaurant, and a neon sign for the Palace Theater. He had forgotten how good it felt to be tired, ocean tired. When her towel landed on his head, he turned to see her in a dry pair of board shorts and a cotton hoodie.

She tossed him a pair of rubber slippers. "Careful, they're worn thin."

"My size. You wear these?"

"In case of a blowout." She dug a dark blue hoodie from behind the truck's bench seat. "And this," she said, handing it to him. "Should be enough for Reubens."

"Nice fit."

"A student castoff. Saved for an emergency."

The hoodie was thick and soft, almost new, with Orchard Isle Surf Shop printed across the back. "Get in," Celeste called, and when she started the truck, a staticky Mick Jagger was singing about his Sweet Black Angel.

"That's an old one," he said.

"Always. 97.1. Home of back-in-the-day and always classic rock." "Want to learn some history."

"Always."

"It's the only political song ever performed by the Stones. Dedicated to Angela Davis."

Peter liked the Rolling Stones and had heard about Angela Davis in lectures at the Academy about the Black Panthers, but he was more interested in hearing about Diego, wondering if he had anything to do with the hoodie and slippers. "Tell me about Diego."

"Big tiger," she said. "15-footer."

"Thanks for telling me."

"I tried. You're a big boy."

Across the street and past a line of parked cars, she stopped n front of Reubens. He followed her into Reubens and felt right at home. Their table wobbled and so did his chair. The linoleum floor was cracked. The lighting dim. And black-light paintings of Mexican heroes and bullfights lined the walls. But the salsa and chips were free, homemade, and thick with onions, chili pepper, and tomatoes.

The guacamole came thick with chunks of avocado. The margarita on the rocks was the best he had ever tasted, which was saying a lot because he considered himself an expert on Mexican food and drinks. In Santa Barbara, he could eat at a different Mexican restaurant every day or night of the week and never hit a bad one. But he wondered about Celeste's eating habits. “It’s not exactly training-table food,” he said, after watching her eat two cheese enchiladas with beans and rice, a fist-full of chips, and downing two margaritas.

“I was raised on this stuff,” she said.

From the looks of her, Mexican was definitely better than Wheaties and wheat germ, so he ordered another margarita to go with his Chile Rellenos, and concentrated on the pleasure of eating, until Celeste leaned back and raised her third margarita in salute, saying, “Yummy. Ono!”

“Delicioso,” Peter said as he dipped a salty, oily chip into chunky salsa.

“I’m glad you don’t like to talk while eating.”

“Makes it easier.”

Peter offered to pay, Celeste said no, and they split the bill

She drove by the soccer fields, the canoe clubs, over a concrete bridge, and parked across the street from the Naniloa. "Hurry,” Celeste said. “I have to get home.”

Without looking back, he ran across the street, through the parking lot and into the hotel. Later that night, he stood on the lanai gazing at the moonlit ocean. The water looked smooth and deep and black. And he was thinking about Celeste Blake.

34.IRON MEN AND BAR STOOLS

Time: September-October 2001
Location: Hilo, Hawaii

Peter lost track of time. He'd start his mornings in the university library. While Celeste taught, he'd begin reading with *Land and Power in Hawaii*, shift to *Kū Kanaka, Stand Tall, A Search for Hawaiian Values,* and move to the basement for a snooze with dreams from *Waikiki Beachboy*. When Celeste first found him there, she said they had time to run fifteen miles. It would be easy, she promised. She was tapering down for a big race, so she was tapering.

They ran from the university to the airport and across the runway to a straight stretch of road through saltwater ponds that reached into the ocean, where waves broke on lava rock. At her halfway mark, he was soaked in sweat, begging for water, so she ran onto a narrow trail over lava rock, thick with shade, as she pointed out Banyan, Hala, and Kukui Nut trees. At the edge of a freshwater pool long enough to swim laps, waves broke on lava rock, splashing them with warm white foam. Without taking off her shoes, she jumped in and let herself sink through water so clear he could see her on the bottom, waving for him to follow.

By the time he jumped, Celeste was shooting to the surface. By the time he pushed off the bottom, she had surfaced. And by the time he reached the surface, she was running over lava rock.

He caught her, stayed with her for a few miles, then gave up, too tired to breathe. They met later at Reubens, where he ate fish tacos while Celeste graded student papers and asked about San Francisco. Had he seen the surf spot under the Golden Gate Bridge? The spot at Seal Rock? Was the saltwater pool still there? Did he know Duke Kahanamoku had set a world record there?

He said yes to the surf spots but didn't tell her the pool had been turned into a parking lot.

Celeste wrote a note in the margins of a typed essay and told him she hadn't seen Sarah Costa. "I guess she has had her own things to do."

The next day, Celeste introduced him to Jerry at the bike shop across from the community college. Peter rented a road bike that he could lift with one hand, and they drove east and up a mountain road past the Volcanoes National Park. On what Celeste called "the dry side" they pedaled on broken asphalt past a locked gate and up a fire-access road. At first, it was a smooth climb shaded by thick trees bending in the wind. He had to stop three times to catch his breath, but Celeste kept going on asphalt, cracked and crumbling and bordered by lava rock until she reached the 7,000-foot level. When he caught her, they flew down in wild s-turns through lava fields and burned out ohia forests.

That night, Celeste ate two helpings of Salmon Alfredo. He bolted down a sausage pizza, a

nd then they sat on the lanai at his hotel and watched a white ocean liner sparkle in the moonlight as tugboats guided it out of the harbor.

The next day, before the bad news, he finished Land and Power, and they swam at Kawamoto Pool in water that felt as cold as the ocean off Santa Barbara. Peter managed 1500 meters between faded lane lights, over cracked and patched concrete, and under a Quonset-hut roof with a center strip open to the sky. Celeste lapped him twice.

They ate at Cafe 100. Celeste ordered her after-workout favorite, a carbo-loading special called Loco Moco, two bowls of it, each a bowl filled with fried rice topped with hamburger steak, a fried egg and thick gravy. "Invented in Hilo," she said, wiping gravy off her chin. "That's history. Don't let anyone tell you different."

Peter promised. She smiled, and when he asked about Sarah Costa, Celeste rolled up her napkin and tossed it in the rubbish can. "No sign of her, and I have bad news. A faculty friend is ill, and I have to replace him as an advisor on a field trip." She touched his hand. "The students need me. If I don't go, the trip is canceled. They can't miss Waipi'o Valley. It's their history." She sighed. She'd be gone for five days. No matter what, she'd be back in time for the Ironman. Would Peter be here when she returned?

Peter didn't know what to say.

"Well, if you are, I'll see you."

Was it the next day?

Forgetting to check the time, Peter called Hitchens and reached him at home, drinking Scotch. Hitchens said that the name Celeste Blake didn't ring a bell, but he'd check around. It sounded familiar, but nothing to do with the Doodler or Lois Lane. He mumbled "Blake" three times and ended with, "I'll check around. When are you coming back?"

Peter tried to reach Ernesto, called his number three times. On the fourth try, Tanya picked up the phone. "Blake?" she asked. "I don't remember any Blakes. It's too early. I'm not awake. Celeste? I'll ask Val. Who is she? You have a girlfriend? Don't tell me. She's attractive? A professor? Forget it. You have a job, not a good one, that's true, but come home. I'll tell Ernesto you called."

"Wait." But she had hung up. A few minutes later, Ernesto called back and asked, "Did you find Sarah?"

"Not yet."

"What you been doing?"

He told her about Celeste. Celeste Blake.

"Try Auntie Kim's Place."

"Wait." But he had hung up.

Was it the next day?

Peter was sitting in a booth where he could see everyone who walked or stumbled through the door of Auntie Kim's Place. A young man in a white dress shirt was tending bar, every booth filled with men in their thirties, forty, or fifties, most of them neatly dressed in slacks and aloha shirts, sitting with smiling young women dressed like bank clerks. The music and chatter were turned down low under a cloud of smoke and aftershave.

A short bruiser with glassy eyes slid into the seat across from him, followed seconds later by Auntie Kim setting a Bud and a shot glass between them. "This is Mr Matsui," she said. "He's a friend, but he's drunk. Forget everything he says."

"That sums it up," Matsui said and watched her go, poured beer into his shot glass, downed it, and held out his hand. "My friends call me JJ. And you must be Special Agent Sieracki."

Peter took the tight, sweaty grip and answered with a nod. "Who told you?"

"I work at the college with Celeste."

"You do? What's with the shot glass?"

"I'm in training." Matsui stuck a cigarette between his lips put it down. "Limiting myself."

For what? Peter wondered. Matsui was maybe 5.6, at least 160, in his late 50s or early 60s. Pasty from breathing bar fumes. Peter nursed his draft, remembering to be nice.

"Where is she?" Matsui asked. "Celeste?"

"She's in Waipi'o."

"Really? She didn't tell me."

"Five days."

"Waipi'o?"

"Yes."

Matsui poured another shot. Downed it. Poured another. "You still looking for the union lady?"

"That's right."

Kawika brought a glass of water, set it in front of Matsui, shook his head, and left.

"He's a good kid," Matsui said.

"A young man."

"Not like his sister."

"Who?"

"I mean their looks. You're not blind. Blue eyes and blond hair, tall and thin, mostly haole. Not like his sister."

"Have another beer."

Matsui drank another shot. Gave up and drained the bottle, waved for Kawika. The bartender came back with a longneck Bud and said, "I've been thinking about enlisting."

"For what?" Matsui asked, lighting his cigarette.

"There's a war."

"Against who?" Matsui asked. "What country?"

Kawika turned to Peter. "What do you think?"

"Don't ask him. He's on vacation. Bring another beer."

"I think the Marines will be good for me."

"Be all you can be," Matsui said.

"That's the army," Kawika said.

They watched him go. "Who is he?" Peter asked. "Why's he asking me?"

"You're his sister's boyfriend."

"Are you stoned? You smell like weed."

"It's the bar. It always smells like this." Matsui sniffed his armpit and stood up. "Have to go to the head."

Kawika returned with two red dogs and two beers, winked at Peter, and left them on Matsui's side of the table. "Get him wasted before the race."

"Who brought these?" Matsui asked, slipping into the booth and picking up a dog. "Kawika? Right? He's trying to help his sister." Matsui bit into the red meat, swallowed beer from a bottle, lit his cigarette, blew smoke, and said, "This doesn't look good, smoking and eating, drinking in a bar." He blew a cloud of smoke laced with red dog at Peter. "Sorry about that." He blew the next cloud at the ceiling.

"No problem."

"It's crazy," Matsui said. "I'm one of those people who can grind all kine grindz, as much as I want, and my body turns it to health food. No joke. I'm good to go. Except for swimming, that's my weak point, if I have a weak point, which I don't." He powered down a beer, set it gently on the table, and picked up another red dog.

Peter remembered a college buddy, a swimmer who smoked weed before and after practice and finished second at the NCAA nationals. With the right genes, a body was capable of great trickery. "Swimming is Celeste's strongest," he said, watching Matsui mulch a mouthful of red dog.

"Don't I know it?" Matsui sucked in smoke through red dog. "She's a good wahine." He swallowed and leaned across the table. "You been up to her place in Volcano? The Blake place? Their house? No? Never mind." He finished his beer, waved for another, and slumped back against the booth. "Sarah Costa can handle."

"Who?"

"Wait. Where's my beer?" Matsui shouted for a beer. Shouted for an order of fries, waved off the fries. Shouted for boiled peanuts. Waved it all off. "Sarah Costa is tough and a little dangerous."

"Where is she?"

"You don't know? I'm not surprised. You FBI folks have a hard time finding your shoes, even when they're on your feet. Don't get me wrong. I respect you folks. I'm all for law and order. Restorative justice. That's me."

"Sarah Costa?"

"Who?"

Auntie Kim handed Matsui a glass of water. "You've had enough. Go home. I'll call a taxi."

Matsui shook his head. "Not water. That's bad luck. Next thing you know, I'll be drowning in it."

"Where is Sarah Costa?"

Matsui pushed the glass of water at Peter. "Forget Sarah Costa. She has memory problems. Can't remember faces. Did she tell you about that? Couldn't remember me. Hell, it's only been twenty years."

"Only?"

"You're right about that."

"Where is she?"

"Since you're FBI, I'll draw you a map. But I'm not going with you. I have a race in day or a couple of days. Maybe three. And don't tell her I told you."

"I will."

"Good. I'll draw you a map." He dug through his pockets, came up with a rental car map of the Big Island, and drew felt-pen arrows on it, reaching east from Hilo, ending at the ocean. "That's Kalapana," he said. "Don't go there." His felt-pen arrows turned left, followed the coast, and stopped, drew a stick figure man pointing at a stick figure house and what looked like an upside-down tree.

Matsui folded the map into a tiny square and handed it to Peter. "Look for the Hala trees and a Volvo station wagon, orange. Only house for miles. No house numbers or street numbers out that way."

"Hala? Remind me, which one are those?"

"Bushy on top with lots of roots sticking out of the trunk. Kinda like bushy tripod trees. And the Volvo is a square, chunky Euro tank. Can't miss it. "

"I know what a Volvo looks like."

"Good. You find it, and you'll find Sarah." Matsui stood up. "I gotta make some calls. Be right back. Wait here. Just a second." He drained Peter's beer, walked out the back door, and didn't come back.

35.UPSIDE DOWN TREES

Time: October 2001
Location: Hilo and Puna

It took three hours, but Peter found his way. When the two-lane road ran into the ocean, he turned left and followed a rough strip of asphalt along the shoreline until he saw a break in the trees and a narrow driveway that led away from the ocean to a station wagon parked in the orange glow of a porch light.

It was too dark to tell the car's color or if the jungle of trees contained any that resembled tripods, so he parked on the ocean side, rolled up his windows, closed his eyes, and waited for morning.

At first light, the trees did, in an odd way, look like tripods, more like multi-pods, with multi-roots shooting out at 45-degree angles. Walking to the front door, he heard a door slam, water running, and dishes tossed in the sink. He smelled coffee brewing and toast burning. A dog barked, and a woman's childlike voice started to sing about a brand-new key. "Perfect timing," he whispered, then knocked on the door.

The dog, a tenor, barked once, then a man's voice asked gently, "Who is it?"

"Sorry. I saw your light." He paused. "I think I'm lost."

"Wait. My hands are full."

"I'm looking for a friend." Peter tucked in his shirt, brushed back his hair, and was checking his zipper when the door opened, just a crack, wide enough for a wire-haired dog, knee-high and rust colored, to peek out. The dog sniffed Peter's shoe, rubbed its head against his ankle, and darted down the driveway.

"Shorty!" A grey-haired man wearing silk pajamas and a 49ers hoodie stepped onto the porch. He was as tall as Peter, with blue eyes and a ragged Fu Manchu mustache. One delicate hand held a bagel with cream cheese, the other an oversized cup of coffee. He looked over Peter's shoulder and said, "Oh, I know who you are." He smiled.

"You do?"

"That's your rental car?"

"Yes."

"You're a tourist?"

"Yes."

"And you're lost."

"Exactly."

"See? That was easy."

"What?"

"It happens a lot out here. Lost tourists."

"Oh."

He looked over Peter's shoulder. "Are you alone?"

"I'm looking for a friend. She lives somewhere on this road, but the houses are set back so far from the road."

"I know what you mean." He bit into his bagel, hid his mouth with his hand, and managed to say, "The next house is a mile that way." He pointed his cup at the trees.

"Does Sarah Costa live there?"

The man shook his head. "I don't know. If Jimmy were here, he could help. But he's not here. He's flying in tomorrow. Or is it the next day?" He sipped his coffee, bit into his bagel, and said, between chews, "I don't know many people here. I'm from Kona. You know?

We're different from Puna people. So I keep to my myself. I'm Brad, Jimmy's house-sitter."

"Peter."

"That's Shorty, Jimmy's dog. He's part terrier."

From somewhere in the trees, Shorty barked once.

"He's very smart," Brad said. "He likes to bark and can hear things miles away."

"That's good."

"We're good friends."

Peter brushed away a fly, slapped at a mosquito. The air smelled of coffee, citrus aftershave, and strong weed. Peter held up his phone. "I tried calling. No bars.'

"Not out here." Brad swallowed and smiled, a gentle cream-cheese-and-bagel smile. "No bars, never. None for drinking or phoning."

Peter pointed at two photographs on the wall behind Brad. "Is that the Golden Gate Bridge? And the Cliff House with the lightning?"

"Could be. You from San Francisco? Don't tell Jimmy, or he'll hug you until you can't breathe. He loves that city, that's where he is now." Brad popped the last bit of the bagel into his mouth.

"Any chance Jimmy has a house phone? A landline?"

"You bet." The morning light lit up Brad's blue eyes. "Come in, come in. I guess there's no harm. Now let's see… the phone."

Peter followed him into the living room. A leather loveseat faced a picture window filled with a jungle of tripod trees. There was a coffee table made of glass in front of two easels, each with pastel impressions of Hala leaves.

"Lauhala," Brad said. "The Hawaiians used it for everything. I get stuck on a subject and can't let it go. It's not my fault. Your people make me do it."

"My people?"

"Tourists. You buy tons of waterfalls, sunsets, ocean scapes, and Hawaiian plants. I'm on Hawaiian plants now."

"Does Jimmy paint?"

Brad smiled. “Gave it up a long time ago. But he has a soft spot for artists. That’s me.”

“He lives out here alone?”

“He loves the quiet.” Brad pulled off his hoodie, saying, “Sorry, it’s already warming up.”

Peter thought 180 pounds, fifty-five years old, lean and long-armed. He could take him in a fight if he had to, but he wished he hadn’t left his Glock in the hotel safe.

“I’m going crazy out here,” Brad said. “Too much solitude drives me crazy. Jimmy says he likes it. It lets him rest, forget the mainland. You know, decompress. Me, I need people. I didn’t think he’d be gone this long. Oh, let’s see, yes, the phone.” He pointed at the stairs. “It’s in the bedroom. I hid it.” He set his coffee cup on the banister, and Peter noticed the cup had been hand-painted with red lettering. “Peace!”

“That’s me,” Brad said. “I did that.”

The stairs led to a huge loft with a king-size bed and a teak dresser. Brad picked up a pair of boxer shorts and tossed them at a rattan hamper.

“Missed,” Peter said.

“Don’t tell Jimmy.” Brad studied the room, picked up a T-shirt, a pair of socks, a beach towel, and an empty champagne bottle. “I know it’s here, somewhere. Let me think.”

“Big party?”

“Just me pretending, if you know what I mean. I’m not supposed to have parties, but when I drink I like to call my mom on the Mainland, so I hide the phone from myself. Long distance, you know what I mean?”

Peter nodded. “Sure.”

“I was supposed to clean up. Instead, I made a mess. It’s so nice having someone to talk to. You don’t mind, I hope. I’ve been out here months. The phone. Look everywhere. It’s cordless.”

“How long have you known Jimmy?”

“Oh, forever.”

“How long is that?”

"Let me think. Okay. Two or three years?"

"That's forever?"

"For here it is. People come and go." He scratched his head, snapped his fingers, pointed at the bed, and threw a rumpled blanket over the rumpled sheets, and turned around. "Mind if I have a smoke? Pakalolo helps my memory."

"I thought that worked the other way," Peter said. "Screwed with short-term memory."

"Not for me. I'm backward." He opened the top drawer of the rattan dresser, found what he was looking for, and used an orange Zippo to light a fat joint. Inhaled twice and offered it to Peter.

"Too early for me."

Holding his breath, Brad said, "Now that you mention it. I think it was four years ago I met Jimmy." A long exhale. "I was working in Kona, in Kona Town, where the tour boats pick up tourists. I was selling my tinies."

"What?"

He tried to make a square with his fingers and thumbs, managed a triangle. "Small kine pictures. Waterfalls. Pastels. Oils on wood scraps. He bought two the first time we met. Then two more. Then one day he drove all the way Kona just to buy a large water color for his place in San Francisco." He leaned back against the wall. "You look beat." Three longs hits off the joint, then holding his breath, "Go ahead, sit on the bed."

"I'm fine."

Brad smiled. "And over drinks, he asked if I would house-sit for him. A couple months out of the year. Just me and the house. What could I do? I was living in a studio with three roommates. The starving artist. Even a house in Puna was better than that." He took another hit, lit a stick of incense, and waved it around the room before tossing the incense and the joint in a jade vase. "Presto, and here I am. House-sitter for the stars. Free rent plus two hundred bucks a week and plent of time to paint."

"Makes sense."

"Sure it does. Lots of snowbirds like him in Puna, but no one likes to leave their house empty even for a few days. And he's one of the good ones. He saved my life."

"Good for you."

"It's not what you think." He pointed at the bed. "Nothing happens. Nothing like that."

"I understand."

"No, you don't." Hands on hips, he smiled. You're so straight… Wait." He slapped his head. "I got it! Check under the bed."

"What?"

"There." Brad was on his knees, reaching under the bed, dragging out a black leather portfolio, and then the phone.

Peter spread the portfolio open on the bed. "Are these yours?"

"Heavens, no. Charcoal, yuck. I can't live without color."

Peter nodded, smelling citrus aftershave, moldy paper, marijuana, and pachouli incense as he paged through the portfolio.

"Poor Jimmy," Brad said, his hand on Peter's shoulder. "Now I see why he gave up painting. Is that a woman?"

Peter had stopped at a fading sketch, a blurry shadow in high heels and a red-cross armband. "Can't tell," he said. Then Shorty was barking, and they heard three heavy knocks at the front door.

"Coming," Brad shouted. "Stay here. I'll be right back.

Peter studied the date below the drawing. Was it 1974? San Francisco? He ripped out the page, folded it in half, in half again, and tucked it inside his shirt as Brad called up from the bottom of the stairs. "Your girlfriend found Shorty. A real peach. She looks absolutely pretty, in a scary way. A little old for you. Hurry down."

36.THE ROAD HOME

Time: October 2001
Location: Puna, Volcano Hawaii

Peter saw a grey-haired woman, short and stocky, in jeans and a sweatshirt, with a dog in her arms.

"Poor thing," Sarah said. "He was running in circles in the middle of the street. And led me right to Peter."

"He's like Lassie," Brad said, taking Shorty and hugging him. "Jimmy would kill me if I lost his dog. How crazy is that?"

"Very crazy," Peter said.

"Was he barking for help? Did he tell you Peter was inside?" Brad laughed and shook his head. "I'm being silly."

Backing away, Sarah said, "We should go, Peter. We're late."

"What about coffee? One good deed deserves another. It's way too early to be without coffee, young lady. Come in."

"That's a thought," Peter said. "Come in."

"Maybe next time." Sarah blew Shorty and Brad a kiss. "Hurry, Peter. Celeste is waiting."

Going uphill, Peter gripped the steering wheel as a howling blur of monster truck, with six pig dogs in a cage made for three, blasted its horn and overtook him in passing lane, its driver flipping him off, cutting him off, and leaving him in a black cloud of oily exhaust. Where was Costa? He drove uphill, past the entrance to the National Park, skidding over wet asphalt under darks skies, until the road dipped down into sunlight and blue skies, and he was about to turn around when he looked left and saw Sarah unlocking a single-bar gate.

She raised her hand, said, “Leave it there.”

In Celeste’s pickup, he sat shotgun, and Sarah drove along fresh asphalt through low-growth Ohia growing from black lava spotted with steam vents until they reached a deserted parking lot. Peter walked with her to the edge of a crater, a four-mile jagged circle of volcanic pit, a thin crust over sleeping lava. He stood beside her, freezing in the wind.

“Kilauea Caldera," Sarah said. “A thousand-foot drop.” She leaned over the ledge. “Scares the hell out of me.”

“It’s beautiful,” Peter said.

“Then, why are you backing up?"

“The truth?”

“Try it.”

“I don't trust you.”

“That works.”

A long way off, the ocean was a thin line of blue under thick white clouds running from the sun. “Why are we here?” Peter asked.

“My father loved this place. He brought me here when he wanted me to listen. I wasn’t always good at listening.”

They felt the earth move.

“He must be here now,” Peter said.

“Don’t kid yourself. The earth is here, not spirits. She reached inside her leather jacket and came out with a half pint of Jim Beam.

“None for me.”

“It’s not for you.” She twisted off the plastic cap, sipped whiskey, and poured the rest on the ground. “For old friends.”

"Is that a Hawaiian thing?"

"No. From the movies, can't remember which one."

They felt the earth move.

"Never mind that," she said. "Sometimes we get a couple hundred tremors a day, a swarm." She capped the empty bottle, tucked it back in her jacket. "Eruptions and lava flows to the left. A crack running along the coastline to the right. The island is building and tearing itself apart at the same time." She faced him. "Tell me something. Did Johnny send you?"

"If he did, he took the long way around." Peter told her how Lois had met him at the parole hearing, drugged him, and stolen his badge.

"And your gun?"

"That too."

"You're in the wrong profession.'

"I got it back."

"Where is it now?"

"Locked in the hotel safe."

"Best place for it." Sarah zipped up her jacket, stuck her hands in her pockets, and said, "Lois always had a thing for guns. I still have one of her souvenirs."

Peter told her what had happened.

"An accident?"

"Maybe."

"She was a good friend."

"That's not what I heard."

"She could be trouble, no doubt about that." She stared into the crater until she heard Peter ask, "When are you taking me to Celeste?" He made a move to go, and Sarah grabbed his arm. "First, a promise. I need you to stay out of this."

"You mean that man in the house? Brad?"

"Never mind him. I'll take care of it."

"What about this?" Peter handed her the charcoal drawing, watched her unfold it, and tuck it in her back pocket. He felt her press her hand to his chest. "I'll take care of him," she said. "You take care of Celeste and let me handle this. Promise me, or you'll lose her. You don't want to touch this one. Believe me. Promise me."

He felt his heart beating against her hand. Didn't understand what she was asking, but said, "Promise."

Peter followed her up the mountain, past fields of lava rock and Ohia to a forest of tall pines, onto a ragged, rutted dirt road walled in by Hapu ferns. Peter saw the brake lights flash. The Toyota stopped as a ragged man stepped into the road, holding up his hands and shouting, "The Lord is coming. Coming soon." Then he crossed himself and wandered off into the Ohia and wild ginger, into a clearing where a blue tarp sheltered a sagging hammock and a moldy cooler hosted a pile of sleeping cats.

The truck spit mud as it sloshed its way uphill onto a dirt driveway between Douglas firs and stopped at a detached garage. Peter parked behind it, next to a single-story house with a tin roof and a wide front porch.

Celeste was waiting on the porch. She hugged Sarah first, then Peter. "Did you see the fourth wise man?" she asked. "Don't mind him. He's been living in the trees for years. Mom is sleeping." She hugged Peter again. "Sorry. I've been busy." She stepped back.

Celeste led them into a long living room. There were three leather couches, a high ceiling, and wood floors. To the right a sitting room with a writing desk, a high-backed chair, and a glass bookcase. To the left a formal dining area with a dark wood table, eight matching chairs, and a centerpiece of purple orchids. "Kitchen's in the back," she said.

Peter felt the earth move gently, then stronger, shaking the house before shuddering to a stop. Celeste shrugged and said, "That's nothing. My father grew up on the San Andreas fault."

They followed her to the sitting room.

"Dad thought earthquakes were great because they kept the price of real estate down. That's why we could afford this house. That and the freezing rain. No one comes to Hawaii to freeze," she laughed. "They want sun and warm." She stopped at a closed door. "Mom's room," she said. "Wait here."

Sarah felt herself slipping back to her hospital days when she would walk through halls smelling disinfectant, exchanging tired words with tired nurses, and speaking to nervous visitors trying to hold back tears.

Sarah spoke to Peter in whispers, told him Celeste's father had passed two years ago. There was only her mother now. There was a chance for a peaceful ending. Even ALS could be gentle near the end. Sarah had seen patients trapped inside themselves fall gently asleep and never wake from their dreams.

Celeste came back and took Peter's hand.

When she opened the door, Peter saw double-hung windows splashing morning light on a hospital bed with an oxygen tank next to its nightstand. The woman in the bed opened her eyes, and Celeste bent down to kiss her gently on the forehead. "Love you, Mom."

A clear oxygen mask covered the lower half of the woman's face. She blinked twice before she closed her eyes. Celeste stepped back. "Mom, this is Peter, Sarah's friend. He came to say hello."

Peter reached down and lifted the woman's hand from the bed, gently held it, and said, "Good morning, Mrs. Blake."

"Costa," Celeste said. "Ms Jane Costa."

Later, Celeste asked Peter if he would go with her. A student needed help to find a safe place to live. "A crazy boyfriend," Celeste said. "We get a lot of that."

"I'll wait in the truck."

Celeste turned to Sarah, kept talking, faster now, saying Kawika would be home after work, and would Sarah take care of her mother. "Her medicine…"

"I know where it is."

When they were gone, Sarah walked through the house, stopped in Celeste's bedroom, and studied the movie posters on the wall. Platoon. Casablanca. True Romance. She touched the trophies for swimming and rubbed her fingers along the row of hardcover books: *Hawaii's Story by Hawaii's Queen, Land and Power in Hawaii,* and *Volcano,* all nonfiction, all about Hawaii, two memoirs about love and loss, and a researched study of political and social corruption. Then came *Crime and Punishment,* a Russian novel, written in 1866, a worn-out paperback that looked out of place on the shelf. Sarah remembered trying to read a similar copy in college, an already tired textbook edition. She had taken it with her after graduation and tried to finish it. Tried again. She liked the title, and tried again, then lost it. At the hospital? At the pool? Or at a hotel or motel somewhere on the road to her next assignment?

Celeste must have found its heart.

Sarah carried the novel to the living room and lit Kiawe wood in the fireplace. Found a bottle of Maker's Mark and left it untouched. Opened the book to a page near the end, bookmarked by a faded black-and-white photograph.

In the photo, two rows of smiling adults were standing on the steps of a Victorian house. In the front row, a smiling Ms Jane cradled a baby to her chest. Sarah turned the photo over and recognized Terrence's handwriting: "People's Temple Nursery, Christmas 1976, a baby girl, Potrero Hill, San Francisco. Parents lost in Jonestown, November 1978."

Sarah replaced the book on the shelf, walked to Ms Jane's bedroom, and sat in the dark, her hand resting on her friend's wrist.

37.IN THE REALM OF HAVA-ITI

Time: October 5, 2001
Location: Volcano, Hawaii

In Puna, Sarah left the memoir on the rental car seat and stepped into the morning air, cool and salty. The Union had called yesterday, urging her to reconsider, to return as quickly as possible, there was work to do. And when she had told them the truth, that she was taking care of a family emergency, the director paused before saying, "Family?"

She pulled a hoodie over her head and walked up the driveway. Clear skies were promising a new day. She stopped at the front door, smelled pot smoke and coffee brewing. When Brad opened the door, Shorty darted out of the shadows and into her arms.

"Oh, no, not you again," Brad said. "Have you lost Peter again? Sorry, please, there's no time. Jimmy's flying in tomorrow morning. Or tonight, and I have tons of work to do."

"Stop talking. It's not safe here."

"You're scaring me," he laughed. "Hey, wait. I was only kidding when I said Jimmy would kill me. He's not like that. He's a good man."

Holding Shorty under her arm like a football, Sarah reached her other hand inside her hoodie. "You're coming with me."

"Is that a gun?"

"It's my finger pretending to be a gun."

"You're kidnapping me?"

"And Shorty."

"I'm too stoned for this."

"Good. Makes it easier."

"The house cleaning?"

"Forget it."

"That's a plus."

"Get your stuff."

Sarah found Peter and Celeste in the kitchen, carbo-loading for the big race the next day, hunched over huge plates of spaghetti topped with vegetarian chili. In between mouthfuls, Celeste looked out the window and said, "Where'd you get the dog? And the stoner?"

"Strays." Sarah said, pouring milk into a wine glass.

Peter tore off a piece of Hawaiian-style bread. "Is that Brad?"

"He needs a ride to Kona."

They watched Brad stretch out under a tree, hands behind his head and gazing up at the sky with Shorty on his chest.

"Tell him to come inside, eat," Celeste said. "There's plenty food."

They ate together, with Brad concentrating on the spaghetti while Shorty waited patiently under the table. When Sarah tossed Shorty the last bit of french bread, Brad and Peter got up to do the dishes. Celeste pointed at the cabinet where her mother's medicine was stored. Pointed again, for the fifth time, at Kawika's work number penciled on the kitchen wall. "Anything happens, you call me and Kawika," she said. "Understand?"

Nodding, they followed Celeste outside, where the air was cool and thick with mist.

Celeste tied her high-top Converse to her bike's handlebars and, with Brad's help, lifted the Varsity into the back of the Toyota next to his easels and boxes of paintings. Peter tossed in a backpack full of bananas, peanut-butter sandwiches, and homemade oat cakes. Brad said Kona water was undrinkable, and Sarah slid in a five-gallon jug of Hilo water, "Straight from the tap at Auntie Kim's."

Celeste rolled a swimsuit, a rubber cap with plastic flowers, and a pair of Speedo goggles in a beach towel, and set it on the front seat.

Sarah watched them play catch with sleeping bags, from Peter to Celeste to Brad, and into the truck. "Bring plenty pictures," Sarah said. "Shots of Matsui finishing last."

"I almost forgot." Celeste ran into the house and returned with a shoe box filled with camera gear. "Dad's old stuff." She handed the box to Sarah. "Check it out for me. See if any of it works."

"Me?"

"It's from your time. But I'm leaving Matsui out of this. Karma will catch up to him. Guys like him always get what they deserve."

Sarah didn't say she knew plenty of people who had dodged karma all their lives. Instead, she sat on the tailgate, settled the shoebox on her lap, and picked out an old Nikon, a black F1 with a 50mm lens. "Your father knew his stuff," she said. She pointed the camera at Celeste and Peter. "Get closer," she said. "Closer. Closer. Nice." At the last second, she clicked the shutter release.

"Like my dad," Celeste said, "Always taking pictures."

"There's no film," Sarah said. "Just wanted to see you two together.." She hadn't used the Nikon since her college days, but she remembered how to advance the film and pressed the shutter release. "Still smooth," she said, holding the camera to her eye, smelling the worn metal where Terrence had scratched his initials into the black steel. "Who's TC?" she asked Celeste. "Do you know?"

"Dad always said he bought his stuff from pawn shops."

Sarah handed Celeste the F1 and picked out an Instamatic, according to Terrence, a model 100, the first Instamatic of its kind. Thirty years ago, Ms Jane had used its peanut flash to light up the Presidio Stockade. Now, Sarah saw the guards in the flash's harsh light and heard Terrence telling her that a prisoner, a mutineer, had been shot and killed at the fence line. And later, on an island in the bay, Lois Lane assuring her that one of the prisoners had escaped to Canada, a boy from California, Lindy Blake, and she could help Terrance do the same. Private Lindy Blake.

Celeste pointed the F1 at Sarah and turned the focus ring on the 50mm lens. "There you are," she said. "Sarah in focus."

"How do I look?"

"Like someone holding an old camera with no film."

Sarah felt the young woman's arms around her, and saw the taxi in front of the Costa home in Daly City. Recognized the driver stepping out, holding the telegram.

"We've got to go," Celeste said and kissed Sarah on both cheeks.

She watched them go. In the old pickup, Celeste at the steering wheel, Peter riding shotgun, and Brad stretched out in the back, waving goodbye with Shorty's paw.

Later, Sarah sat beside Ms Jane's bed. "Blake," she said. "I should've guessed. Terrence's idea?"

Ms Jane saw the camera equipment in Sarah's lap and wanted to tell her friend about the movies Terrence had made when they first came to Hawaii. Her friend would love the ones of Celeste on the beach at Hapuna and her running on the grass in front of their home in Volcano. She wished Sarah could see Terrence trying to hold the camera steady for David's birth, unexpected after years of trying. David's first steps, his first birthday. The two of them together, a brother for Celeste.

Ms Jane searched her friend's face and saw her standing in the glow of the Falcon's headlights with her arm around David. Saw her at the hospital with Cappy. She wanted to tell her that Cappy had saved them that night on Morse Street. It was Cappy who had helped her return the baby girl to the Presidio. Poor Cappy. Poor Vincent, who had lost his son to Jones. Poor Val, who had taken Celeste's from her mother's hands and promised to care for her child until her mother returned or could convince the Reverend Jones to send for her chid.

But most of all, she wanted to hold Sarah in her arms, hold her close and tight, and ask her forgiveness.

38.RESCUES

Time: October 6, 2001
Location: Hawaii

In the morning, Sarah folded back Ms Jane's comforter. Her friend's eyes were closed, her breathing good. She kissed Ms Jane's forehead, felt her pulse, and told her everything would be good. Her children would be home soon.

Outside, she wrapped herself in a blanket and sat on the front steps. As the sunrise rushed over her, she made the call and heard herself say, "I think I can help you."

Celeste had exchanged her board shorts and t-shirt for a black Speedo and a pair of goggles. After using a black felt pen to ink "808" on each arm, she topped off her official look with a flowered bathing cap.

"Are you sure about that cap?" Peter asked.

"It's mom's. Her good luck charm."

"Then it's perfect."

Celeste pulled the cap tight over her ears, climbed over the rocks, and slipped into the water, stopping when she was waist-deep to ask, "Can you see him?"

Peter used his binoculars. "Are you kidding? It's a feeding frenzy."

Seconds later, a cannon shot sent 1,500 swimmers crashing toward orange buoys.

Sarah pedaled her bike across Highway 11 to the park's service entrance. In her field jacket and jeans, she walked her bike past the locked gate, coasted through morning mist and sulfur fumes, telling herself there was more than one way to save a drowning man.

As the sun pushed back the clouds, she stopped at the Kilauea Overlook, rested her bike against the railing, and tried to forget the black-and-white photographs. To stop wondering how the police technician had found the strength to hold the camera steady. To stop counting the victims. In 1974, 130 homicides in San Francisco. In 1975, 132.

She remembered Hitchens offering her his flask. Remembered saying she didn't drink wine, not anymore, and asking for anything stronger. They were standing over a body. Six feet, 148 pounds, in a blue jacket, multi-colored shirt, blue jeans, brown socks, and brown shoes. Multiple stab wounds. Discovered by a woman in her nineties while walking her dog. When two policemen, surprised by her calm demeanor, asked her if she had seen many bodies, she closed her eyes and rolled up her sleeve, exposing five numbers.

Now, the sound of a car's brakes made Sarah look up. She was standing at the edge of the caldera, the air cold and harsh, running on memories. In the parking lot, a man in a heavy jacket and sock cap stepped out of a Volvo, closed the door gently, turned to check the road, and walked toward her.

Celeste swam toward the stragglers. The ocean off Kona, unlike Hilo Bay, was clear and blue. She could see flickering yellow coral heads and stretches of rippled white sand dropping off to deep blue. She lifted her head out of the water and checked for a path through a tangle of thrashing arms and propeller legs.

The sun felt warm on her face. She wanted to go easy and enjoy the view, but the the churning school of crashing bodies forced her to keep moving or be gouged, kicked, or forced under. It would only last a moment, she told herself. Soon the misguided would wear themselves out kicking and elbowing each other to gain a few yards. Then the pack would thin out, and all she had to do was swim to the pier, find her bike, pedal a hundred miles, and run a marathon in her high-tops. No problem.

A safety paddler looked her way, and she dove under, rolled over, and watched a heavyweight swim over her, swinging his arms like hammers, trying to beat his way to the pier. When a patch of sunlight appeared, she kicked to the sky, inhaled cool morning air, and watched the safety paddler veer toward the leaders. Behind her, the stragglers were spreading out, and in their wake, one of them had stopped, was waving, slapping the water, then slipping under.

He was shorter than Sarah remembered. Heavier, older, in his fifties, worn down and tired. He leaned over the railing and shook his head. "Jesus, that's a drop. All these years, and I've never been out here. Hell of a drop."

"It'll do the job."

Still looking down, he said, "I know you, but I don't remember the name."

"Costa," she said. "We met a long time ago."

"At Finocchio's."

"In the seventies."

"Way back."

"I had a friend who worked there. Cappy. A nurse and Navy vet."

He nodded. “I knew him.”

“There were others.”

He closed his eyes. “Yes. I introduced them to him. But I didn’t know.”

She slipped her hand into her jacket pocket. Moved closer, until she could smell him, soapy clean in the sharp wind.

He leaned back against the railing, looked past her at the mountains, one dead, one dying. “I loved him,” he said. “More than anything. But I didn’t know what he was. I didn’t know.”

“Where is he?”

He shook his head. “We’re safe now. Understand? I had to do it.”

He turned to the caldera, and for a second she thought he was going to climb the railing and jump, wipe clean his memories. But he turned to her instead, and handed her a a wrinkled envelope. “Finish it,” he said, reaching for her. “Do it now.”

Celeste thought she saw Matsui pop to the surface, shouting for help, wide-eyed, and reaching for her. She jack-knifed under him, found his knees, turned him, and guided her hands up his body until she could reach over his shoulder, across his chest, and grab his armpit. With her hip jammed against the small of his back, she kicked toward the surface, thinking Matsui seemed thinner, taller, even wiry. Then she broke into the sunlight.

The stragglers were leaving them behind, but the shore was close, maybe, a hundred yards away. They could make it if Matsui would help. But seeing his face now, she realized this wasn’t Matsui. “Relax,” she shouted. “Relax. I got you. Just kick.”

“Friggin cramp. Can’t breathe.”

She switched to egg-beater kick. “Lay flat, don’t move, try to float.” She supported his head with one hand, her other under his back. “Just float. Relax and float.”

Sarah swore at her bad luck. Matsui’s years of beer drinking and with a belly to match would have made him an easy rescue, a floater.

Instead, this fellow was all muscle and bone, a sinker. "Relax. Look at the sky. I got you."

One arm across his chest, her hip in his back, Celeste switched to a scissor kick, with her free arm reaching and pulling underwater. She thought they had a chance, until she felt him kick, tense up, and twist. "Crap." He spit water. "Help. I can't breathe."

She switched to eggbeater, checked his breathing, kicked toward shore, felt the swell, pinched his nose and covered his mouth with her free hand. The waved lifted them up and rolled them toward shore. She kicked to the surface, shouted for help, blew air into his mouth, kicked a coral head, stepped on a slippery rock, and saw a yellow kayak paddling toward her.

On the road, Sarah pedaled past the naked man, heard him shout, "He's coming soon. Born again. The star in the sky. Follow the star. This way."

She stood up on the pedals to make the climb past a hammock sagging with cats.

At home, she sat in the dark, with the note in her hand. A name, a date of birth, and a number on a police report and a cause of death. Near midnight Peter called to say Celeste was a mile from the finish line, and race officials were packing up there equipment. They had asked two police officers to kindly remove her, citing safety and insurance concerns. But the officers, ex-students from the community college, had returned, reporting that there was nothing they could do to stop a citizen from running at night. Even a crazy one running barefoot. The officials shrugged and kept packing, while one of the officers, in dark blues and on his way to the patrol car, stopped to tell Peter, "Professor Celeste is one one tough wahine."

39.NO DEATH PENALTY IN HAWAII

Time: December 25, 2001
Location: San Francisco Bay

On her way to the airport, Sarah asked the driver for music then glanced down at the Tribune's sports page. A three-column photo featured a triathlete on a stretcher. In bold, a headline took a shot at the truth: "Visitor from Colorado rescues local triathlete."

Sarah looked up, surprised to hear the radio tuned to HPR and a commentator saying Robert S. McNamara, the Secretary of Defense during the Vietnam War, would be in San Francisco to discuss recent events in Afghanistan.

Her cellphone rang, and Matsui said, "What, no goodbye?"

"What happened to you?"

"Stopped at Auntie Kim's for breakfast. Had a few drinks."

"Maybe next year."

"Not me. Forget it. Life's too short. Why kill myself?"

Sarah looked out the window, saw the road to the airport.

Matsui said, "Too bad you're leaving. Peter tells me he'll be staying for a couple more weeks. The Park Service asked for FBI assistance with an investigation. Someone in DC volunteered him."

"What kine investigation?"

"A suicide. Maybe an overdose? Nothing suspicious. An old guy, a snowbird in his car at the Overlook. It's federal land, so paper work must be created, boxes checked."

"SOP."

"And you, where to now?"

"Setting sail. Take care of yourself, soldier."

"Same to you."

"No worries. I saved the baby Jesus. That has to count for something."

The next day, Sarah was leaning over the railing of the MS Golden Gate. A crew member, a friend of Ms. Jane's from the old days, had told her to relax, not to worry. Be cool. There'd be plenty of time.

Violin music drifted up from the main cabin, where uniformed waiters served trays of glittering mimosas. As the ferry moved away from the dock, a stocky young man in a dark suit stepped through the hatchway. He offered Sarah a polite smile, mentioned security concerns, and asked if he could check her bag, the one underneath the bench.

"Never mind her," Special Agent Jonathan Smith called from the hatchway. He waved off security, told him to wait in the main cabin, then walked across the deck to stand beside Sarah. Shoulder to shoulder, they watched the city grow smaller.

"What's all the fuss?' she asked.

"McNamara's downstairs. Special party. You didn't know?"

"I may have heard something."

Fog crossed the Golden Gate, covered city's edge.

"How's our boy doing?"

"You should know."

"I thought he could use the work. Keep him from getting lost in paradise."

"He found a history teacher."

"Good for him. Anyone we know?"

Sarah shook her head. “Local girl.”

“Lucky man. Any sign of Terrence and Miss Jane?”

“Nothing.”

“Doodler?”

“Another dead end.” She picked up her gear bag, set it on the bench.

“Going somewhere?”

“Have to get in the water.”

“Still trying?”

Sarah nodded, sat down, and unlaced her boots. “Maybe McNamara wants to come with me.” She kicked off her boots. Unzipped her jacket. “He still owes the ocean a swim.”

“You won’t let me forget?”

“No way.” Sarah stripped down to her bathing suit and stuffed her clothes in her gear bag. When she turned to face him, she was holding Lois Lane’s .38. For a second she tested its weight and balance, then held it by the barrel, and said, “The luck went out of this thing long ago.” Then she threw it as far as she could into the Golden Gate’s wake.”

Special Agent Smith said, “She asked for my help.”

“Victim Services?”

“For an old friend.”

“You always were a softy.”

The ferry’s engines throttled back, and Agent Smith looked up, surprised to see Alcatraz. “We’re here.” When he turned around, Sarah was gone. “Be careful,” he said. “The tide’s going out fast.”

Sarah had dropped into the dark water and drifted down into David’s arms. Now she was swimming with him, together toward the shore, gliding over the living and the dead.

READING LIST

While writing *Saving McNamara,* I went where my characters, fantasies, and memories led me. If you are interested in a nonfiction approach, you may find the following reading list helpful. Joseph Stanton's poem "Unforgiven" follows this list.

1. Alternative Considerations of Jonestown & People's Temple. Website **jonestown.sdsu.edu** hosted by the Special Collections of Library and Information Access at San Diego State University, first posted January 5, 2013

2. Double Play, The Hidden Passions Behind the Double Assassination of George Moscone and Harvey Milk. Mike Weiss, 1984, Vince Emery Productions.

3. Every Secret Thing. Patricia Campbell Hearst, 1982 Doubleday. (Hearst's account of her kidnapping by the Symbionese Liberation Army. LZ)

4. Imaginary Museum, Poems on Art. Joseph Stanton, 1999, Time Being Books.

5. Island, Poetry and History of Chinese Immigrants on Angel Island 1910-1940. Him Mark Lai, Genny Lim, and Judy Young, 2014,University of Washington Press.

6. J. Edgar Hoover, The Man and the Secrets. Curt Gentry, 1991, W.W. Norton.

7. Kill Anything That Moves, The Real American War in Vietnam. Nick Turse, 2013, Metropolitan Books.

8. Ku Kanaka, Stand Tall, A search for Hawaiian Values. George Hu'eu Sanford Kanahele, 1986, A Kolowalu Book, University of Hawaii Press and Waiaha Foundation.

9.Land and Power in Hawaii, The Democratic Years. George Cooper and Gavan Daws, 1990, University of Hawaii Press.

10. Manual for Draft-Age Immigrants to Canada. Mark Satin, 1968, House of Anansi

11. Season of the Witch, Enchantment, Terror, and Deliverance in the City of Love. David Talbot, 2012, Free Press.

12. Stayin' Alive, The 1970s and the Last Days of the Working Class. Jefferson Cowie, 2010, The New Press.

13. Ten Years that Shook the City, San Francisco 1968-1978. Edited by Chris Carlsson and Lisa Ruth Elliott, 2010, City Lights Foundation Books.

14. The Doodler, A renewed hunt for a forgotten serial killer. Podcast by San Francisco Chronicle reporter Kevin Fagan, produced in partnership with Ugly Duckling Films and Neon Hum Media, first airing March 16, 2021 and available through podcast apps.

15. The Life We Were Given, Operation Babylift, International Adoption, and the Children of the War in Vietnam. Dana Sachs, 2010, Beacon Press.

16. The Mayor of Castro Street, The Life and Times of Harvey Milk. Randy Shilts, 1982, St.Martin's Press.

17. The New Exiles, American War Resisters in Canada. Roger Neville Williams, 1971, Liveright Publishers.

18. The New Winter Soldiers, GI and Veteran Dissent During the Vietnam War. Richard Moser, 1996, Rutgers University Press.

19. The Unlawful Concert, An Account of the Presidio Muting Case. Fred Gardner, 1970, TheViking Press.

20. The Untold Story of the Doodler Murders. Elon Green, December 11, 2014, online essay with numerous sources listed, found at theawl.com. (https://www.theawl.com/2014/12/the-untold-story-of-the-doodler-murders/)

21. The Zebra Murders: A Season of Killing, Racial Madness and Civil Rights. Earl Sanders and Bennett Cohen, 2006, Arcade Publishing.

21. Waikiki Beachboy. Grady Timmons, 1982, Editions Ltd.

22. When an Artist, In Vietnam Era, Tried to Drown Robert

McNamara — and Nearly Did It. Greg Mitchell, August 7, 2009, updated May 25, 2011, Huffington Post, identifying Paul Hendrickson as the reporter/writer helping to uncover the incident and featuring it in his 1995 book: **The Living and the Dead**: Robert McNamara and Five Lives of a Lost War.

23. Volcano, A Memoir of Hawaii. Garrett Hongo, 1993, Alfred Knopf Inc.

24. Zebra: The True Account of the 179 Days of Terror in San Francisco. Clark Howard, 1979, Richard Marek Publishers

Unforgiven

Ratty little Mister Beauchamp,
a moot, inglorious Milton,
fabulist as parasite and chump,
author of *The Duke of Death*
(renamed *The Duck of Death by Little Bill),*
will write nothing of this,
nothing of the real matter here,
nothing of the moral etched in blood and pain.

Mutter this with William Munny, out of Missouri,
in silhouette against the sky's clotted blue:
"It's a hell of a thing killin' a man."
Here's a sun settled on a dark horizon
of Golden Rule, where we must understand
that killing's hard, for most of us, to do —

the point at last so simple, so humane
(after all those years
of cartoony killfest cowboy flicks).
These frames,
so stunningly (at last) cinematic,
click back the hammer,
revolve the cylinder
from reel to real,
and squeeze off
that one
            last
              painstaking
                shot
right between the eyes.

by Joseph Stanton from Imaginary Museum

www.ingramcontent.com/pod-product-compliance
Lightning Source LLC
Chambersburg PA
CBHW030535310726
48979CB00010B/1913/J

* 9 7 8 0 9 9 8 5 5 0 4 6 6 *